Undercover Hearts

SEALs of Love Romance

Lilly Grace Nash

Published by Janice Lam, 2024.

UNDERCOVER HEARTS

First edition. April 28, 2024.

Copyright © 2024 Lilly Grace Nash.

ISBN: 979-8224628629

Written by Lilly Grace Nash.

Also by Lilly Grace Nash

SEALs of Love Romance
Undercover Hearts

Watch for more at https://lillygracenash.com.

Table of Contents

To my beloved husband,

whose unwavering support, endless encouragement,

and steadfast belief in me

have been the guiding light throughout my journey.

Your love is the foundation upon which I build my dreams.

Prologue: The Mission

The secure briefing room within the naval base was stark and utilitarian, the air thick with tension. Fluorescent lights hummed overhead, casting a cold glow on the faces of those gathered around the table. At the head stood Captain Marcus Elliott, a man whose service stripes bore witness to decades of dedication to his country. His gaze swept across the room, settling finally on Jake Thompson, who sat straight-backed and attentive, the quiet intensity in his eyes belying the turmoil within.

"Thompson," Captain Elliott began, his voice grave, "we've got a situation that requires someone with your unique skill set. It's sensitive, and it's on home soil."

Jake nodded, his mind racing. Missions on home soil were rare, and their nature was invariably complex and fraught with danger.

"Your hometown, to be precise," Captain Elliott added, his eyes locking onto Jake's with a gravity that immediately heightened the sense of urgency in the room. The mention of his hometown, a place imbued with memories of simpler times, sent a shockwave through Jake, a mixture of disbelief and a sinking feeling of inevitability.

Captain Elliott leaned forward, folding his hands on the table. "Thompson, your primary AO will be the town and its surrounding areas. The Black Oak Militia has established a significant foothold there. Intel suggests they're operating out of a compound in the dense forest to the north, but we've got SIGINT that places key members within the town at regular intervals."

Jake nodded, familiar with the terminology. AO, area of operation; SIGINT, signals intelligence. The specifics grounded him, reminded him of the countless briefings he'd sat through before, though none quite like this.

The town he remembered, with its tree-lined streets, friendly faces, and the tranquil pace of life, seemed an unlikely backdrop for a threat of this magnitude. It was a place where community meant everything, where neighbors gathered for summer barbecues and cheered on the local high school football team under the Friday night lights. The thought of such darkness infiltrating the very heart of his childhood sanctuary was both surreal and deeply unsettling.

"This isn't just any mission, Thompson," Elliott continued, breaking through Jake's momentary daze. "It's personal. The Black Oak Militia has been growing right under the noses of your friends and family. They're well-organized, heavily armed, and from what we've gathered, they're planning something big. Something dangerous."

The complexity of the situation lay not only in the nature of the threat but in the emotional terrain Jake would have to navigate. Returning to his hometown as an undercover operative meant facing the past he had left behind, including relationships paused mid-sentence and the shadows of what-ifs that lingered in the corners of his heart. The place that had shaped him, that held the echoes of his first love and the dreams of youth, was now a battleground where the lines between friend and foe might blur dangerously.

"We're operating under ROE that prioritize stealth and information gathering over direct engagement," Elliott continued. "Your insertion will be low-key—no fanfare, no backup. You're going in soft, Thompson. Civilian clothes, civilian demeanor. We need eyes and ears on the ground, not a show of force." "The risks are high," Elliott said, his voice a solemn echo in the sterile room. "You'll be walking into an environment filled with potential hostilities, and your cover is everything. If your true mission is compromised, it won't just be your life at risk. It could endanger those you care about."

As Captain Elliott detailed the mission specifics, the complexity of Jake's task became increasingly clear. "Thompson, given your history and connections within the town, an assumed identity is off the table. You're going back as yourself, but with a twist," Elliott stated, a stern seriousness in his gaze. "You'll be portraying a version of yourself that has grown disillusioned with the government, particularly its treatment of veterans. It's a narrative that's unfortunately all too common and believable. It will serve as your inroad to the Black Oak Militia."

Jake absorbed the captain's words, the gravity of the situation sinking in. Going back not under the guise of an alias but as a shadowed version of himself was a strategy fraught with personal risk and moral ambiguity. It meant airing views and grievances that were antithetical to his true beliefs, playing the part of a man who felt abandoned by the country he had sworn to protect.

"The militia is recruiting, and they're targeting individuals exactly like the persona you'll be adopting—veterans who feel let down and forgotten. Your dissatisfaction will be your cover, and your military background will make you an attractive recruit to them," Elliott continued, his eyes locked onto Jake's, ensuring the gravity of the situation was fully understood.

The operation's success hinged on Jake's ability to convincingly inhabit this disillusioned persona, to walk a fine line where he could draw the militia out without compromising his principles or mission. "It's crucial that you gain their trust, Thompson. We need intel on their leadership structure, planned activities, and any potential targets. But remember, these people are wary of outsiders. Any hint that you're not fully committed to their cause could blow your cover."

Jake felt a cold resolve settle over him. The mission demanded that he navigate the delicate balance of infiltrating the militia without losing himself in the process. The thought of returning to his hometown, a place of childhood innocence and cherished memories, now as a man on a mission to expose a hidden threat, was a stark reminder of the sacrifices his duty required.

"Your connections in town, your reputation—they will get you through the door, but it's your ability to sell this disillusioned version of yourself that will keep you there," Elliott emphasized. "This is about more than just gathering intel; it's about protecting your community from within. We're counting on you to tread carefully, Thompson. The risks are high, but the potential cost of inaction is higher."

With a heavy heart but a steadfast spirit, Jake committed himself to the task. The safety of his hometown, the preservation of its peace and innocence, depended on his ability to walk among those who sought to disrupt it, to uncover their plans, and to help put an end to their machinations before they could inflict irreparable harm. It was a mission unlike any other, one that would test not just his skills as a SEAL, but the very fabric of his identity.

Captain Elliott nodded, a gesture of both approval and acknowledgment of the gravity of the task at hand. "We're counting on you, Thompson. Your knowledge of the area, your connections—they could be key to infiltrating the militia and gathering the intel we need to take them down. But remember, this mission requires more than just your skills as a SEAL. It demands discretion, tact, and a level of emotional resilience that will be tested at every turn."

"We've been tracking the members and who we believe to be their leader, Mark Dalton." the captain continued, clicking a remote to bring up aerial images of dense woodland, within which were scattered clusters of buildings and vehicles. "They've been operating under the radar in your hometown. Recent intel suggests they're ramping up their activities—stockpiling weapons, recruiting aggressively, and we've got chatter that suggests a large-scale operation might be imminent."

Captain Elliott's gaze hardened as he clicked to the next slide, the room's atmosphere growing even more somber. The image displayed appeared innocuous at first glance—a grainy photo of a local community center's charred remains. However, the story behind it was anything but.

"Two months ago," Elliott began, his voice carrying a weight that demanded attention, "the community center in the heart of town was gutted by a fire. Officially, it was an accident. Unofficially, we believe the Black Oak Militia was sending a message."

Jake leaned forward, his focus sharpening. He remembered the community center well; it was where he'd attended countless town meetings and where his high school basketball team celebrated their championship victory years ago. The idea that it could be a target...

"A message?" Jake asked, the words tight. "What kind of message?"

Elliott sighed, the lines on his face deepening. "A warning, to anyone who might oppose them. We intercepted communications shortly after the incident. They didn't claim responsibility outright, but the timing and the language used in their chatter..." He paused, choosing his next words carefully. "It suggests they're escalating, ready to move from intimidation to direct action."

The room fell silent as the implication hung heavy in the air. Jake felt a chill run down his spine. The community center wasn't just a building; it was a symbol of the town's unity and spirit. Attacking it, even indirectly, was a declaration of war against everything the town stood for.

"How certain are we about this connection?" Jake pressed, needing to understand the scope of the threat.

"We're not dealing with certainties, Thompson," Elliott replied, meeting his gaze squarely. "We're dealing with probabilities, and every piece of intel points to the Black Oak Militia. That's why you're here. That's why you're going back."

Jake nodded, the mission's stakes crystallizing in his mind. The loss of the community center was more than just property damage;

it was an assault on the town's heart. If the militia was willing to go that far, there was no telling what their next move might be.

As Captain Elliott continued outlining the mission, Jake's resolve hardened. He wasn't just fighting to infiltrate an extremist group; he was fighting to protect his home, to safeguard the memories and values embedded in every corner of the town. The incident at the community center was a stark reminder of what was at risk, and Jake knew there was no turning back.

The room fell silent as the implications of the captain's words sank in. Jake felt a chill run down his spine. The town he remembered as a peaceful community was now the backdrop for a domestic terrorist threat.

"Our intel is limited," Elliott admitted, his expression grim. "We know they're well-armed and well-funded, but their exact agenda is still unclear. That's where you come in, Thompson."

Jake listened intently as the captain outlined the mission. He was to infiltrate the Black Oak Militia under the guise of a disillusioned veteran seeking camaraderie and purpose. His objective was to gather intelligence on the militia's leadership, their operational capabilities, and their targets. It was a role that would exploit Jake's combat experience and his intimate knowledge of the town, but it also placed him in grave danger. Infiltrating a militia group was fraught with risks, and discovery would almost certainly mean death.

"You were chosen for this mission not just because of your skills as a SEAL, but because you're a hometown boy. You understand the people there, the geography. You blend in," Elliott said, locking eyes with Jake. "But make no mistake, this is going to be dangerous. You'll be working alone, without backup. We need someone on the inside, and you're the best fit for the job."

"What's our endgame, sir?" Jake asked, his voice steady.

"We stop them, by any means necessary," Elliott replied, his tone leaving no room for doubt. "We need to know what they're planning, and we need to dismantle their operation before they can act. You're our eyes and ears on the ground, Thompson. You find us the intel we need to take them down."

Jake nodded, a sense of resolve settling over him. This was more than a mission; it was a chance to protect his home from a threat that lurked in the shadows. He was no stranger to the horrors that men could inflict upon one another, but the thought of such darkness touching the streets where he had grown up was unfathomable.

"I'll do it," Jake said, the words firm and without hesitation.

Captain Elliott gave a curt nod, the ghost of a smile touching his lips. "I knew I could count on you, Thompson. Gear up. You have a lot to learn and a short time before you deploy."

As the briefing concluded, Jake was left to grapple with the weight of his assignment. The challenge before him was immense: to return to the familiar streets of his childhood, not as a prodigal son, but as a man on a mission to root out darkness from within. He would need to draw on every ounce of his training, his understanding of the town, and, most crucially, his moral compass, to navigate the perilous path ahead.

But beyond the danger, beyond the tactical challenges of his mission, lay the deeper, more personal battle he would face. Returning to his hometown as a ghost, hiding his true purpose behind a mask of camaraderie, would test him in ways he couldn't yet foresee. As he stood to leave, his resolve was clear. Whatever it took, he would protect his home from the darkness that threatened it. The mission was more than an assignment; it was a calling—one he would answer with his life, if necessary.

Crossroads of Duty and Home

Jake

The fluorescent lights of the briefing room flickered overhead, casting stark shadows across the maps and photographs strewn across the table. Captain Elliott stood at the head of the table, his gaze fixed on me.

"Thompson, this isn't going to be like any mission you've been on before," Captain Elliott began, his voice carrying the kind of gravity that commanded absolute attention. "You're heading back to your roots, to a place where you're not just a Navy SEAL, but where you're Jake Thompson."

I nodded, the weight of his words settling on my shoulders. Returning to my hometown for a mission had a surreal feel to it, blending the boundaries of my professional and personal lives in ways I had never anticipated.

"The Black Oak Militia," he continued, shifting the images on the screen to display several rugged-looking individuals, "has embedded itself deep within the community. Your task is to infiltrate them, gather intel, and identify their plan of action. And you'll be doing it all under the guise of Jake Thompson, hometown hero."

The room felt smaller as the reality of the mission sank in. I was to walk the streets I grew up on, not with the innocence of youth, but with the purpose of a man on a mission, a protector moving unseen among those he sought to defend.

"How do you suggest I approach this, sir?" I asked, already running through potential strategies in my mind. "They know me there. I can't just waltz in as someone else."

"That's precisely why you're perfect for this, Thompson," Elliott said, a hint of a smile breaking through his otherwise stern demeanor. "You're going in as yourself. But, we're spinning your narrative. You're disillusioned, a veteran who's seen too much and questions whether it was all worth it. That's your in."

The thought of playing up a version of myself that was disillusioned didn't sit well with me, but I understood the necessity. It was a role I would have to play convincingly, drawing on darker moments I'd faced to lend authenticity to the guise.

"Your first point of contact will be with Mitch Larson," Elliott added, pulling up a profile of a man I recognized from my youth. "He's been seen with militia members and seems to be a sympathizer. Your shared history might make him more inclined to open doors for you."

Mitch Larson. I hadn't thought about him in years. We played football together in high school, shared victories and losses. It was hard to reconcile that image with the man Elliott described, but I knew the mission came first.

"And if I'm made?" I asked, the question hanging heavy between us.

Elliott's gaze met mine, steady and unwavering. "You know the risks, Thompson. But we have every confidence in your abilities. You're not just fighting as a SEAL; you're fighting for your hometown, for the safety of people you grew up with."

Silence filled the room as the weight of the mission settled over me. It was more than duty; it was personal. I was not only the Navy's weapon but also the town's shield. The dual nature of this mission, bridging my past and present, was daunting, but I knew my resolve had to be ironclad.

"Understood, sir. I won't let you down."

As the briefing concluded and I made my way out, the challenge ahead seemed monumental, a delicate balance of blending in while standing apart, of protecting without revealing. But amid the complexities, my determination was clear. This was my mission, my fight. For my country, my town, and for the peace of those unknowingly resting on the brink of danger.

In the days that followed the briefing, I was thrust into an intensive training regimen tailored specifically for undercover work. The facility, a nondescript compound far from prying eyes, became my world—a place where the boundaries of my abilities were tested and expanded.

Each day was a grueling marathon of physical and mental challenges. Mornings started before the sun rose, with physical conditioning that pushed me to my limits, followed by classes that felt more like mental gymnastics than anything else. I learned the art of blending in—not just changing my appearance, but adopting mannerisms and speech patterns that would make me indistinguishable from any other disillusioned veteran.

"Remember, Thompson, the key to deep cover isn't just about not standing out—it's about fitting in so seamlessly that you become invisible," my instructor, a former undercover agent whose name I never learned, would say. His lessons were punctuated with stories from the field, real-life tales of close calls and the importance of psychological manipulation in gaining and maintaining trust.

In the afternoons, we practiced counter-surveillance techniques in mock urban environments, learning to spot tails and evade detection. "Always assume you're being watched," another instructor drilled into us. "Your life—and the mission—depends on it."

In a small, dimly lit room adorned with nothing but a table and a few chairs, I sat down with a team of intelligence officers. The air was thick with anticipation and the weight of the task ahead. These were the people who would help me weave my new identity, one that would stand up to the scrutiny of the Black Oak Militia and anyone else who might question my presence back in town.

"We've got to make this believable, Thompson," one of the officers, a woman with sharp eyes and a no-nonsense demeanor named Agent Harris, began. "Your cover story isn't just a shield—it's your weapon in this environment. It needs to be bulletproof."

We started with the basics, the framework of my identity that would remain unchanged—I was Jake Thompson, a Navy SEAL returning home. But the reasons for my return, the layers of my supposed disillusionment, needed to be crafted with care.

"You've seen combat, experienced loss, and faced the complexities of modern warfare," another officer, Agent Martinez, chimed in, flipping through my file. "Let's build on that. You're coming home because you're searching for a sense of peace, something you couldn't find in the military."

It was a narrative close enough to the truth that it stung. I had seen too much, lost too much, but my mission was far from a quest for personal peace. Still, it was a story I could tell convincingly because, in some ways, it mirrored the inner conflicts I had grappled with in silence.

"We'll say you've grown disillusioned not with the ideals of service, but with the institution itself—the bureaucracy, the politics, the sense of being a small cog in a vast and often indifferent machine," Agent Harris added, her pen flying across her notebook as she spoke.

As we dove deeper, integrating elements of my real background into the cover story, the line between the persona I was adopting and my true self began to blur. We discussed how I'd talk about my time in the SEALs, focusing on the camaraderie and the sense of brotherhood, subtly implying that it was something I sought but ultimately found lacking in the broader context of the military.

Agent Martinez suggested adding a personal project to my narrative—a reason for my prolonged stay in town that would seem innocuous but provide cover for my activities. "Maybe you're fixing up your late grandfather's house," he proposed. "It gives you a reason to be here, a connection to the community, and it's a solitary project that would believably occupy your time."

That hit close to home. My grandfather, a veteran himself, had been one of my greatest influences, and his passing had left a void in my life. Incorporating him into my cover story felt like both a tribute and a deception.

As the meeting drew to a close, we had outlined a comprehensive cover story, complete with details about my supposed disillusionment, my reasons for returning home, and my activities in town. It was a narrative woven from threads of truth and fiction, designed to protect me and further the mission.

Stepping out of the room, I felt armed and ready, but also heavy with the knowledge that every interaction from here on out would be a performance. The story we'd crafted was my armor, but it also served as a constant reminder of the stakes. I was no longer just Jake Thompson, Navy SEAL; I was Jake Thompson, the prodigal son searching for meaning in the ashes of his past, walking a tightrope between two worlds.

But it was the evenings, in the solitude of my quarters, that the full weight of the mission settled on me. I'd sit alone, poring over maps of my hometown, memorizing faces of known militia members, and rehearsing my backstory until it felt like a second skin. It was during these moments of solitude that doubts would creep in, whispering fears about what awaited me. Could I really infiltrate the militia without being discovered? What if my actions put the very people I was trying to protect in danger?

Yet, with each passing day, my resolve hardened. The personal stakes of this mission went beyond any I had faced before. This wasn't just about national security; it was about protecting my home, the people who had shaped me into the man I was. The thought of the militia's ideology taking root in the streets where I played as a kid, threatening the peace of the community that raised me, fueled my determination.

I found a renewed focus in my training, a clarity of purpose. I wasn't just preparing for a mission; I was preparing to defend my past, my memories, and the future of my hometown. The skills I honed, from blending in to psychological manipulation, weren't just tools for infiltration; they were my weapons in the fight to come.

As the final days of training drew to a close, I felt a transformation within me. The man who arrived at the compound, a SEAL trained for combat, had evolved into someone far more complex—a warrior equipped not just with physical prowess but with the subtlety and nuance required for the shadow war I was about to enter.

The night before my return to the town that had shaped me, I found myself alone with my thoughts, the cover story carefully crafted with the intelligence team echoing in my mind. It was a solid plan, one that leveraged my real experiences and emotions, making it all the more convincing—and all the more difficult to bear.

Sitting in the sparse room provided for me at the base, I turned over the dog tags in my hand, a tangible link to my past and a constant reminder of the weight of the duty I carried. The quiet of the night allowed my thoughts to drift, inevitably, to what awaited me in the town I once called home. Memories long boxed away began to surface: the sound of laughter echoing down high school hallways, the thrill of Friday night football games, and the peace of early morning fishing trips before the world woke up. Each memory carried a bittersweet edge, a reminder of what I was fighting to protect but also what I had lost.

Among those memories was Emily—vibrant, passionate Emily, whose dreams had always been too big for our small town. Our breakup, though mutual, had left unresolved feelings that time had never fully erased. The thought of seeing her again, of potentially putting her in danger, added a layer of personal risk to the mission that I hadn't fully anticipated. It wasn't just the physical dangers of infiltrating the Black Oak Militia that I had to navigate; it was the emotional minefield of my past.

In the silence of my room, I acknowledged the dual roles I was about to undertake: the protector, committed to safeguarding the community from a threat they didn't even know existed, and the man, Jake Thompson, who couldn't help but feel the pull of his roots and the unresolved chapters of his life.

I realized then that my emotional preparation was as crucial as the physical and tactical training I had undergone. Steeling my mind, I focused on the mission, reminding myself of the stakes. The safety of the town, the protection of its people, was paramount. Any personal feelings, any lingering regrets or what-ifs, had to be secondary. My role as a protector demanded nothing less.

Yet, acknowledging the emotional challenges didn't diminish them; it only made me more aware of the tightrope I would be walking. Every interaction, every decision, would be fraught with the tension of my dual identity. I would need to navigate not only the dangers posed by the militia but also the complexities of returning to a life I had left behind.

As the night deepened, I made a quiet vow to myself. No matter what lay ahead, no matter the personal cost, I would fulfill my duty. I would protect my town, confront my past, and face whatever feelings arose with the same determination and courage that had defined my career as a SEAL.

The dawn found me resolute, ready to face the challenges of the mission. The emotional turmoil, the anticipation of confronting my past, had been acknowledged, but it would not deter me. I was a SEAL, trained to face any adversity, but I was also Jake Thompson, coming home with a purpose. The duality of my role was my strength, not my weakness, and I was ready to embrace whatever lay ahead.

Shadows and Warnings

Emily

The early morning light filtered through the dusty blinds of the small office, casting a warm glow over the cluttered desk that once belonged to my father. Surrounded by stacks of old newspapers, the sound of the aging clock on the wall ticked in sync with my heartbeat. Here, amidst the remnants of stories told and untold, I found my sanctuary.

I ran my fingers over the edges of the yellowed clippings that adorned the walls, each one a testament to my father's legacy—a legacy of truth, of fighting for the underdog, of never backing down no matter the cost. His articles covered the walls like wallpaper, stories that had shaken the foundations of our small town and, sometimes, even beyond.

As I settled into the chair that seemed molded from years of his presence, I couldn't help but feel a surge of pride mixed with a twinge of sorrow. He had been more than a journalist; he was a beacon of integrity in a world that often felt overshadowed by deceit and corruption. And now, with his pen passed down to me, the weight of expectation hung heavy in the air.

Today, like many days before, I was reminded of why I chose this path. Not for the accolades or the recognition, but because, through these articles, through his relentless pursuit of the truth, my father had made a difference. He had given a voice to those who had none, and in doing so, had taught me the value of words, of stories, of the truth.

I opened my laptop, the screen illuminating the collection of notes and leads I had compiled over the weeks. Top of my list was the Black Oak Militia, a shadow that had been growing over our town, unseen yet palpably present. Rumors had been swirling, whispers of meetings in the dead of night, of plans that could endanger the very fabric of our community.

My father had once said, "Journalism is not about writing stories; it's about telling the truth, no matter how uncomfortable it may be." It was a mantra I lived by, one that had guided me through every story, every investigation. And as I stared at the blinking cursor on the screen, I knew that uncovering the truth about the militia would be my most challenging story yet.

But I was determined. Because to step back, to ignore the growing unrest, would be a disservice to the legacy my father left behind. This desk, these clippings, were not just reminders of the past; they were a call to action—a call to continue the fight for truth, for justice.

With a deep breath, I began to type, each word a step forward in the shadow of my father's legacy. The path ahead was uncertain, fraught with challenges and dangers I could only begin to imagine. But one thing was clear: I was ready to face whatever lay ahead, armed with nothing but my words and the unyielding spirit my father had instilled in me.

The journey of a thousand stories begins with a single truth, and for me, that truth lay in the heart of my hometown, waiting to be uncovered. And as the sun rose higher, casting light into the darkest corners of the room, I felt a renewed sense of purpose. I was Emily Harris, journalist, seeker of truth, and my story was just beginning.

Stepping out of the newspaper office into the bustling streets of our small town felt like stepping back in time. The town, with its quaint shops and friendly faces, hadn't changed much over the years, but I had.

"Emily! Just the person I wanted to see," Mrs. Jenkins called out from her bakery, the aroma of fresh bread wafting into the street. She waved me over with a flour-dusted hand. "When are you going to settle down and give your mother some grandchildren? You know, before it's too late."

I forced a smile, the familiar question echoing the sentiments of a town stuck in time. "I'm not sure, Mrs. Jenkins. There's so much I want to do first," I replied, my voice trailing off as I caught the bemused look on her face.

"Oh, honey," she sighed, shaking her head as if my ambitions were a quaint, misguided dream. "You're such a bright girl. It'd be a shame to see all that go to waste."

As I excused myself, her words lingered in my mind, a stark reminder of the expectations placed on me. To many in town, my worth was measured by milestones I had no interest in rushing toward.

Walking further, I ran into Mr. Carlson, the high school history teacher. "Emily, still chasing stories, I see. Your father was a good journalist, but don't you think it's time to think about a real career?"

"A real career," I mused, the words stinging. To them, journalism was just a hobby, a phase. They couldn't understand that to me, it was a calling.

Each interaction was a gentle, sometimes not-so-gentle, nudge towards the life they envisioned for me—one of domestic bliss and conformity. But beneath the surface of their well-meaning advice lay an undercurrent of expectation that I found suffocating.

In the privacy of my thoughts, I rebelled against their visions for my future. My ambitions stretched far beyond the town's borders, fueled by a desire to make an impact, to tell stories that mattered. I wanted to follow in my father's footsteps, not to tread the well-worn path laid out before me by tradition.

As I continued my walk, the contrast between the community's expectations and my personal ambitions became even more apparent. I wasn't content with the status quo; I yearned for more—more challenges, more growth, more opportunities to make a difference. My resolve to transcend small-town roles and make my mark on the world through journalism only grew stronger with each passing conversation.

These interactions, while disheartening, served as a reminder of why my work was so important. In a town where the unconventional was often met with skepticism, my pursuit of truth and justice through journalism was an act of defiance—a declaration of my independence and a testament to my determination to carve my own path.

And so, with each step, I reaffirmed my commitment to my craft, to uncovering the stories that lay hidden beneath the surface of our seemingly idyllic town. My ambition to impact the world beyond through journalism was undiminished by the expectations that sought to hold me back. I was Emily Harris, and I had a story to tell—a story that would transcend the confines of this small town and echo far beyond its borders.

***

The quaint little café at the corner of Main and Elm was buzzing with the usual morning crowd when I overheard it—the whispered conversation that would change the course of my next big story. Tucked away at a small table near the back, nursing a cup of coffee that had long gone cold, I was lost in thought over my next article when the murmurs caught my attention.

"...and they say it's the Black Oak Militia behind it," a voice said, barely above a whisper.

"The militia?" another voice questioned, skepticism lacing their tone. "Here? You're pulling my leg."

"No, seriously," the first voice insisted. "Mark Dalton was seen around, and you know his type. They're planning something big, or so I've heard."

Mark Dalton. The name wasn't unfamiliar. Rumors about him and his fringe beliefs had circulated before, but the mention of the Black Oak Militia was new—and alarming. My journalistic instincts kicked in, my previous apathy towards my coffee forgotten. I pretended to focus on my laptop, but my ears were tuned to the conversation, absorbing every detail.

As the voices lowered further, straining to catch more became futile. I closed my laptop, my mind racing with questions. The Black Oak Militia's presence in our town was a significant development, one that could have far-reaching implications for the safety and stability of our community.

I paid for my coffee and left the café, the seed of curiosity firmly planted. My first stop was the newspaper office, where I scoured our archives for any mention of the militia or Mark Dalton. Finding nothing, I realized we were potentially facing a story that had flown under everyone's radar—a story that, if true, needed to be brought to light.

The rest of the day I worked on this. I dialed the familiar number of Sergeant Reynolds, a contact within the local police department who had always been a reliable source of information. The line rang twice before he picked up, his voice carrying the weary undertone of a man stretched thin.

"Reynolds speaking."

"Sergeant Reynolds, it's Emily Harris," I began, trying to inject a note of casualness into my voice. "I'm looking into some activity around town, thought you might have some insights. Anything on the Black Oak Militia?"

There was a pause on the line, a moment of silence that spoke volumes. "Emily, that's a delicate topic," he finally replied, his tone guarded. "Why the sudden interest in them?"

I leaned forward, sensing the reluctance in his voice. "Rumors are swirling, and if there's a story, I intend to find it. Anything you can share would be helpful."

Another pause, longer this time. "Look, Emily, I'm not at liberty to discuss ongoing investigations, but I'll say this—be careful. This isn't your typical story. The Black Oak Militia... they're not just local troublemakers. There's more at play here, and it's dangerous."

The warning sent a chill down my spine, but it also steeled my resolve. "I understand the risks, Sergeant. But the community has a right to know if there's a threat. Any guidance you can offer would be invaluable."

Reynolds sighed, a sound heavy with unspoken concerns. "Just... keep your eyes open, and don't dive too deep. And Emily, watch your back. These people, they don't take kindly to prying eyes."

The call ended with a click, leaving me staring at the phone in my hand, the weight of his words settling around me like a cloak. It was the first of many conversations that day, each call weaving a tapestry of caution and veiled warnings.

I reached out to Deputy Mayor Thompson next, hoping for a political angle or perhaps a less restrained perspective. But the response was eerily similar, a mixture of concern for my safety and a palpable tension whenever the militia's name was mentioned. "It's a sensitive issue, Emily," Thompson had said, his voice tight. "We're working on it, but for now, it's best left alone."

The pattern continued as I called other contacts—old classmates now in law enforcement, a few reluctant sources within the town hall, and even a couple of off-the-record chats with folks I knew had their ear close to the ground. Each conversation added layers of complexity to the story but also heightened my sense of unease.

The sun had long since set by the time I finished my calls, the darkness outside mirroring the shadowy nature of the investigation before me. The warnings to tread carefully, to not dig too deep, echoed in my mind, a chorus of voices united by fear and concern.

But alongside the caution, there was also a thread of defiance, a shared recognition of the importance of bringing the truth to light. The Black Oak Militia, a group shrouded in secrecy and rumor, had become a palpable presence in our town, and the implications of their activities were too significant to ignore.

As I sat in the dim light of my office, surrounded by notes and half-formed leads, I realized that this story was more than a challenge—it was a test of my resolve, of my commitment to journalism and to the town that had shaped me. The warnings had made one thing clear: the path ahead would be fraught with danger, but the story of the Black Oak Militia needed to be told, and I was the one to tell it.

Frustrated but undeterred, I decided to widen my net. The town's library was my next destination, where historical records and local newspaper archives from years past could provide context or clues. Hours passed as I dug through old documents, piecing together fragments of information that hinted at a network of discontent simmering beneath the surface of our town's placid exterior.

By the end of the day, I had more questions than answers, but my determination had only solidified. The Black Oak Militia's activities were more than just idle gossip; they were a story that demanded investigation. And I, Emily Harris, was going to uncover it.

As I organized my notes and planned my next steps, I felt the familiar thrill of the hunt, the drive to pursue the truth wherever it led. This wasn't just another article; it was a mission to expose the shadows lurking in our midst, to protect my community by bringing its potential threats into the light.

The whispers in the café had opened a door to a hidden world, and I was stepping through it, armed with nothing but my pen and my resolve. The Black Oak Militia didn't know it yet, but their days of operating in the dark were numbered. I was on their trail, and I wouldn't rest until their story was told.

The glow of my computer screen was the only light in the room as night enveloped the town outside. Armed with a determination to peel back the layers of secrecy surrounding the Black Oak Militia, I dove into the depths of my investigation, starting with the digital world. Online forums, social media groups, and obscure websites became my initial hunting grounds, places where whispers and rumors often found a voice.

I sifted through countless posts and threads, deciphering coded language and piecing together fragmented information. It was like assembling a puzzle without the picture on the box as a guide. Every mention of the militia, every veiled reference to their activities, added another piece to the increasingly complex image I was constructing.

The digital trail led me next to the local archives, a treasure trove of historical documents and past editions of our town's newspaper. Here, in the musty air filled with the scent of old paper, I searched for any precedent, any past mentions that might shed light on the militia's origins or objectives. Hours turned into days as I combed through records, my eyes scanning microfiche screens and yellowed pages for any clue.

Among the routine announcements and local news, I found it—a series of articles from decades ago, hinting at a group with similar ideologies to the militia's current rhetoric. These weren't direct references to the Black Oak Militia itself but to a seed of discontent that had seemingly found fertile ground in recent years.

With a growing sense of unease, I turned to police reports, requesting information under the guise of following up on community safety concerns. The responses were guarded, the details scant, but the underlying message was clear: there was a hesitance, perhaps even a fear, regarding the militia's growing presence.

Each step of my investigation, each hour spent in the digital and physical archives, deepened my understanding but also my concern. The Black Oak Militia was more than just a group of disillusioned individuals; it was an organized entity with a reach and influence that had silently permeated my hometown.

My notes began to form a daunting picture, one that hinted at preparations for something significant, something potentially dangerous. The absence of concrete evidence was frustrating, but the implications of my findings were impossible to ignore. The militia was planning something, and the lack of transparency, the whispers of clandestine meetings, all pointed to an event that could disrupt the very fabric of our community.

As I leaned back in my chair, the weight of my discovery pressing down on me, I realized the magnitude of the story unfolding before me. This wasn't just another article; it was a call to action. The people of my town deserved to know the truth about the forces moving in the shadows, and I was determined to bring that truth to light.

My initial investigation had laid the groundwork, but it was clear that uncovering the full extent of the Black Oak Militia's influence would require more than just digging through records and reports. It would require confronting the militia head-on, piecing together the scattered whispers into a narrative that could no longer be ignored.

Determined and more focused than ever, I prepared for the next phase of my investigation. The path ahead was uncertain, fraught with challenges and risks, but I was undeterred. Armed with my findings and fueled by a sense of duty to my community, I was ready to delve deeper into the shadows, to expose the Black Oak Militia and the threat they posed. The truth was out there, and I, Emily Harris, was going to find it.

Jake's Return

Jake

The familiar outline of my hometown emerged on the horizon, a tapestry of memories and emotions intertwined with the mission at hand. As I drove the familiar roads, the weight of my dual identity settled heavily on me. I was Jake Thompson, Navy SEAL turned undercover operative, returning to a place that once defined me, now armed with a purpose far removed from the carefree days of my youth.

Turning off the main road, I passed the old high school, its brick facade a silent witness to years gone by. I couldn't help but glance at the football field, where echoes of past victories still lingered in my mind. Yet, the nostalgia was quickly overshadowed by the task ahead. The town that had once been my entire world seemed smaller now, its boundaries more defined against the backdrop of my experiences beyond.

My first stop was Larson's Auto, a place that held no significance to the mission but was pivotal for my cover. Mitch Larson, once a high school teammate, now a potential link to the Black Oak Militia. The bell above the door jingled as I stepped inside, the familiar scent of oil and metal greeting me.

"Jake Thompson, as I live and breathe," Mitch exclaimed, genuine surprise in his voice as he emerged from behind a car. "Never thought I'd see you back here."

"Life's full of surprises," I replied, forcing a smile as I extended my hand. The handshake was firm, the interaction laced with unspoken questions.

"What brings you back, man?" Mitch asked, wiping his hands on a rag.

"Just needed a break from everything. Figured it was time to come home, you know?" I answered, sticking to the script we had crafted. The half-truth felt heavy on my tongue.

Mitch nodded, a knowing look in his eyes. "Well, you picked an interesting time to come back. Things have been... different around here."

His vague statement piqued my interest, a hint of the underlying tensions I had been briefed on. "Different how?"

"Just the usual small-town drama, magnified. You'll see," he said, quickly changing the subject. "Anyway, if you're sticking around, we should catch up. Grab a beer, talk about the old times."

I agreed, seeing an opportunity to glean more information. "Sounds good, Mitch. I'll take you up on that."

Leaving Larson's Auto, I couldn't shake the feeling of unease that Mitch's words had stirred. The town might look the same on the surface, but the undercurrents of change were palpable. I continued my reconnaissance, driving through neighborhoods and past landmarks that were etched in my memory. Each turn revealed more about the town's current state—the boarded-up shops downtown, the new security cameras outside the bank, the tension in people's faces as they went about their day.

It was clear that the Black Oak Militia's influence had seeped into the very fabric of the community, altering its rhythm, its mood. And amidst this familiar yet now foreign landscape, I found myself grappling with my own transformation. The streets where I once roamed without a care were now arenas of observation, each interaction a measure of the distance between who I was and who I needed to be.

It was in this moment of quiet reflection, with the mission pressing heavily on my mind, that thoughts of Emily began to surface unbidden. Emily Harris—her image was as clear in my mind as if I had seen her just yesterday, not years ago.

I wondered, with a mix of anticipation and apprehension, if she was still around, if her dreams had taken her far from this place or if our paths might cross once again on these all-too-familiar streets. Emily, with her fiery determination and passion for truth, had always seemed destined for more than what our small town could offer. Yet, the thought of her still being here, perhaps even investigating the same shadows that I was sent to infiltrate, added a layer of complexity to my return that I hadn't fully anticipated.

As I drove through the town earlier, I found myself scanning the faces of passersby, half-expecting, half-dreading to see her among them. Would she recognize me, the Jake Thompson she once knew, beneath the guise of my undercover persona? And more importantly, how would I reconcile the flood of emotions her presence would undoubtedly stir with the focus required for my mission?

These thoughts of Emily, mixed with the memories of what we once shared, were a stark reminder of the life I had left behind. They underscored the duality of my return—not just as a protector of my hometown but as a man confronting the remnants of his past. The possibility of seeing Emily again, of having to navigate the intricate dance of reconnecting while concealing my true purpose, was a complication I hadn't fully considered.

Yet, as the night settled in, enveloping the town in darkness, I realized that thoughts of Emily could not distract me from the task at hand. If she was still here, involved in some way with the unfolding events, our paths would inevitably cross. Until then, I needed to focus on the mission, on the reason I had come back to this place that held so many memories.

The town had changed, and so had I. The person Emily knew, the person I was, had been shaped by experiences and duties far beyond these town limits. I couldn't afford to let my guard down, to let past affections cloud my judgment. The stakes were too high.

With a deep breath, I started the car and pulled away from the overlook, the town spread out below me like a map of intertwined destinies. Whether or not Emily and I would cross paths remained to be seen, but for now, my mission—and the protection of our hometown—had to be my sole focus. The days ahead promised to reveal much, about the Black Oak Militia, about the town, and perhaps, about myself and Emily too.

Under the cloak of night, the town felt different, its familiar contours shadowed by the mission that lay heavy on my shoulders. I had driven aimlessly, lost in thought, until I found myself parked outside the Rusty Anchor, a local bar that had always been a gathering spot for townsfolk. It was here, I decided, that I would begin my cautious dance with danger, taking my first deliberate steps towards infiltrating the Black Oak Militia.

Stepping into the dimly lit interior, the murmur of conversations and the clink of glasses greeted me like an old friend. Scanning the room, I recognized a few faces, nods of acknowledgment exchanged, but my attention was drawn to a figure seated alone at the far end of the bar. Even from a distance, there was something familiar about him, and as I approached, the recognition clicked. It was Derek Simmons, a name that had come up in my briefing as a known associate of the militia.

"Derek Simmons," I called out as I approached, keeping my tone casual, "it's been a long time."

He looked up, his expression one of surprise that shifted quickly to suspicion. "Jake Thompson? Well, I'll be damned. What brings you back to town?"

"Just needed a change of scenery," I replied, taking a seat beside him, my heart rate steady despite the adrenaline coursing through my veins. "Heard you've been keeping busy," I added, watching for his reaction.

Derek's eyes narrowed slightly, a guarded look settling in. "You could say that. Times are changing, Jake. Not everyone's happy with the way things are going."

His words were laced with an undertone of defiance, a hint at the unrest simmering beneath the surface. I nodded, feigning a shared understanding. "I've seen a lot, been a lot of places. Makes you think about what you're fighting for, you know?"

Derek took a sip of his drink, his gaze still fixed on me. "And what are you fighting for, Thompson?"

The question was a test, a moment of truth that would either solidify my cover or expose me before I even began. "Peace, I guess," I said, letting a hint of disillusionment color my voice. "A place where a man can live without being told how to think, how to be. Seems like that's getting harder to find."

A slow nod from Derek, and I sensed a thawing, the first crack in the barrier he had erected. "You might be onto something there, Jake. Maybe there's more for you to find here than you think."

As the conversation shifted to more neutral topics, I knew I had passed the initial test. But this was just the beginning, the first cautious step into the murky waters of infiltration. Derek Simmons, with his links to the militia, could be my in, but every interaction was a risk, every word exchanged a potential slip in the intricate dance of deception.

Leaving the Rusty Anchor that night, the cool air felt sharper against my skin, a reminder of the thin ice upon which I tread. The encounter with Derek had set the stage for the complex mission ahead, a mission that would require all my skills in observation, deception, and reconnaissance. The path forward was fraught with danger, but I was committed. For my town, for the people unaware of the shadow growing among them, I would walk this tightrope.

And as I drove away, the bar fading into the rearview mirror, I couldn't help but feel the gravity of what lay ahead. The game had begun, and there was no turning back. The night had marked my first contact with the world I sought to infiltrate, a world that would test my resolve, my identity, and my heart in ways I had yet to imagine.

***

Leaving this place, I had been a boy fueled by a fervent desire to serve, inspired by my grandfather's tales of valor and sacrifice. His stories, woven from the threads of war and heroism, had sculpted my ambitions, instilling in me a profound sense of duty that had propelled me into the arms of the Navy, and eventually, the SEALs. There, I found a purpose and a brotherhood that tested and tempered my spirit. Yet, this new belonging, while fulfilling, had ensconced my heart within walls thickened by necessity, isolating me within a fortress of my own making.

The return to my roots, to this bastion of my formative years, was not merely a physical journey but an emotional pilgrimage, a trek across the intricate landscape of my own heart. The tranquility of the town, so at odds with the turmoil within me, served as a mirror, reflecting the chasm between the boy who left with dreams of heroism and the man who returned, burdened by the realities of the duty he had so eagerly embraced.

As I crossed the threshold into the town, the weight of my grandfather's legacy felt both comforting and constrictive, a mantle that had guided me but also set me apart. The camaraderie and purpose I found in the SEALs, precious and revered, had also forged a barrier between me and the world I left behind, a barrier now made all the more palpable by my return.

Now, leaving the dim warmth of the Rusty Anchor behind, I stepped out into the crisp night air, the encounter with Derek Simmons echoing in my mind. It was a beginning, fraught with the tension of what lay ahead. I slid into the driver's seat of my car, the engine coming to life with a comforting rumble, and pulled away from the curb, my thoughts already turning to the next phase of my mission.

The drive to my grandfather's house took me through the heart of town, past landmarks steeped in personal history. Each street corner, each faded storefront held a piece of my past, a reminder of days long gone. But it was the house at the end of Maple Street that held the deepest significance, the place where my story for returning had rooted itself—in the home of a man who had shaped so much of who I had become.

The house stood silent in the moonlight, its familiar silhouette a stark contrast against the night sky. My grandfather, a man of strength and quiet dignity, had passed away while I was deployed, leaving the house empty, a shell of the memories it once held. As I parked the car and stepped out, the weight of those memories settled around me like a cloak.

Walking up the path, I could almost hear his voice, feel the roughness of his hands as he taught me to fix things, to build, to create. He was the one who had instilled in me the values of service and sacrifice, who had inspired my path to becoming a Navy SEAL. Now, his house, neglected and in disrepair, stood as my cover story and my reason for returning. It was a story grounded in truth, the pain of loss and the duty to honor his memory woven into the very fabric of my mission.

As I unlocked the door and stepped inside, the stillness of the house enveloped me. Dust motes danced in the beam of my flashlight, the air heavy with the scent of disuse. Each room held echoes of laughter, of conversations long past, of moments frozen in time. It was as if the house was holding its breath, waiting for life to return to its empty halls.

Standing there, in the home that had once been a beacon of warmth and love, I felt the full force of my emotions. The sadness for my grandfather's passing, the longing for simpler times, and the stark reality of my current situation merged into a poignant sense of purpose. I was here to protect, to serve, to fight against the shadows that threatened this town, but I was also here to reconnect with my roots, to honor the memory of the man who had taught me what it meant to be courageous.

Fixing up the house would not only serve as a convincing cover for my presence in town but would also be my tribute to him, a way to keep his spirit alive even as I navigated the dangerous waters of my mission. It was a tangible link to my past, a reminder of why I was fighting, and a beacon of hope in the darkness that loomed ahead.

As I closed the door behind me, stepping further into the darkness, I resolved to face the challenges ahead with the same strength and integrity my grandfather had exemplified. The road ahead was uncertain, fraught with danger and deceit, but I was determined to see it through. For my town, for my grandfather, and for the legacy he had left behind.

Later, as I stood on the porch, the night had cloaked the town in a mantle of tranquility, the kind of peace that seemed almost alien after years spent in the clutches of chaos. Below, the town lay sprawled, a mosaic of light and shadow, its serenity belying the storm that brewed beneath the surface. In this moment of solitude, I allowed myself a moment of reflection on the dual purpose of my return. On paper, I was a soldier on leave, seeking the solace of familiar sights and the comfort of family to salve the wounds wrought by war. Yet, beneath this benign facade, a more ominous objective lurked, casting a long shadow over my intentions.

My mission, assigned with the weighty assurance of necessity, was to infiltrate the Black Oak Militia, a task that summoned a maelstrom of conflict within me. This group, veiled in secrecy and driven by ideals antithetical to the values I had sworn to protect, posed a clear and present danger not just to the national security I had dedicated my life to safeguard, but to the very heart of this community. The thought of the Black Oak woods, once a sanctuary of innocent escapades and whispered promises, now a bastion for those who sought to tear apart the fabric of our society, filled me with a profound sense of betrayal.

As I gazed out into the night, the weight of what lay ahead pressed down on me with an almost physical force. The irony of my position was not lost on me. I had left this town as a young man eager to defend my country, only to return as a shadow, tasked with rooting out an enemy nestled within the bosom of my own home. The lines between duty and deception blurred, weaving a complex tapestry of moral quandaries that I struggled to navigate.

The Black Oak Militia, with its insidious agenda cloaked in the guise of patriotism, represented a perversion of the ideals I held dear. My role, to infiltrate their ranks and expose their machinations, felt akin to walking a tightrope suspended over an abyss. Each step forward brought me closer to my objective, yet the risk of losing myself in the darkness that I sought to combat loomed ever larger.

The tranquility of the night, once a source of comfort, now echoed with the silent screams of potential futures destroyed by the actions of the few. The realization that my efforts, if successful, could prevent such loss, provided a cold comfort, a beacon of purpose in the enveloping darkness. Yet, the cost of this mission, the potential rifts it could create within this community and within my own soul, cast a long shadow over the path I had chosen to walk.

As the night deepened, and the lights of the town flickered like stars grounded to the earth, I wrestled with the enormity of my task. The role I had to play, that of a prodigal son returned, belied the truth of my presence, a truth that if revealed, could shatter the fragile peace of this place I once called home. The burden of this knowledge, of the double life I was forced to lead, weighed heavily upon me, a constant reminder of the sacrifices demanded by duty, and the price of secrets kept in the service of a greater good.

The thought of Emily wove itself through the fabric of my musings, a thread of gold amid the darker strands of my mission's purpose. Our history, rich with the vibrant hues of first love and the deep shadows of parting, painted a complex portrait of what we once were to each other. Those days, when our biggest concerns were the whispers of the wind through the Black Oak woods and the promises we etched into the bark of ancient trees, seemed like relics of another lifetime, artifacts of a simpler age. Yet, the mere possibility of crossing paths with her again sent ripples of anticipation through the still waters of my heart.

This blend of excitement and dread was a paradox I struggled to reconcile. On one hand, the thought of reconnecting with Emily, of rediscovering the cadence of her laugh and the warmth of her smile, ignited a spark of hope within me, a yearning for a sliver of light in the midst of the shadows that had become my constant companions. The idea of sharing even a moment with her, to see if the connection that once bound us could still exist, was a thrilling prospect.

Yet, entwined with this anticipation was a coil of apprehension, tightening around my heart with the knowledge of the danger my presence here represented. My mission, should it be exposed, could thrust Emily into a maelstrom of peril, her life endangered simply by association. The thought of her being targeted, of the brightness in her eyes dimming with fear, was a specter that haunted my every step. This dread, this fear for her safety, cast a long shadow over the flicker of excitement, reminding me of the stakes at play.

Emily had always possessed a fierce determination and a boundless capacity for compassion, qualities that no doubt propelled her forward in her pursuit of truth as a journalist. Her knack for unearthing stories that lay hidden beneath the surface made her admirable, but in the context of my mission, it also made her vulnerable. The thought of her inadvertently stumbling upon the web of deceit I was weaving, of her journalistic instincts leading her into the crosshairs of the very danger I sought to contain, was a possibility that chilled me to the core.

Moreover, the complexity of our past, the unresolved threads of our story, added layers to my apprehension. The ember of our connection, never fully extinguished, now threatened to ignite amidst the most dangerous of circumstances. The prospect of rekindling what we had, under the shadow of my secrets and lies, felt like a betrayal of the honesty that had once defined us. The exhilaration of potentially reconnecting with Emily was thus tempered by the reality of my mission, a balancing act between the desire to reach out and the necessity of maintaining distance.

As I stood there, overlooking the town that cradled both my past and my perilous present, the silhouette of Emily in my mind's eye was both a beacon of hope and a harbinger of potential heartbreak. The complexity of these emotions, the intertwining of longing and fear, underscored the duality of my return. It was a reminder that every step I took was fraught with implications, not just for me, but for the people who were once my entire world.

Emily's Lead

Emily

Walking away from the diner the next morning, I couldn't help but feel the shift in the air. Main Street, with its cozy storefronts and the gentle sway of the old oak trees lining the sidewalks, had always represented a haven of predictability. Yet now, an undercurrent of unease seemed to thread through the familiar, a subtle disruption in the fabric of our everyday lives.

The conversations I had inadvertently become a part of over my morning coffee yesterday weren't the usual fare of small-town gossip. They were laced with an edge of concern, a sense of something amiss that the community was not yet fully willing to confront. The mention of military-grade equipment and secretive gatherings wasn't meant for the ears of a casual listener; it was shared in hushed tones, a testament to the growing anxiety among the townsfolk.

The journalist in me knew that rumors and hearsay were not enough. Solid reporting required evidence, corroboration, and a deep understanding of the story's implications. The snippets of conversation from the diner were a starting point, but they were just the tip of the iceberg. What was the militia's agenda? Who were its members, and what drove them to seek out military-grade equipment? Were these secretive meetings a sign of something sinister, or merely the misunderstood gatherings of a few enthusiasts?

These questions formed the backbone of my investigation. Each piece of the puzzle needed to be meticulously uncovered, examined, and fitted into place. My approach had to be methodical, starting with the most accessible sources and branching out into the more elusive. The gun shop, with its recent spike in unusual sales, was a logical next step. But beyond that, the woods themselves beckoned, a silent witness to the meetings that had set the rumor mill ablaze.

As I walked, my mind buzzed with the potential angles of this story, the paths my investigation could take, and the impact it could have on our community. The challenge was invigorating, a reminder of why I had chosen this path. Journalism was not just about reporting facts; it was about understanding the heart of a story and its significance to those whose lives it touched. It was about holding a mirror up to society and asking the hard questions, even when the answers might disturb the reflection staring back.

With my father's lessons etched deep in my heart, I felt a responsibility to pull at the threads of this emerging story, to shed light on the darkness that seemed to be encroaching upon our town. The thought of a militia group operating in our midst was both alarming and infuriating. This was my home, a place where children played in the streets and neighbors looked out for one another. The idea that such a group could shatter the peace and safety of our community was unacceptable.

Armed with determination and a notepad filled with questions, I set out to gather information. Walking into the local gun shop felt like stepping into another world. The walls were lined with rifles and hunting equipment, the air tinged with the metallic scent of gun oil. Behind the counter stood Frank Miller, the shop's owner, a man whose rugged exterior was matched only by his knowledge of everything firearms. I had known Frank since I was a kid, coming in with my father on occasional Saturdays. Back then, his tall tales of government overreach and his slightly paranoid conspiracy theories were more entertaining than concerning. Today, however, I needed the journalist in me to take the forefront, not the nostalgic child.

"Morning, Frank," I greeted, approaching the counter with a casualness I didn't quite feel. "Busy day?"

Frank glanced up from his ledger, a hint of recognition flashing in his eyes before he masked it with his usual gruff demeanor. "Emily Harris," he said, his voice a mix of surprise and something akin to wariness. "Don't see much of you around here."

"I guess I don't have much need for a hunting rifle in my line of work," I replied, forcing a smile. My eyes quickly scanned the shop, noting the conspicuous absence of customers. "Actually, I'm here on business. Mind if I ask you a few questions?"

Frank's expression hardened, a clear sign that he understood this wasn't a social call. "Depends on the questions," he grunted, leaning back against the shelves.

I pulled out my notepad, my resolve firming. "It's about the recent uptick in sales," I began, watching his reaction closely. "I've heard rumors about unusual purchases—tactical gear, firearms not typically used for hunting. Anything you can tell me about that?"

For a moment, Frank looked as if he would kick me out of his shop, his affinity for privacy and skepticism of the press well-known. But as he studied my face, perhaps seeing the sincere concern and determination there, something shifted.

"It's not the regulars," he admitted after a heavy silence, his voice lowering to a whisper as if the very walls might be listening. "New faces, mostly. They come in asking for bulk orders of tactical gear, semi-automatics... the kind of stuff you don't use to hunt deer."

His confirmation sent a chill down my spine, but I pressed on. "Any idea who they are? Or what they're planning with that kind of equipment?"

Frank shook his head, a trace of his own concern flickering across his features. "Don't know much about who they are. They don't talk, and I don't ask. Cash transactions, no names. But," he paused, glancing around the empty shop before continuing, "there's talk, you know? Whispers about a group in the woods. Training for something big. But you didn't hear that from me."

The implication of his words hung heavily between us, a tangible cloud of foreboding. "Frank, this is serious. If there's a group preparing for... for whatever it is, we need to know. The community has a right to be aware, to be safe."

He sighed, the weight of the situation pressing down on him. "I know, Em. I just... I sell guns. I don't get involved in politics or whatever crazy stuff these folks are planning. But be careful, alright? These aren't your run-of-the-mill hunters."

Leaving the shop, Frank's warnings and the information he'd reluctantly shared replayed in my mind. The story was bigger and potentially more dangerous than I had imagined. The thought of a militia group, armed and training in secrecy, was a threat that couldn't be ignored. My journalistic instincts were alight with the urgency of the investigation, but Frank's cautionary words also reminded me of the risks involved. This wasn't just about getting a story anymore; it was about uncovering a threat nestled within the very heart of my hometown.

Refocusing my efforts, I turned away from the increasingly unyielding doors of local law enforcement and sought alternative avenues. My next step was to reach out directly to those on the fringes, those whose stories could shed light on the militia's activities from angles the police might not see—or choose not to.

I arranged to meet with an old school friend, Lara, who had become involved in community activism. Over coffee in a secluded corner of the library café, I shared my concerns and the resistance I'd encountered. Lara's face was a picture of empathy, but her words carried a warning. "Emily, some of these militia guys are woven into the fabric of our town. They're not just outsiders; they're people we grew up with. Be careful how you tread," she advised, her voice low.

Her caution did little to deter me; if anything, it highlighted the importance of my investigation. Lara provided names of individuals who had expressed quiet dissent towards the militia's growing presence. "They might talk to you, Emily. They trust you," she said, scribbling down contact information on a piece of napkin.

Each conversation was a delicate dance, a balancing act of probing for information without pushing too far, too fast. From a retired veteran who muttered about the militia's distortion of patriotism, to a concerned mother whose son had been approached by militia members, the stories began to form a mosaic of unease and manipulation.

Armed with these testimonies, I dove into public records, seeking permits for rallies the militia might have held or businesses they might be connected to. The digital breadcrumbs were sparse, but they painted a picture of a group trying to legitimize their presence under the guise of community service and protection.

I also revisited the online forums, this time with a keener eye for the subtext in the messages. The coded language, once cryptic, began to reveal patterns and hints of the militia's plans and ideologies. Screen captures and notes piled up, each piece a thread in the larger tapestry of the story unfolding before me.

The deeper I dug, the clearer the scope of my investigation became. This wasn't just about a group of extremists; it was about the undercurrents of dissatisfaction and fear that allowed such a group to flourish. It was about the challenges of confronting ideologies that had taken root in the very community I loved.

One evening, after a day of fruitless research, I received an anonymous email. "Look into the property records along the old mill stream," it read, void of any other context. The cryptic message sent a shiver down my spine, but it was a lead I couldn't ignore. The next day, I found myself wading through property deeds and transfer records, uncovering a series of purchases under shell companies that could very well be linked to the militia.

Each step of this journey reaffirmed the complexities of the story I was chasing. The obstacles weren't just external; they were also internal—a battle between the desire to expose the truth and the fear of what that truth might mean for my town.

Frustration simmered within me, but it was only the beginning. Later, as I made calls and visited sources, the pattern continued. A cryptic warning left on my voicemail chilled me to the bone: "Stay away from the militia story, Emily. It's bigger than you, and it's not worth your life." The voice was distorted, unrecognizable, but the message was clear—someone was watching, and they didn't want this story told.

Even more disheartening was the social pushback. At the grocery store, whispers followed me down the aisles, and what were once friendly faces now looked away, their expressions a mix of fear and disapproval. It seemed that the militia, with its insidious influence, had not only infiltrated the fabric of our community but had also sown seeds of sympathy among its members.

"Emily, you're stirring up trouble," Mrs. Harper, a family friend, whispered to me outside the post office. "Some stones are best left unturned."

The lack of cooperation from official channels, the veiled threats, and the cautionary tales from those who still dared to speak, all served to harden my resolve. The truth was a puzzle, and I was slowly piecing it together, driven by a sense of duty not just as a journalist, but as a member of this community. The Black Oak Militia had cast a long shadow over our town, and I was determined to bring it into the light.

As the distance to the local newspaper office shortened with every step, my mind raced, piecing together the fragments of a story that seemed to grow darker with each thought. The image of strangers, their faces obscured not just from Frank and others, but from the very community they were infiltrating, lingered at the forefront of my thoughts. These individuals, who moved with a purpose shrouded in secrecy, were arming themselves in a manner that went beyond the needs of personal protection or recreational hunting. The very notion of it—a militia, gathering in the shadows of the Black Oak woods, stockpiling weapons that had no place in our peaceful town—sent a shiver down my spine.

With every breath of the crisp, autumn air, my resolve deepened. This wasn't merely a story to chase; it was a looming threat to the safety and unity of the place I called home. The town, with its sleepy streets and close-knit community, was a place where children's laughter filled the parks, where neighbors met for weekly potlucks, and where the biggest event of the year was the fall harvest festival. The thought of that tranquility being shattered by the sound of gunfire, of families being torn apart by ideologies they didn't subscribe to, fueled a fire within me.

My pace quickened, driven by the urgency of the situation. The need for more information, for tangible evidence, was imperative. Yet, as the office came into view, a niggling sense of apprehension tugged at the edges of my determination. Delving into the heart of this brewing storm meant drawing the attention of those who wished to remain hidden. The danger wasn't just to myself; it was a shadow that could extend to my colleagues, my friends, and my family.

Stepping into the office, the chatter of keyboards and the murmur of phone conversations momentarily grounded me in the familiar. Yet, the sense of foreboding refused to be dismissed. As I sat at my desk, the screen of my computer a blank canvas awaiting the first strokes of this emerging story, the weight of responsibility settled on my shoulders. The strangers buying up tactical gear, their faces unknown but their intentions increasingly clear, were a puzzle I needed to solve.

But it wasn't just the who and the what that concerned me; it was the why. Why here, in our town? What was it about this community that drew them in, that made them believe they could operate with impunity? And more importantly, what could be done to stop them before their preparations turned into actions that could not be undone?

The quest for answers was no longer just professional; it was personal. This town, with its every flaw and beauty, was a part of me, as much as I was a part of it. The people here, with their simple lives and complex stories, deserved peace and safety. The children playing in the schoolyard, the families planning their futures, the elders sharing tales of the past—they were all unwitting participants in a game they didn't choose to play.

Sitting at my cluttered desk, the soft hum of the office around me, Jake Thompson's image infiltrated my thoughts like a shadow crossing the sun. It was odd, really, how the mind could bridge years in mere seconds, pulling from the depths of memory feelings and faces one thought were securely anchored in the past. Jake and I weren't just a fleeting high school romance; we were the embodiment of young love full of promise and naiveté. We shared everything from secret dreams whispered under the starlit sky in the Black Oak woods to the mundane routines of school life. Our connection was deep, rooted in a mutual understanding and respect that seemed destined to withstand time.

But time, as it turned out, was both a healer and a divider. When Jake announced his decision to join the Navy, it felt as though the ground beneath us shifted. I understood his reasons—the sense of duty inherited from a lineage of military service was not just a calling but a legacy he felt compelled to honor. His quiet strength and determination, qualities I had fallen in love with, were the very things that propelled him toward a life filled with danger and uncertainty.

His departure was a watershed moment in our lives, marking the end of our shared journey and the beginning of individual paths that would take us in wildly different directions. The chasm that formed between us was not born of anger or betrayal, but of silent acceptance that our futures lay apart. My pursuit of journalism, driven by a passion to unearth truths and give voice to the silenced, became my solace, filling the void left by his absence with purpose and resolve.

Now, as I found myself entangled in the web of an investigation that bore the hallmarks of the very world Jake had immersed himself in, the distance between our lives seemed more pronounced than ever. His realm was one of covert operations and classified missions, a world where information was guarded like a treasure and every action had life-or-death stakes. My world, though fraught with its own dangers, thrived on transparency and the pursuit of knowledge meant to be shared, not hidden.

Reflecting on what Jake might think of the emerging militia story, I couldn't help but feel a pang of longing for the simplicity of our past conversations. Would he view the situation with the calculated eye of a soldier, assessing threats and strategizing responses? Or would his connection to our hometown stir in him a protective instinct, compelling him to stand in defense of the community we both cherished?

The irony was not lost on me that, in some ways, our chosen paths mirrored the conflict at the heart of my investigation—a clash between secrecy and disclosure, between guarding and revealing. Despite the years and the silence that had grown between us, I found myself wishing I could talk to Jake about it all, to hear his perspective and perhaps to bridge, even momentarily, the vast expanse that had opened up between our worlds.

But such thoughts were a luxury I couldn't afford, not with the shadow of the militia looming ever larger over our town. Still, as I turned my attention back to the screen before me, the ghost of a smile tugged at my lips. Jake had always been a fighter, and so was I. In our own ways, we were both striving to protect and serve, bound by a sense of duty that, despite everything, still connected us across the miles and the silence.

Shaking off the distraction, I refocused on the task at hand. The story of the militia wasn't just another article; it was a call to action, a chance to use my voice to protect the community I loved. And as I followed the trail of clues, my determination only grew. This was more than an investigation; it was a battle for the soul of our town, and I was ready to fight it with every tool at my disposal.

Echoes of the Past

Jake

The local diner, with its retro décor and the comforting aroma of coffee and fried eggs, hadn't changed much over the years. It still felt like a relic from a simpler time, a place where the town's heartbeat could be felt most strongly. As I stepped inside, the bell above the door announced my arrival, drawing a few curious glances my way.

I spotted them in a booth at the back, a group of my old high school friends, seemingly frozen in time. Their faces were older, sure, but the easy laughter and camaraderie that I remembered so fondly were as vibrant as ever. For a moment, I hesitated, the weight of my mission pressing down on me. But as they waved me over, any reservations were momentarily pushed aside.

"Jake Thompson, as I live and breathe!" exclaimed Dave, standing up to pull me into a rough embrace. "We thought you'd forgotten all about us!"

The warmth of their welcome was disarming, and for a brief moment, I allowed myself to forget the reason I had come back. We slid into the familiar banter of old times, reminiscing about the high school football games where victory seemed as vital as life itself, the pranks that had become the stuff of legend, and the teachers who had tried (and often failed) to keep us in line.

As the conversation flowed, I found myself playing the part I had rehearsed so many times, the disillusioned veteran who had seen too much of the world and found it wanting. "Yeah, things sure didn't turn out the way I thought they would," I mused, stirring my coffee absentmindedly. "You grow up thinking you're fighting for something big, something important. But in the end, you start wondering what it was all for."

My words hung in the air, a subtle but deliberate planting of my cover story. To my relief, they were met with nods of understanding rather than suspicion.

"Man, that's rough, Jake," said Mike, his expression somber. "We always thought you were out there living the dream, being the hero."

"Hero's just a word," I shrugged, trying to keep my tone light despite the heaviness of the conversation. "Turns out the world's a lot more complicated than we thought back in high school."

The talk then turned to the town, to the changes and the undercurrents of dissatisfaction that had begun to surface. They spoke of jobs lost, of families struggling, of a sense of security that seemed to be slipping away. And as they did, I listened, my mind racing, cataloging every piece of information that might relate to the militia's influence.

"It's like we don't recognize this place anymore," Dave said, a sentiment echoed by the others. "Feels like we're standing on the brink of something, but nobody's quite sure what."

Their words struck a chord with me, not just as Jake Thompson, the hometown boy made good, but as the operative tasked with uncovering and neutralizing a threat to this very community. Here, amidst the laughter and nostalgia, was a tangible sense of the discontent the Black Oak Militia was likely exploiting.

As we parted ways, promises to catch up again soon exchanged with hearty backslaps and handshakes, I stepped out into the sunlight, feeling the weight of my dual roles more acutely than ever. The casual reunion had offered invaluable insights into the town's mood, but it had also reminded me of what I was fighting to protect. These were more than just operations and objectives; they were about real people, my people, caught in the crossfire of ideologies they might not even understand.

I found myself walking down memory lane, both literally and metaphorically. The familiarity of each storefront, each bend in the sidewalk, was comforting, yet each step was a reminder of the mission that had brought me back. It was during this reflective walk that I spotted Mrs. Greene, my former English teacher, stepping out of the library with a stack of books cradled in her arms.

"Mrs. Greene!" I called out, quickening my pace to catch up to her.

She paused, peering over her glasses with a momentary look of confusion that quickly turned to recognition. "Jake Thompson," she exclaimed, a warm smile spreading across her face. "My, how you've changed!"

Her comment, meant as a simple greeting, carried a weight that only those who had seen me grow up could truly understand. "It's been a long time, Mrs. Greene," I replied, offering to carry her books.

As we walked, she asked about my time since leaving town, about the adventures she assumed I had embarked upon. "I always knew you'd go on to do great things, Jake. You had such potential," she said, her tone laced with pride.

I felt a twinge of something akin to guilt at her words, knowing the narrative I was about to spin. "I did see a lot, Mrs. Greene," I began, carefully choosing my words. "But the world out there...it's not all I thought it would be. Serving seemed clear-cut when I was here, learning about heroes in your class. Out there, though, it's all shades of gray."

Her expression softened with empathy as she listened. "I can only imagine the things you've been through, the tragedies of war," she said quietly. "It must have been so hard."

The term 'tragedies of war' resonated with me more than she could know, opening a door to further solidify my cover. "Harder than I ever thought it would be," I confessed, allowing a shadow of my true feelings to surface. "Makes you question a lot of things...like what you're really fighting for, and if it's all worth it in the end."

Mrs. Greene nodded, her gaze thoughtful. "That's a heavy burden to carry, Jake. I'm sorry it's been so tough. But you're home now. Maybe here, you can find some of that clarity you've been searching for."

Our conversation continued a little while longer, touching on lighter topics before we parted ways outside the grocery store, but her words stayed with me. They were a reminder of the innocence and hope with which I'd left this town, a stark contrast to the person I had become.

As I walked away, I couldn't help but marvel at how seamlessly the fabrications woven into my cover story melded with the genuine pieces of my own disillusionment. It was a necessary deception, yet speaking those words aloud to someone who had once inspired me felt like a betrayal of sorts.

Yet, this interaction, like the ones before it, was a crucial step in blending back into the community, in building a believable facade that would allow me to move undetected among those I was here to observe. Mrs. Greene, with her memories of the young man I once was, had unwittingly reinforced my cover, making Jake Thompson, the disillusioned veteran, even more real to those who might be watching.

The local memorial park, nestled on the edge of town, had always been a place of reflection and remembrance. As I walked along the winding paths, the crisp autumn air filled my lungs, carrying with it the whispers of the past. The park, with its meticulously kept gardens and benches donated by families in memory of loved ones, held a sacred place in the heart of the community. It was here that we celebrated victories, mourned losses, and came together in moments of national pride or tragedy.

Approaching the veterans' memorial, a solemn structure of granite etched with the names of those who had served and sacrificed, I felt a familiar tug at my heart. Among those names were friends, classmates, and relatives—people I had grown up with, whose dreams had been cut short by the harsh realities of war. As I traced the cold, hard letters with my fingertips, the weight of my own experiences bore down on me, a heavy cloak of grief and guilt.

Standing there, surrounded by the echoes of their courage, I was confronted with the intensity of my emotional ties to this town and its people. Memories of laughter and camaraderie, of shared hopes and aspirations, clashed with the darker shadows of loss and regret. It was a poignant reminder of why I had chosen to serve, of the ideals and values I had sought to protect. But it also underscored the profound cost of that service, both to myself and to those left behind.

As I moved from one name to the next, the reality of my current mission came into sharp focus. I was here to root out a threat from within, to protect this community from those who sought to exploit its vulnerabilities. Yet, the very connections that bound me to this place also threatened to undermine my objectivity, to cloud my judgment with personal bias and emotion.

The doubts began to creep in, insidious and unsettling. Could I truly remain detached enough to complete my mission effectively? Was it possible to navigate the murky waters of espionage and counterterrorism without losing sight of who I was, of the values I held dear?

The internal conflict raged within me as I sat on a nearby bench, the names on the memorial standing as silent witnesses to my turmoil. It was a struggle between duty and heart, between the call to protect and the instinct to preserve the sanctity of those memories.

In that moment of quiet reflection, I realized that my emotional ties to the town, rather than being a liability, could also be my greatest strength. They provided a context, a deeper understanding of what was at stake. My connection to this place and its people was a reminder of the real, human cost of failure.

Rising from the bench, I took one last look at the memorial, a silent vow forming in my mind. I would use my ties to this community as a compass, guiding my actions with a clear understanding of the consequences. The mission was not just about tactics and intelligence; it was about safeguarding a way of life, about protecting the very essence of what made this town home.

With renewed determination, I stepped away from the memorial, the names of the fallen etched not just in granite, but in my heart. Their sacrifice would not be in vain. I would complete my mission, not in spite of my emotional ties, but because of them. For in those ties lay the true reason for my fight: not just to win, but to preserve what was most precious.

***

The Harvest Home Festival had always been a highlight in the town's calendar, a celebration that marked the change of seasons with its array of colors, scents, and the laughter of families gathered together in the spirit of community. As I navigated through the bustling streets, lined with stalls selling everything from homemade pies to handcrafted jewelry, the atmosphere was electric, infused with a warmth that seemed to temporarily suspend the undercurrent of tension I had been so focused on.

It was amidst this vibrant chaos, as I paused to watch a group of children darting around a hay bale maze, that I saw her. Emily Harris, as radiant as I remembered, her hair catching the sunlight in glints of gold, was interviewing a local farmer about his pumpkin crop. The sight of her, so unexpectedly, sent a jolt through me, reigniting a tumult of emotions I thought I had long since mastered.

I watched, momentarily transfixed, as she laughed at something the farmer said, her notebook clasped in one hand, a pen in the other. It was a scene so quintessentially Emily, her curiosity and passion for storytelling as vibrant as ever. The connection between us, dormant yet undiminished by time and distance, pulsed to life, a reminder of the depth of what we once shared.

Compelled by a force I couldn't resist, I found myself moving towards her, each step a battle between desire and duty. As I approached, her gaze lifted, locking onto mine with an intensity that halted me in my tracks. The recognition in her eyes was immediate, a spark that acknowledged our shared past even as it questioned the years that lay between.

"Jake," she breathed, her voice a mix of surprise and something indefinable. "You're back."

"Emily," I managed, the familiarity of her name on my lips unleashing a flood of memories. "It's been a long time."

The conversation that followed was a delicate dance of superficialities, a verbal sparring that skirted around the depth of our history. I complimented her on the article she had written about the festival, carefully maintaining my cover as a man who had simply come home to find some peace. Yet, every word, every glance, was charged with an undercurrent of unspoken truths and unresolved feelings.

The peril my return might cast upon her was starkly clear in my mind. Rumors had reached me, whispers that Emily was delving into matters that weren't looked upon favorably. The militia, with their vigilant scrutiny and expanding sway, would hardly welcome her probing or my unexpected reconnection with her. My mission necessitated a level of detachment that proved challenging in her presence; every second spent near Emily underscored the high risks involved. Thus, with a heavy heart, I murmured an excuse about urgent matters needing my attention and reluctantly took my leave.

As I moved away from my encounter with Emily, the festival's cheerful cacophony enveloped me once more. Yet, the brief interlude had sharpened my senses, refocusing my attention on the underlying currents that flowed beneath the surface of the town's festive veneer.

With the weight of my mission pressing heavily on my mind, I began to observe the crowd through the lens of my training, alert to the subtleties that might betray the militia's presence. It didn't take long to notice them: quiet conversations that ceased abruptly as I walked past, the exchange of glances that spoke volumes in their silence. Here, amidst the laughter and celebration, the Black Oak Militia's influence was a whisper, an undercurrent that stirred just beneath the surface. I spotted a pair of men standing off to the side of the main thoroughfare, their heads bent together in earnest discussion. As I approached, one of them slipped a folded piece of paper into the other's hand—a flyer, if my guess was correct, likely bearing the militia's call to arms or announcing a clandestine meeting.

Their eyes caught mine, and for a moment, there was a flash of recognition, a spark of defiance, before they turned away, melting back into the crowd. I resisted the urge to follow, to confront them then and there. Instead, I filed away their faces, mental notes in the growing dossier of my mind.

Further along, I paused to admire a display of local craftsmanship, my gaze lingering on the intricate work. But it was the vendor's offhand comment to a prospective buyer that caught my attention. "You know, there are folks around here looking to take things back to how they used to be. Good folks, doing what needs to be done." The implication was clear, and the nod he received in return was a silent acknowledgment of shared beliefs.

Even the children, caught up in the joy of the festival, were not untouched by the militia's reach. I overheard a snippet of conversation between two boys as they compared the badges pinned to their backpacks. "My dad got this one at a meeting," one said proudly, pointing to a symbol that I recognized as being associated with the militia. It was a stark reminder of how deeply the group had embedded itself into the fabric of the community, spreading its ideology even to the youngest members.

Each observation, each overheard word, added another layer to my understanding of the militia's influence. They were here, hidden in plain sight, weaving their narrative into the fabric of the town's daily life. And while the festival continued around me, a celebration of harvest and homecoming, the seeds being sown by the militia promised a harvest of a very different kind.

The contrast between the town's festive atmosphere and the quiet machinations of the militia was jarring. Emily's focused curiosity, so intent on capturing the joy and unity of the festival, stood in stark relief against the backdrop of my own mission. Her pursuit of stories that celebrated the community was a reminder of what we were all fighting to preserve, yet it also underscored the urgency of my task.

As the festival began to wind down, with vendors packing up and families making their way home, I found myself once again in Emily's orbit. The crowd had thinned, creating an intimate space amidst the remnants of celebration. She approached me, a thoughtful look on her face, illuminated by the soft glow of the remaining festival lights. It was a look I recognized, one that had always preluded deep conversations between us.

"Jake, can we talk?" she asked, her voice lower than the festive din that surrounded us. There was a seriousness in her tone that drew me in, despite the alarms sounding in my head, warning of the danger my proximity posed to her.

We found a quiet spot away from the last of the festival-goers, near the edge of the park where the sound of the river provided a gentle backdrop to our conversation. It was here, in this secluded enclave, that Emily's questioning gaze found me, searching, probing for the truth beneath the surface.

"You've changed, Jake," she started, her voice tinged with a mix of concern and curiosity. "I mean, I always knew you'd come back different... war does that to people. But there's something more, something you're not saying. Can you tell me what's going on?"

Her intuition, always sharp, cut a little too close to the bone. I was faced with a choice—reveal the truth of my mission, of the dangers that lurked in the shadows, or maintain my cover, keeping her at arm's length for her own safety. The latter won out, necessity dictating the preservation of my role over the yearning for openness.

"It's just... the things I've seen, the experiences I've had, they change a person," I said, choosing my words with care. "You're right, I'm not the same guy who left all those years ago. The world's a lot more complicated than I thought it was, and I guess I'm still trying to find my place in it."

Emily's gaze held mine, a myriad of emotions flickering across her face—understanding, sadness, and a hint of frustration. "I just wish you'd let me in, Jake. Whatever it is, we can face it together, like we used to."

The sentiment, so earnest and full of the trust we'd once shared, twisted in my chest. The irony of her words wasn't lost on me; here I was, surrounded by a town full of my past, engaged in a mission that required me to stand apart, isolated by secrets and lies. The fear that my presence, my mission, could bring harm to Emily and those I cared about was a constant shadow, one that darkened our interaction.

"I appreciate that, Em, I really do," I managed, my voice steady despite the turmoil within. "Right now, I just need to figure some things out on my own. But it means a lot, knowing you're here."

As we parted ways, the distance between us felt more profound than mere physical space. It was a chasm wrought by circumstances and choices, by the path I had chosen to walk. Emily's questioning glance, filled with concern and the remnants of a connection that refused to be severed, stayed with me long after the festival lights had dimmed.

Alone, perched on the tailgate of my truck parked on a hill overlooking the town, I found myself engulfed in a sea of reflection. The festival's laughter and music had faded into the night, leaving behind a silence that was as comforting as it was haunting. Below, the town lay shrouded in darkness, its familiar outlines a soft glow against the night sky. It was a view I had seen countless times before, one that spoke of home and belonging. Yet, tonight, it felt different—weighted with a significance I had never felt so acutely.

The day's encounters replayed in my mind, each interaction a thread weaving the complex tapestry of my return. My old friends' easy camaraderie, Mrs. Greene's pride and sorrow, and most of all, Emily's intuitive concern. These were the connections that rooted me to this place, that defined who I was and who I had become. They were also the ties that complicated my mission, infusing it with a personal dimension that I hadn't fully anticipated.

As I gazed out over the town, I couldn't help but question my ability to carry out my orders without causing harm to the very fabric of this community. The mission, clear-cut in its inception, had morphed into a labyrinth of moral and ethical dilemmas. The people I was here to protect were not just names in a briefing folder; they were my friends, my teachers, my first love. How could I navigate this delicate balance between duty and the bonds of my past?

The fear that my actions, however well-intentioned, could inadvertently endanger those I cared about weighed heavily on me. It was a burden I had not fully appreciated when I accepted the mission, a burden that now seemed insurmountable in the quiet of the night. The thought of the town, so vibrant and full of life during the day, becoming a battleground for hidden conflicts and unseen dangers was a stark reminder of what was at stake.

My reflection deepened as I considered the implications of my presence here. Every move I made, every word I spoke, had to be measured, calculated to avoid detection or suspicion. Yet, the more I immersed myself in the role I had to play, the more I felt the lines between the soldier and the man blurring. Was it possible to remain detached, to view this place and its people through the impersonal lens of a mission? Or had I already crossed a threshold, entangling my fate with that of the town in ways that could not be easily untangled?

In the solitude of the night, with the town spread out before me, I grappled with these questions, the doubts swirling in my mind like leaves caught in an autumn breeze. The mission, with its clear objectives and defined parameters, suddenly seemed far more complex, a test not only of my skills as a SEAL but of my integrity and resolve as a person.

Yet, amidst the turmoil of doubt and reflection, a resolve began to crystallize within me. The very connections that made this mission so challenging also imbued it with a profound sense of purpose. I wasn't just fighting for abstract ideals or distant goals; I was fighting for my home, for the people who had shaped me, for a way of life that deserved to be protected.

As I climbed back into my truck, the night around me felt a little less oppressive, the path ahead a little clearer. The challenges remained, as did the doubts, but I knew now that my emotional ties to this town were not a weakness, but a source of strength. They grounded me, reminded me of why I was here, and who I was ultimately fighting for.

Driving back to my grandfather's house, the night enveloped me, a cloak that offered neither comfort nor concealment from my thoughts. The encounter with Emily, her intuitive probing, and my necessary deflection, underscored the complexity of my situation. It was a reminder of the stakes, of the delicate balance between duty and personal connection that I was forced to navigate. In protecting her, in safeguarding the town from the shadows that threatened it, I had to remain aloof, distanced by the very mission that had brought me home.

Rekindled Flames

Emily

The Harvest Home Festival, a yearly celebration marking the end of summer and the bounty of the fall, had always been a highlight in the calendar for the residents of our small town. It was a day when the community came together, when the air buzzed with laughter and music, and the scent of apple pies and roasted corn filled the streets. As I navigated through the bustling crowds, notebook in hand, ready to capture the spirit of the festival for the local newspaper, I was lost in the vibrancy of it all.

Then, I saw him. Jake Thompson.

He was standing near the old oak tree that marked the heart of the festival grounds, looking so much like the Jake of my memories yet undeniably changed. The sight of him was like a jolt to my system, stirring a whirlwind of emotions I thought I had long since navigated and compartmentalized. There was surprise, of course—his return to our hometown had been the subject of quiet speculation, but I hadn't truly believed it until now. But there was also a resurgence of... something else. A flicker of the old flame that had once burned so brightly between us.

My heart raced as nostalgia washed over me, mingling with a sharp pang of curiosity. What had brought Jake back after all these years? He had left for the Navy with dreams of heroism in his eyes, leaving a void in his wake that had never quite been filled. And now, here he was, a ghost from the past made flesh and blood once more.

I watched him for a moment, unnoticed. He seemed lost in thought, his gaze distant, as if he were seeing something beyond the festival's gaiety. The years had sculpted his features with new lines, lending him a maturity that the boy I remembered lacked. But it was the intensity in his eyes, that familiar determined spark, which struck a chord deep within me.

A part of me wanted to approach him right then, to bridge the gap of years with a simple hello. But another part hesitated, held back by a tangle of unresolved feelings and the fear of reopening old wounds. It was a peculiar sensation, standing there on the precipice of the past and present, my reporter's instincts warring with the remnants of a high school sweetheart's heartache.

So, I took a deep breath, steadied my racing heart, and decided to observe from a distance for a little longer. Jake hadn't seen me yet, and I needed a moment to collect myself, to prepare for the inevitable collision of our worlds. As I watched him move through the festival crowd, an enigmatic figure shrouded in the familiarity of home, I couldn't shake the feeling that Jake Thompson's return was going to be the start of something significant.

For now, though, I tucked away the rush of emotions his presence had evoked. There was a story here, I was sure of it. Not just the tale of a hometown hero's return, but something deeper, something that stirred the journalist in me to uncover. But first, I needed to confront the past that stood, quite literally, before me.

And so, with a mixture of trepidation and resolve, I started to make my way through the crowd towards him, ready to face whatever this unexpected reunion might bring.

As I approached Jake, threading my way through families and groups of friends who were engrossed in the festival's joyous chaos, the distance between us seemed to shrink with each step, yet felt infinitely vast in the emotional gulf it represented. When I finally reached him, standing near the oak tree that had witnessed countless festivals and personal milestones of our youth, he turned, his gaze meeting mine in a moment laden with the weight of years gone by.

"Emily," he said, his voice carrying a mixture of surprise and something else—perhaps a hint of the same tumultuous blend of feelings swirling within me. His use of my name, simple and familiar, sent a wave of memories crashing over me, evoking a sense of intimacy that the passage of time had not entirely eroded.

"Jake," I managed to reply, my voice steady despite the whirlwind of emotions his presence stirred. "I didn't know you were back in town."

For a moment, we simply looked at each other, the air around us charged with a palpable tension that spoke of unresolved pasts and unspoken questions. It was as if the festival's vibrant energy had coalesced around us, heightening the sense of a connection that had once been unbreakable.

"It's been a long time," he said, his eyes not leaving mine. In them, I saw shadows of the boy I had known, the one who had shared dreams and secrets with me under these very trees. But there was also the presence of the man he had become, marked by experiences I could only guess at.

The chemistry between us, a force that had once drawn us irresistibly together, made itself known once again, as undeniable as it was unexpected. It was a connection that time and distance had failed to sever, manifesting now in the way our conversation seemed to flow naturally, despite the awkwardness of the reunion.

"How have you been, Jake?" I asked, a part of me wanting to bridge the gap between us, to return to a familiarity that was as comforting as it was complicated.

"I've been... around," he answered, a cryptic response that hinted at stories untold. "And you? Still uncovering the town's secrets?"

His reference to my passion for journalism, a career path I had chosen with a determination to make a difference, brought a small smile to my lips. "Always," I affirmed, the professional in me briefly overtaking the emotional turmoil of the moment. "There's always a story waiting to be told."

As Jake and I delved into the treasury of our shared past, each memory painted in the vivid hues of youth and unbridled ambition, a subtle shift in the air between us became increasingly apparent. His laughter, though genuine, carried a timbre of reservation, and his eyes—those familiar windows to his once open soul—held back chapters of his story that remained untold. The Jake I remembered, whose spirit seemed as free and expansive as the sky above our hometown, now seemed to navigate our conversation with a careful, almost meticulous, guard over his emotions.

"Remember the homecoming game our senior year?" Jake prompted, his smile a ghost of the carefree expressions I recalled. "Your article nearly landed the team in hot water. I think that was the moment I realized just how powerful your words could be."

The memory brought a genuine smile to my face, a brief respite from the growing realization of the changes in Jake. "I prefer to think of it as 'creative enthusiasm,'" I corrected, attempting to steer us back to familiar, less fraught territory. "Besides, it all worked out, didn't it?" There was a comfort in recalling these moments of shared history, yet each laugh and anecdote seemed to underscore not just the distance time had placed between us, but the barriers experience had erected around Jake.

"And the night we watched the meteor shower from the school roof," I ventured further, the memory bright with the innocence and adventure of our teenage years. "I'm surprised we never got caught." It was a tender recollection, one that had always symbolized the purity of our connection.

Jake's response, a mixture of nostalgia and something akin to melancholy, echoed back to me. "That was all you. I was merely in the orbit of your audacity," he said, a line that once would have been delivered with an effortless charm now seemed weighed down by an invisible burden.

In the midst of our walk down memory lane, a sudden shift in Jake's demeanor caught me off guard. His laughter, which had moments ago filled the air with echoes of our shared past, faltered, and the warmth in his eyes cooled to a measured distance. The transformation was subtle, yet unmistakable—a wall coming up, a door closing.

"I, uh, I should probably get going," Jake interjected abruptly, his voice tight, the casual ease of our conversation evaporating as if it had never been. "There's something I need to take care of."

The words hung between us, a sudden chill on what had been a warm, nostalgic breeze. My heart, momentarily buoyed by the rekindling of old connections, sank with confusion and a dawning concern. This wasn't the Jake I remembered, the one who could spend hours debating and laughing without a care in the world. This Jake was a stranger in some ways, his sudden need to leave a stark reminder of the unseen forces at play in his life.

"Is everything okay?" I asked, reaching out in a gesture that was part inquiry, part plea for the truth behind his hastily erected barriers. My voice betrayed a hint of the turmoil his abrupt departure stirred within me, a mix of disappointment and worry.

Jake hesitated, his gaze meeting mine in a moment laden with unspoken words and uncharted depths. "Yeah, everything's fine. Just remembered a...a project I've been putting off," he managed, the explanation falling flat, a poorly disguised mask over reasons he wasn't ready to share.

The excuse, transparent and evasive, left more questions than answers. The Jake I knew was never one to shy away from confrontation or honesty, yet here he stood, a portrait of evasion. As he turned to leave, a part of me wanted to call him back, to demand the truth, to bridge the growing gap with the stubborn tenacity that had once defined us both.

But I held back, the words unspoken, the questions unasked. In that moment, I realized the depth of the chasm that had grown between us, a divide not just of time and distance, but of experiences too heavy to share on a whim. Jake's sudden departure was a reminder of the complexities we now navigated, a painful acknowledgment of the individuals we had become—shaped by life's relentless tide, holding onto pieces of a past that seemed increasingly like a dream.

As he walked away, the connection that had once seemed indestructible felt fragile, a thread stretched thin by the weight of untold stories and hidden wounds. Left standing alone, I couldn't help but wonder what battles Jake was fighting alone, what burdens he carried that forced him to retreat behind a veil of secrecy. The festivity of the Harvest Home Festival continued around me, but its colors seemed dimmed, its laughter a distant echo against the backdrop of my swirling thoughts.

In the wake of Jake's abrupt departure, I found myself adrift in a sea of conflicting emotions, the remnants of our encounter swirling around me like leaves caught in an autumn gust. The festival, with its kaleidoscope of sounds and colors, continued unabated, but I barely noticed the joy and laughter that filled the air. Instead, I was ensnared in a reflective solitude, pondering the complex web of feelings that Jake's sudden return had unraveled within me.

As I meandered aimlessly through the festival grounds, the echoes of our past interactions played in my mind like a familiar melody, each note resonating with the warmth and closeness we once shared. There was a comfort in the nostalgia, a bittersweet reminder of a time when our lives were inextricably intertwined, when our futures seemed as one. The sudden resurgence of those long-dormant emotions was both exhilarating and disarming, a testament to the enduring connection that time had failed to sever.

Yet, Jake's hasty excuse and swift departure cast a shadow over the fledgling flames of rekindled warmth. It was a stark reminder of the chasm that now lay between us, a gap widened by years of silence and separation. The Jake who had stood before me was both familiar and foreign, his presence a bridge to the past, but his guardedness a barrier to understanding who he had become.

In the solitude of my reflections, I grappled with the duality of my feelings. On one hand, there was an undeniable joy in seeing Jake again, a spark rekindled from the embers of our shared history. On the other, there was confusion and a sense of loss, a mourning for the straightforward intimacy that had once defined us, now complicated by the layers of experience and secrecy that enveloped him.

The festival around me felt distant, a backdrop to the tumultuous inner dialogue that consumed my thoughts. Questions without answers whirled through my mind, each one probing the depths of Jake's sudden reclusiveness. What had happened to him during our years apart? What burdens did he bear that compelled him to retreat behind a facade of evasiveness? And, perhaps most poignantly, where did I fit into the tapestry of his life now?

As the night drew on and the festival lights began to dim, I found a quiet bench away from the throng of revelers. Seated there, amidst the dwindling festivities, I allowed myself a moment of vulnerability, a pause in the rush of the day to truly feel the weight of Jake's return. It was a moment of introspection, a time to acknowledge the resurgence of old feelings and the uncertainties of new realities.

The reflective solitude offered no easy answers, but it did provide a clarity of sorts. Jake's return had reopened a chapter of my life that I thought had been closed, stirring a tumult of emotions and memories. Yet, it also underscored the undeniable truth that we were no longer the people we once were. The challenge now was to navigate this new landscape of our rekindled connection, to explore the possibilities and limits of what lay ahead, armed with the knowledge that the path forward was as uncertain as it was inevitable.

In the quiet of the night, as the final notes of the festival faded into silence, I rose from the bench, a resolve settling over me. The journey ahead would require patience, understanding, and perhaps most of all, the courage to face whatever truths lay hidden behind Jake's guarded return. With a deep breath, I stepped back into the night, the festival behind me, and the promise of tomorrow—a day filled with both old memories and new beginnings—stretching out ahead. The resolve crystallized within me as I saw Jake, a solitary figure against the backdrop of the park's muted twilight. He sat on a bench, lost in thought, the very image of isolation amidst the sprawling expanse of green and shadows. The sight of him, so alone, fueled my determination to bridge the distance that had grown between us, to pierce the veil of mystery that had enveloped him since his return.

Taking a deep breath, I approached, my footsteps soft on the grass, my heart a tumult of anticipation and apprehension. As I drew near, Jake looked up, his expression a mix of surprise and something indefinable, a complexity of emotions that mirrored my own. The air between us was charged, a tangible current of unresolved history and unspoken questions.

"Jake," I began, my voice steady despite the turmoil within. "We need to talk. I can't pretend that your return doesn't affect me, that I'm not worried about you. There's so much I don't understand, so much you're not saying."

The tension between us was palpable, a living thing that thrummed with the beat of our racing hearts. Jake's gaze held mine, a storm of conflict and reluctance warring in his eyes. The moment stretched, a lifetime of memories and emotions hanging in the balance.

Then, without warning, the distance between us closed, the barriers we had erected crumbling under the weight of our shared past. Jake's arms enveloped me, pulling me into an embrace that was both a sanctuary and a flame, igniting the passion that had lain dormant between us. Our lips met in a kiss that was an explosion of sensation, a confluence of every unspoken word and pent-up emotion. It was a kiss that defied the years apart, that spoke of longing, of love, of the inextricable tie that bound us together.

But as quickly as the fire had ignited, it was doused, Jake pulling away with a suddenness that left me reeling. The warmth of his embrace was replaced by a cold absence, his face etched with a conflict that ran deeper than I could fathom.

"I can't," he whispered, the words a pained exhalation. "Emily, I... This isn't safe. For you. There's so much you don't know, so much I can't explain. I can't drag you into this, into my world. It's better if we keep our distance."

The finality in his voice struck a chord of fear in my heart, a realization of the gravity of whatever shadows haunted him. The passionate embrace that had promised a rekindling of old flames now felt like a farewell, a bitter echo of the intimacy we had once shared.

In the silence that followed, a chasm opened between us, a void filled with unasked questions and unshed tears. Jake's decision to pull away, to shield me from the undisclosed dangers of his mission, was a testament to the depth of his concern. Yet, it also laid bare the complexity of our situation, the impossible choice between yielding to our emotions and facing the realities that kept us apart.

Standing there, in the fading light of the park, the remnants of our embrace lingering like a phantom touch, I was left to grapple with the aftermath of our aborted connection. Jake's abrupt withdrawal, driven by a desire to protect me, only deepened the mystery of his return, leaving me with a heart full of questions and a resolve to uncover the truth, no matter the cost. The decision to confront had led us to the brink of revelation, only to be pulled back by the invisible forces that governed Jake's life, a reminder of the perilous ground upon which we stood.

Undercover Beginnings

Jake

The local diner, with its familiar red booths and the ever-present aroma of brewing coffee, hadn't changed much over the years. It still felt like a snapshot of my youth, a reminder of simpler times. I found myself at a corner table, a black coffee in hand, gazing out the window at the small-town scene unfolding outside. The sight of kids racing down the sidewalk on their bikes and couples strolling hand in hand was starkly at odds with the reason for my return.

As I took a sip of the bitter coffee, memories flooded back. This diner had been our spot—mine and Emily's. It was where we'd plan our future adventures, where we'd laugh until our sides hurt, where we'd dream about escaping the confines of our small town. Now, sitting here alone, those dreams felt like a distant echo, overshadowed by the weight of my current mission.

The contrast couldn't have been more jarring. Back then, I was Jake Thompson, high school athlete with a penchant for trouble, full of life and ambition. Today, I was Lieutenant Jake Thompson, Navy SEAL, trained in the art of war and espionage, back home with orders to infiltrate a domestic militia group that threatened the safety of the community I once knew so well.

I couldn't help but wonder what Emily would think if she knew the true reason behind my return. Would she understand? Would she see it as a betrayal of the life we once envisioned together? The pang of guilt was immediate, a sharp reminder of the unresolved feelings that lingered between us.

The reality of my situation set in as I observed the diner's other patrons, wondering if any of them suspected the danger lurking within their own community. To them, I was just Jake Thompson, hometown hero who'd made good and returned from service. They couldn't know the burden I carried, the secrets I had to keep, or the lies I had to live.

As the last of my coffee disappeared, I steeled myself for the task ahead. My training had prepared me for this—how to blend in, how to gather intelligence without arousing suspicion, how to fight if it came down to it. Yet, no amount of training could fully prepare me for the emotional turmoil of navigating my past while undercover.

The diner, once a haven of comfort and nostalgia, now felt like a staging ground for the dual life I was forced to lead. Leaving a tip on the table, I stood, casting one last look around the place that held so many memories. It was time to leave the past where it belonged and focus on the mission at hand.

Stepping out into the bright light of day, the cool air hit me with a clarity of purpose. The town I loved, the people I cared about, they were all counting on me, even if they didn't know it. The internal conflict would always be there, but for now, the soldier in me took precedence. It was time to infiltrate the Black Oak Militia and ensure the safety of my hometown, no matter the personal cost.

Walking towards the old school auditorium, the building used for most meetings now that the community center had been burned, I could feel the familiar crunch of gravel under my boots, a sound that oddly grounded me. The building itself, a modest, single-story structure surrounded by well-kept lawns and autumn-touched trees, looked as benign as ever. Yet tonight, it was the venue for a meeting that the locals believed was just another community gathering, unaware of the underlying currents that flowed beneath.

As I entered the dimly lit hall, the murmur of voices and the scent of stale coffee hit me. Scanning the room, I recognized a few faces from my past—a high school teacher, a couple of parents of old friends, people who represented the fabric of this community. Their presence here, at a meeting that served as a façade for militia recruitment, underscored the complex web of discontent and disillusionment that the Black Oak Militia had tapped into.

Adopting the persona of a disillusioned veteran wasn't difficult; part of me resonated with the narrative. The disillusionment was real, a byproduct of the things I'd seen and done in the name of duty. But tonight, it was also my cover, a means to an end.

I found a spot at the back, leaning against a wall, my posture deliberately casual. As the meeting commenced, the speakers touched on topics of community and solidarity, but it wasn't long before the underlying themes emerged—government overreach, loss of freedoms, the need to stand up for 'true American values'. The language was coded, but the message was clear, especially to someone trained to read between the lines.

During a break, I seized the opportunity to mingle, introducing myself to a few attendees. "Jake Thompson," I offered, with a handshake that was firm but weary. "Just got back to town, trying to find my footing again."

The story I spun was one of disenchantment. "Served my country, but now I find myself questioning what I was fighting for," I said, the words tasting bitter in my mouth. My narrative struck a chord, as I had known it would. Nods of understanding and sympathetic claps on the back followed my every word. It was unsettling how easily people accepted the disillusioned soldier act, how eager they were to bring me into the fold.

One introduction led to another until I found myself face to face with Mitch Larson, a connection from my past and a known sympathizer of the militia. The recognition was mutual, and the surprise in his eyes quickly turned into something akin to respect.

"Thompson, " he said, a cautious warmth in his tone. "Didn't expect to see you here."

"Life's full of surprises, Mitch," I replied, keeping my voice even. "Figured it's time to stand up for what I believe in, now more than ever."

Our conversation veered into safe territory for a while, reminiscing about old times, but it wasn't long before Mitch leaned in closer, his voice dropping to a whisper. "You're looking for purpose, Jake? You might just find it with us. There's a lot more to these meetings than just talk."

The invitation was veiled, but the implication was clear. I had made my first successful contact, a foot in the door to the deeper, darker workings of the Black Oak Militia. As the meeting disbanded, plans were made to meet again, this time in a setting that promised to reveal the true nature of the militia's activities.

As the community meeting unfolded, I found myself slipping seamlessly into the role of observer, a skill honed through countless hours of training and fieldwork. The room, with its array of local faces, might have looked innocuous to an untrained eye, but beneath the surface, the dynamics were far more complex.

My gaze drifted across the gathered individuals, noting the subtle cues that differentiated the average town resident from those with deeper connections to the Black Oak Militia. There was a language in the way certain individuals interacted, a familiarity that spoke of shared secrets and common goals. These were the people I needed to watch, the ones who held the threads of the larger web I was here to untangle.

Among them, one figure stood out—not by being overly conspicuous, but rather by the quiet authority he wielded. Mark Dalton, the man I'd been briefed on, the charismatic leader of the Black Oak Militia. He didn't take the floor to speak; he didn't need to. His presence alone seemed to command attention, with others gravitating towards him during breaks, seeking approval or guidance.

Dalton was a study in contrasts. His demeanor was that of a concerned citizen, passionate about community and freedom, yet there was a hardness in his eyes, a determination that suggested he was accustomed to being in control, to directing the narrative to suit his agenda. Watching him interact with others, I could see the charisma that made him a compelling figure to those disillusioned with the status quo. He was the kind of leader who could inspire loyalty, making him both a valuable ally and a dangerous enemy.

As the evening progressed, my military training kicked into high gear. I found myself cataloging exits, estimating the number of attendees with potential military backgrounds, and identifying the subtle signs of hierarchy within the group. This wasn't just a gathering of discontented citizens; it was a recruitment ground, a place where the militia could find and foster the kind of loyalty they needed to expand their influence.

Yet, even as I took mental notes on the meeting's dynamics, I couldn't help but feel a pang of regret. Each piece of information I gathered was a step further into the heart of the militia, but it was also a step away from the person I used to be. The simple act of observing, of analyzing, put a distance between me and the community I had grown up in, transforming familiar faces into potential threats or assets.

Despite the internal conflict, I understood the necessity of my role. The information I collected tonight—on the militia's recruitment tactics, their key players, and most importantly, on Mark Dalton—was invaluable. It would shape my next moves, guiding me deeper into the heart of the militia with a clear understanding of the risks involved.

As the meeting concluded and people began to disperse, I lingered for a moment, taking in the scene one last time. My mind was already racing with plans and contingencies, ways to leverage what I had learned tonight to gain further access to the militia's inner circle. Yet, amidst the strategizing, there was also a sense of isolation, a realization that with each step forward in my mission, I was also stepping further away from the very people I was here to protect.

The drive back to my grandfather's house was a quiet one, the night around me a blank canvas for my thoughts. I was in deep now, playing a dangerous game that required every ounce of my training and resolve. But beyond the tactics and the strategies, beyond the role I had to play, there was a deeper motivation driving me. This wasn't just about completing a mission; it was about safeguarding my home, about protecting a community that, despite everything, I still considered my own.

In the days following the community meeting, I found myself weaving through the social fabric of my hometown with a singular focus: to ingratiate myself with members of the Black Oak Militia. Each interaction was a step in a meticulously choreographed dance, one where every word, every gesture, was imbued with the purpose of building trust.

I started frequenting places known to be militia haunts—dusty bars on the outskirts of town, local diners where conversations flowed as freely as the coffee, and even the occasional backyard barbecue, to which I was invited under the guise of rekindling old acquaintances. In these settings, surrounded by the hum of day-to-day life, I played the part of the disillusioned veteran, a role that, while distasteful, provided a valuable cover.

"My time in the service taught me a lot," I'd say, nursing a beer while seated at a bar that seemed to have weathered as many storms as I had. "But the biggest lesson was that the folks making the decisions aren't the ones paying the price." My words were met with nods of agreement, the murmurs of assent from those around me fueling my resolve.

As conversations deepened, I'd steer them subtly towards topics of freedom, government overreach, and the right to bear arms—themes that resonated with the militia's ideology. "Seems to me like we're losing grip on the very freedoms we fought for," I'd muse aloud, watching carefully for reactions, for signs of alignment or dissent.

With each encounter, I dropped hints of my supposed dissatisfaction with the government, careful to toe the line between genuine grievance and overt radicalism. It was a delicate balance, one that required not just a deep understanding of the militia's grievances but also an ability to mirror back their frustrations without fully committing to their cause.

The reactions varied—some were skeptical, their eyes narrowing in suspicion as they weighed my words; others were more forthcoming, their own disillusionment serving as a bridge between my fabricated narrative and their reality. But with each interaction, the seeds of trust were sown, watered by shared stories of service and sacrifice, by the unspoken bond that forms between those who feel abandoned by the system they once served.

Mark Dalton, ever the observant leader, watched from the periphery, his keen gaze missing nothing. Our paths crossed occasionally, each encounter marked by a careful exchange of words, a testing of waters. "Heard you've been making quite the impression," he remarked one evening, his voice neutral but probing.

"I'm just speaking my truth," I responded, meeting his gaze squarely. "Seems to resonate with folks around here."

He studied me for a moment longer, as if trying to peer beneath the surface. "We need more people with your experience, Jake. People who understand what it means to fight for something bigger than themselves."

His words were an invitation, but also a challenge—a call to step further into the shadows that shrouded the militia's operations. Accepting would mean gaining the access I needed to dismantle their plans from within. It would also mean diving deeper into the deception, further entangling myself in a web of lies that stretched over the town like a dark canopy.

As I left that evening, Dalton's words echoed in my mind, a reminder of the mission that had brought me back to this place. Building trust with the militia was not just a tactical necessity; it was a strategic maneuver, one that positioned me closer to the heart of the threat looming over my hometown. With each step forward, I carried the weight of my dual identity—not just as Jake Thompson, the disillusioned veteran, but as a SEAL committed to protecting the community that had raised him, no matter the personal cost.

Navigating the shadowy undercurrents of my mission, I found myself ensnared in a constant battle between duty and distraction. The specter of Emily haunted the peripheries of my mind, her image surfacing at the least opportune moments—when the sunlight glinted off the river in a way that reminded me of afternoons spent by her side or when I passed by the old high school where our paths had so often intertwined.

It was during a solitary walk through the town's quiet streets, under the expansive canopy of the night sky, that the weight of these thoughts felt most oppressive. The town, with its familiar landmarks bathed in the soft glow of streetlights, whispered echoes of a past that seemed both incredibly distant and painfully close. Each step brought a flood of memories, each one tinged with a sense of what had been and what could never be again.

My mission required a razor-sharp focus, a clarity of purpose that left no room for personal entanglements or emotional turmoil. Yet, thoughts of Emily pierced that focus with unsettling frequency. It wasn't just the warmth of old affections that troubled me; it was the gnawing fear for her safety. Her inquisitive nature, her relentless pursuit of truth, had always been qualities I admired. Now, they were sources of deep concern. In a town where shadows lengthened and dangers multiplied, her quest for answers could make her a target.

The unresolved tension between us only compounded my distraction. Our chance encounters, though brief, had reignited a connection I'd thought long extinguished. The chemistry, the undeniable pull between us, was as strong as ever, a reminder of the depth of our shared history and the complexities of our present circumstances. Yet, each encounter ended with a palpable sense of unfinished business, of words left unsaid and feelings unexplored, adding layers of emotional complexity to an already challenging mission.

Amidst the operational planning and covert surveillance, I found my thoughts drifting to Emily with alarming regularity. I worried about the dangers her investigation into the militia might uncover, about the lengths they might go to protect their secrets. The thought of her coming to harm because of my inability to maintain distance was a constant shadow, darkening even the most routine aspects of my mission.

These emotional complications were a liability, a layer of distraction I could ill afford. Yet, they were also undeniably human, a testament to the bonds that tied me to this town and its people. As much as I tried to compartmentalize, to separate the soldier from the man, the lines blurred, leaving me to navigate a maze of duty, affection, and concern.

In the quiet of the night, with only the sound of my footsteps for company, I acknowledged the depth of my dilemma. The mission to protect my hometown from the insidious reach of the militia was clear. But so too was the need to protect Emily, not just from the physical dangers that lurked in the shadows, but from the emotional fallout of our tangled past and uncertain future.

As I made my way back to the safe house, the resolve that had guided me thus far felt tinged with a newfound vulnerability. The challenges ahead were not just tactical but deeply personal, a complex weave of professional duty and emotional entanglement.

Navigating this terrain would require not just skill and strategy, but a level of emotional resilience I was only beginning to understand.

In the days that followed, my cautious dance around the peripheries of the Black Oak Militia began to yield results. A tentative acceptance from some of its fringe members led to whispers of a gathering—a more clandestine meeting than the community fronts I had so far navigated. It was an opportunity I couldn't pass up, a chance to delve deeper into the heart of the militia's operations and intentions.

The invitation came through Mitch Larson, the old high school acquaintance who'd become my unwitting link to the militia's inner circle. "There's a meeting this weekend, out at the old Henderson farm," he said, a hint of caution in his voice. "They're wary of newcomers, but I've vouched for you. Don't make me regret it."

As I drove to the rendezvous point, the weight of the moment settled heavily on me. This was no ordinary gathering. It was a step into the shadows, where the militia's true colors would likely be on display. My role required a delicate balance of engagement and detachment, a challenge to every ounce of my training and resolve.

The Henderson farm was secluded, a forgotten piece of land that time and progress had bypassed. As I arrived, the isolation of the location struck me as emblematic of the militia itself—removed from the mainstream, hidden in plain sight. The gathering was small, a dozen figures clustered around a flickering bonfire, their faces alternately illuminated and obscured by the flames.

Mark Dalton, the militia's charismatic leader, was holding court as I approached. His rhetoric was fervent, a mixture of passionate conviction and dangerous ideology. The topics ranged from government overreach to the erosion of fundamental liberties, each point punctuated by nods of agreement from his audience.

As the discussion turned to plans for action, the air grew thick with a mix of anticipation and tension. Proposals were voiced in vague terms, coded language hinting at acts designed to shake the complacent from their slumber. My role as the disillusioned veteran found its testing ground here, among men and women who saw themselves as patriots on the brink of a necessary revolution.

"Jake, you've seen firsthand what we're up against," Dalton said, turning his piercing gaze upon me. "The corruption, the lies. It's veterans like you who understand the cost of freedom. What say you?"

Every fiber of my being screamed caution as I weighed my response. To show too little enthusiasm would raise suspicion; too much could entangle me in plans I had no intention of supporting. "I'm here because I believe in what you're fighting for," I began, choosing my words with care. "But I also know that recklessness only serves our enemies. Whatever we do, it has to be smart, calculated."

My answer seemed to satisfy Dalton, a nod of acknowledgment granting me a continued place at the fire. But the line I walked was razor-thin, each step forward into their confidence a step closer to the precipice of moral compromise.

As the meeting disbanded, plans still cloaked in the ambiguity of 'when the time is right,' I was left to reflect on the evening's revelations. The militia was more organized, more radical than I had anticipated. Their talk of action was not mere bravado; it was a promise of things to come.

Driving back from the farm, the night seemed darker, the path ahead more uncertain. My infiltration had deepened, but so too had the complexities of my mission. Balancing the need for information against the ethical boundaries of my role had never felt more daunting.

Yet, amid the doubts, my resolve hardened. The militia's plans, whatever they might be, posed a clear and present danger to the community I had sworn to protect. My emotional ties to the town, to Emily, and to the simple yet profound memories of my past, were both a vulnerability and a source of strength—a reminder of why failure was not an option.

The drive back from the Henderson farm was a solitary journey through the darkened country roads, a physical distance that mirrored the growing chasm within me. My mind, a whirlwind of thoughts and emotions, grappled with the dichotomy of my identity—Jake Thompson, the Navy SEAL, versus Jake Thompson, the man entangled in the complex web of his past and present.

Memories of my SEAL training surged to the forefront, vivid recollections of grueling exercises and the relentless push beyond physical and mental limits. These flashbacks were not just echoes of my past; they were reminders of the core values instilled in me: honor, courage, commitment. Values that defined me as a soldier and guided me as a man.

Yet, as I navigated the familiar streets of my hometown, those very values were tested. The undercover work, essential as it was to my mission, forced me into a role that blurred the lines of right and wrong. Each step deeper into the militia's confidence was a step away from the man I wanted to be, from the clarity of purpose that had once seemed unassailable.

The internal conflict was a relentless tide, washing over me in waves of doubt and determination. How could I reconcile the soldier's discipline and the man's heart? Was it possible to uphold my duty without betraying the essence of who I was?

Lost in this turmoil, I found myself pulling over at the edge of the old town park, drawn by a force I couldn't resist. The park, with its sprawling oaks and winding paths, had been a sanctuary of simpler times, of childhood dreams and youthful promises. And there, carved into the trunk of an ancient oak, were the initials "J.T. + E.H."—a testament to a love that had once seemed as enduring as the tree itself.

Standing before our initials, the weight of my current duplicity bore down on me with a crushing intensity. The carving, a symbol of innocence and hope, stood in stark contrast to the man I had become—a man ensnared in a mission that demanded deception and secrecy. The pain of that realization was sharp, a poignant reminder of the distance between the person I was and the person I needed to be.

The personal cost of my mission, illuminated by the soft glow of moonlight on the carved initials, was suddenly, painfully clear. Was protecting my hometown, uncovering the militia's plans, worth the erosion of my own integrity? Could the ends truly justify the means, or was I losing a part of myself in the pursuit of a greater good?

In that moment of doubt, with the cool night air whispering through the leaves, I questioned everything. The mission, my role within it, the potential fallout for those I cared about—especially Emily. The thought of her, of the potential danger my actions could bring to her doorstep, added a layer of fear to the already complex tapestry of my emotions.

As I left the park, the echo of my footsteps a solitary sound in the quiet night, I carried with me a heavy heart. The resolve to complete my mission remained, but it was tempered by a newfound awareness of its personal cost. The soldier within me was ready to fight, to protect at all costs. But the man I was, the man I hoped to be, knew the road ahead would be one of the hardest I'd ever walked.

Digging Deeper

Emily

In the hushed quiet of the early hours, the glow from my desk lamp cast long shadows across the walls, turning my cluttered workspace into a solitary island of light. Surrounded by stacks of old newspapers, their pages yellowed with time, and the cold glow of my computer screen, I felt like a detective from another era, piecing together clues to solve a mystery that threatened the very heart of my community.

As I sifted through article after article, forum post after forum post, a picture began to emerge from the shadows. The Black Oak Militia's activities were no longer random, disjointed events in my mind but parts of a larger, more sinister plan. Like dark clouds gathering before a storm, each piece of information added weight to the looming threat.

My fingers flew over the keyboard, tracing the digital breadcrumbs left by the militia. The anonymity of the internet could not hide the escalation of their plans. It wasn't just angry rhetoric; there were logistics, discussions of meetings and movements that hinted at something tangible, something imminent.

The deeper I dug, the heavier the silence around me felt, broken only by the occasional creak of the old chair or the distant sound of a car passing by. The urgency of my mission pressed down on me, a tangible weight that made the task ahead seem both vital and overwhelming.

Every forum post I decrypted, every anonymous tip I followed, painted a clearer picture of a group far more dangerous than I had initially believed. What had once seemed like a local oddity was now a clear and present danger, a shadow creeping across the town I loved.

The night wore on, and I found myself leaning back in my chair, exhausted but unable to stop. My eyes burned from the screen's glare, from reading between the lines of coded messages and veiled threats. The pattern of the militia's activities unfolded before me, a timeline that spoke of radicalization and a crescendo of ambition.

Sitting in the dim glow of the desk lamp, I couldn't help but lean back, letting the chair take the weight of not just my body but the heavy cloak of responsibility I'd wrapped around myself. My eyes, tired from hours of scrutinizing data and decrypting the hidden messages of the Black Oak Militia, closed for a moment, seeking respite in the darkness behind my lids.

It was during these moments, in the silence of the early hours, that memories of my college years surfaced. Back then, armed with nothing but a notepad, a pen, and an insatiable curiosity, I had embarked on a journey to become a journalist. I remembered the challenges, the late nights spent pouring over textbooks and articles, learning the craft that I hoped would one day allow me to make a difference in the world.

College had been a crucible, shaping and testing my resolve. It was there that I learned the true value of persistence, the importance of digging beneath the surface to uncover the truth hidden in the shadows. Each assignment, each project, had been a step on the path that led me here, to this moment, to this mission that felt larger than anything I had faced before.

As I sat in the quiet of my office, surrounded by the evidence of my current investigation, I couldn't help but draw strength from those early experiences. They reminded me that the essence of journalism was not just in the telling of stories but in the revealing of truths, in the shedding of light on the dark corners of our world.

The challenges I faced back then, the doubts and fears, were not so different from what I felt now. But just as I had persevered then, I would persevere now. The Black Oak Militia, with their veiled threats and hidden agendas, would not deter me. I had a duty, not just as a journalist but as a member of this community, to continue the work I had started, to follow the trail wherever it led, no matter the danger.

***

With a deep breath, I opened my eyes, the darkness of reflection giving way to the determined focus of action. The early morning light, now spilling through the blinds, brought with it a new day, a new opportunity to pursue the truth. My resolve, forged in the fires of my past, was unbreakable. I was ready to face whatever the day brought, armed with persistence, determination, and the unwavering belief in the power of the truth.

I had arranged to meet the informant, a shadow of a figure who had once stood proudly among the ranks of the Black Oak Militia, at an old diner on the edge of town. It was the kind of place that seemed to exist out of time, where the coffee was always strong and the booths held the secrets of a thousand hushed conversations. As I pushed open the door, the bell chimed a greeting, echoing off the faded walls adorned with relics of a bygone era.

He was already there, seated in the farthest booth from the door, his back to the wall, eyes scanning the room with a nervous energy that betrayed his outward calm. I slid into the seat across from him, noting the way his hands trembled slightly as he reached for his cup. The diner was nearly empty, save for a couple of late-night stragglers at the counter, giving us a bubble of privacy in the otherwise silent space.

"Thank you for meeting me," I started, keeping my voice low, conscious of the weight of this moment. The informant nodded, his gaze darting around the room before settling back on me.

"It's not safe, talking like this," he whispered, his voice barely audible over the hum of the old fluorescent lights above. "They're everywhere, watching, listening. You don't know what they're capable of."

I leaned in, my recorder hidden beneath the table, capturing every word. "Tell me about the militia," I urged. "Why did you leave?"

He sighed, a sound heavy with regret and fear. "It wasn't supposed to be like this," he began, his words coming faster now, a dam breaking. "It started as a group of folks concerned about where the country was headed, about protecting our way of life. But it's... it's changed. They've become radicalized, talking about actions that..." He trailed off, shaking his head.

"Actions that what?" I pressed, sensing the significance of his hesitation.

"Actions that could hurt a lot of innocent people," he finished, his eyes haunted. "Plans that, if carried out, could change this community forever."

The gravity of his words settled between us, a tangible presence in the booth. "Why come forward now?" I asked.

"Because it's gone too far," he answered, a firm resolve underlying his fear. "Because maybe, just maybe, someone can stop them before it's too late."

As we continued to talk, he outlined the militia's recent movements, their recruitment strategies, and the alarming shift in their rhetoric. It was a portrait of radicalization that chilled me to the bone, a story of a group teetering on the edge of violence against their own community.

When we parted ways, the informant melting into the shadows of the early dawn, I was left with a notebook filled with the kind of information that could either break the story wide open or put me in immense danger. The realization that I was now a marked woman, a threat to the militia's shadowy agenda, was sobering.

But more than fear, I felt a surge of resolve. This was why I became a journalist, to shine a light on the darkest corners of our society, to give voice to the voiceless and hold the powerful accountable. The informant's words, his warnings, had only sharpened my determination.

As I drove back to the office I knew what I had to do. The story of the Black Oak Militia, their plans, and the danger they posed, needed to be told. It was no longer just an assignment; it was a mission, a duty to my community and to the principles of truth and justice that had guided my entire career.

This breakthrough, while marking me as a target, also solidified my resolve. I was no longer just a reporter; I was a guardian of the truth, ready to face whatever threats lay ahead to bring this story to light.

While delving deeper into the Black Oak Militia, I stumble across echoes of Jake's past, a juxtaposition that gnaws at me. The locals, when they're not cautiously sidestepping questions about the militia, speak of Jake with a warmth that's palpable. "Jake Thompson? Oh, he was always up to something good around here," Mr. Davidson, the owner of the local hardware store, recalls with a chuckle. "Helped build that gazebo in the park, volunteered everywhere... a real community guy."

Hearing these stories, I can't help but wonder about the man who left versus the one who returned. The Jake of the past, the one who smiled easily and lent a hand without hesitation, seems at odds with the guarded, distant figure I encountered at the festival. This duality perplexes me, stirring a cocktail of nostalgia and concern within.

Mrs. Henderson, the librarian, adds her own recollection, her eyes softening as she speaks. "Jake and Emily, you two were inseparable. Always plotting some project or other. He had such high hopes... for himself, for you, for this town." Her words, meant to comfort, instead cast a shadow of doubt. The Jake I knew was full of dreams and determination, a stark contrast to the man shrouded in mystery now walking our streets.

These reflections, these snippets of a shared past, highlight a divide. They paint a picture of a young man deeply woven into the fabric of our community, his aspirations as boundless as the sky above our small town. Yet, the Jake who has returned carries a weight, a sense of disillusionment that seems to cloud his once-clear eyes.

As I gather these stories, piecing together the image of Jake from the echoes left in his wake, I'm confronted with my own conflicted feelings. The man who stands before me now, enigmatic and withdrawn, is both familiar and foreign. The connection we once shared, rooted in shared dreams and mutual respect, now feels fractured by time and experience.

These tales of Jake's involvement in local projects before his departure serve as a poignant reminder of what once was, adding layers of complexity to the turmoil of emotions I find myself navigating. The contrast between the Jake of then and the Jake of now is stark, leaving me to ponder the journey that has led to such a transformation.

My pursuit of the truth about the Black Oak Militia hasn't gone unnoticed. The subtle signs of surveillance begin to accumulate, a silent testament to the fact that my investigations are stepping on sensitive toes. Shadows seem to linger a bit too long in my periphery, unfamiliar faces appear too frequently in my usual haunts, their glances darting away the moment our eyes meet.

One morning, arriving at the office, I find a note slipped under my door, its message stark in its simplicity: "Stop digging." The handwriting is unfamiliar, but the intent is clear, sending a shiver down my spine. It's an anonymous threat, but the danger it implies is all too real.

The phone calls start soon after. Always when I'm alone in the office, the caller hangs up after a few seconds, their silence on the other end of the line more menacing than any words could be. But then, one voice breaks the pattern, raspy and distorted, as if speaking through a filter, "You're in over your head. Leave it alone." The line goes dead before I can respond, the dial tone echoing in the suddenly oppressive silence of my workspace.

These incidents, unsettling in their ambiguity, make one thing unmistakably clear: someone is watching me. My efforts to uncover the militia's activities have made me a target. Each veiled warning, each shadowed figure, serves as a stark reminder of the risks involved in chasing this story.

Yet, with each attempt to intimidate me, my resolve only hardens. The dangers I'm facing, rather than deterring me, only serve to underscore the importance of my work. If the militia, or those sympathetic to their cause, are going to these lengths to scare me off, then what I'm close to uncovering must truly matter.

The growing attention, far from scaring me into silence, ignites a fire within me. I'm a journalist, after all. Exposing the truth, especially when it's being guarded by threats and shadows, is not just my job but my calling. The realization that I'm being watched, that my pursuit of the story has drawn the militia's gaze, only reinforces my determination.

I won't be intimidated. I won't back down. The people of this town deserve to know what's brewing in the shadows, and I'm going to be the one to tell them. The dangers I face are real, but so is my commitment to shining a light on the dark corners of our community. With every veiled threat and every anonymous warning, I'm reminded of the stakes—both for myself and for the town I call home.

Conflicted Hearts

Jake

Standing at the edge of the old fishing pier, I could feel the cool breeze coming off the river, carrying with it the faint scent of moss and the promise of an impending autumn. This place, with its weathered wood and the gentle sound of water lapping against the supports, had always been a sanctuary of sorts—a place where my grandfather and I would spend hours in silence, waiting for a bite, lost in our own thoughts.

The memories were as clear as the waters below, each one a reminder of the lessons learned on this very pier. My grandfather, a stoic man shaped by his own experiences in war, often spoke of duty and sacrifice, though more often through actions than words. It was here, amidst the quiet patience of fishing, that he imparted the values that would later drive me to join the Navy, to strive to be a SEAL.

As I gazed out over the river, the reflection of the early morning sun shimmering on the surface, I couldn't help but feel the weight of those lessons bearing down on me. The simplicity of those days stood in stark contrast to the complexity of the mission I now faced. A mission that had brought me back to my roots, to a town brimming with memories, now shadowed by the presence of the Black Oak Militia.

The solitude offered by the pier allowed me a moment to strip away the layers of the operative, the disguise of the disillusioned veteran, and just be Jake Thompson for a brief moment. It was a necessary respite, a chance to gather my thoughts and steel my resolve. The mission, with all its dangers and moral quandaries, was not just a matter of national security; it was personal, a defense of the very community that had shaped me.

In the stillness of the morning, with only the occasional call of a bird to break the silence, I found a renewed sense of purpose. The foundational values instilled in me by my grandfather, the dedication to duty and the willingness to make sacrifices, were as relevant now as they had ever been. They were a beacon, guiding me through the murky waters of undercover work, reminding me of the importance of the task at hand.

As the sun climbed higher, casting long shadows across the pier, I knew that the time for reflection was over. The day ahead would be filled with challenges, each one a test of my training, my resolve, and my ability to navigate the dangerous path I had chosen. But the lessons of this place, the quiet strength of my grandfather's teachings, would remain with me, a steady compass in the tumultuous journey ahead.

With one last look at the river, a silent tribute to the memories and the man who had helped shape me, I turned away from the pier. The world beyond awaited, with its conflicts and complexities, but I was ready. The values forged in the simplicity of childhood, reinforced by the rigor of SEAL training, would guide my actions. I was Jake Thompson, SEAL and protector, and I would not falter.

The tranquility of the morning was abruptly shattered by a voice, unmistakably hers, calling my name. "Jake?" The surprise in Emily's tone mirrored my own as I turned to find her standing at the entrance to the pier, a silhouette against the brightening sky. How long had she been there? Had she witnessed my solitary reflection?

"Emily," I managed, my voice steadier than I felt. The sight of her here, in a place so laden with personal history, felt like worlds colliding. "What are you doing here?"

She took a few hesitant steps forward, her gaze searching mine. "I saw you leaving the diner," she began, a slight tremble in her voice betraying her calm exterior. "I... I just had to know why you're really back."

The tension between us was palpable, a taut line stretched to its breaking point by questions and half-truths. I could see the concern etched in her features, the curiosity that had always driven her now focused intently on me. But beneath that, there was something else—something that stirred memories of a time when honesty was our only currency.

"I told you, I'm here to settle some personal matters," I said, the lie tasting bitter on my tongue. Maintaining my cover in front of Emily, of all people, felt like a betrayal of the bond we once shared. Yet, divulging the truth, exposing her to the danger that shadowed my every move, was a risk I couldn't afford to take.

Her brow furrowed, a silent challenge to my evasion. "Jake, I know you. There's more to it than that. You've changed... and I'm worried about you."

The conversation with Emily teetered on the edge of truths I yearned to divulge. Each question she posed, laced with concern and unyielding curiosity, tempted me to break my silence, to share the weight of the secret mission that brought me back to our shared past. The air between us was charged with an intensity that harked back to days when honesty was our unspoken pact, a foundation upon which our relationship was built.

"Emily, there's so much I wish I could tell you," I confessed, the words slipping out in a moment of vulnerability. Her eyes, wide and expectant, fixed on me, as if willing me to continue. It was a pivotal moment, one that could alter the course of our rekindled connection.

But as the words hovered on the tip of my tongue, a sharp clarity cut through the swirling emotions. The dangers of my mission, the shadowy presence of the militia that I was here to dismantle, loomed large in my mind. Emily, with her relentless pursuit of the story behind the militia, had unwittingly positioned herself in the crosshairs of a threat she didn't fully comprehend. The consequences of her investigation, coupled with any perceived association with me, could place her in grave danger.

Swallowing the confession that had nearly breached my lips, I steadied my resolve. "But I can't. Not now." The words were a physical effort, a deliberate restraint of the truth that ached to be shared. The look of frustration and hurt that flashed across Emily's face was a stab to my conscience, a reminder of the cost of the double life I was forced to lead.

"It's not that I don't trust you, Em," I continued, each word measured and heavy with unspoken apologies. "It's just... complicated. The less you know, the safer you'll be." The justification felt hollow, even to my own ears, but it was a truth she needed to understand, even if it couldn't be fully explained.

The tension between us shifted, a new barrier erected by my refusal to confide in her. Emily's stance, once open and seeking, now held a guarded edge, a protective shield against the partial truths I offered. "I get it, Jake. Duty first, right?" Her voice held a note of resignation, laced with a bitterness that pained me to hear.

The tranquility of our encounter was abruptly pierced by the distant clamor of voices, an undercurrent of tension that swept towards us like a cold front. The sudden intrusion of this discord into our secluded moment by the pier jolted me back to reality, a stark reminder of the volatile undercurrents flowing beneath the town's seemingly calm surface.

Instinctively, my gaze swept towards the source of the disturbance, identifying the telltale signs of militia activity. The subtle, yet unmistakable, movement among the shadows near the edge of the wooded area adjacent to the pier sent a clear signal—danger was closer than I had realized.

Without hesitation, my protective instincts surged to the forefront. "We need to go, Emily," I urged, my voice low but insistent. The confusion in her eyes pained me, but there was no time to explain. I grasped her hand, feeling the tension of the moment intertwine with the warmth of her touch, an odd juxtaposition against the urgency of our departure.

As we hastily retreated from the pier, I kept a vigilant eye on our surroundings, the trained part of my brain cataloging escape routes and potential threats. Emily's presence at my side, her safety now my immediate concern, added a layer of personal risk to an already dangerous situation.

The encounter with the militia, though unseen by Emily, was a glaring indicator of the risks she unknowingly faced. My mission, aimed at infiltrating and undermining the militia from within, had suddenly intersected with my personal life in a way I had hoped to avoid. The reality that Emily could become a target by association, or simply by being in the wrong place at the wrong time, was a possibility I couldn't ignore.

Once we were a safe distance away, the adrenaline that had fueled our swift departure began to ebb, leaving behind a heavy silence. Emily's questions hung in the air, unasked yet palpable, as she tried to make sense of the sudden shift in our evening. My explanations were vague, crafted to provide comfort without revealing too much. "Just a precaution, Em. It's better to be safe," I offered, hating the evasion even as I spoke the words.

The close call served as a stark reminder of the dangers my presence brought to those around me, especially to Emily. The balance I had been striving to maintain between my personal connections and my professional obligations had been upended, revealing the precarious nature of my dual existence.

***

Alone in the dimly lit confines of my grandfather's house, the day's events played back in my mind with vivid clarity. The serenity of the old fishing pier, momentarily reclaimed in Emily's presence, now felt like a distant memory, overshadowed by the harsh intrusion of my mission's reality. The close encounter with the militia near the pier, though unseen by Emily, was a jarring reminder of the delicate balance I was forced to maintain.

Ensuring Emily's safety had been instinctual, a non-negotiable priority that had momentarily unified the conflicting aspects of my life. But as I replayed our hasty retreat, the implications of our encounter with the militia loomed large. The risk of exposure, of drawing unwanted attention to Emily because of her proximity to me, was a variable I had hoped to control more effectively.

The solitude of the house offered no comfort, only the space to confront the complexities of my situation. My dual existence as Jake Thompson, the hometown hero, and the undercover operative tasked with dismantling a growing domestic threat, had never felt more at odds. The personal connections that anchored me to this town, that provided both motivation and cover for my mission, now seemed like liabilities—avenues through which harm could come to those I cared about.

The weight of my mission and the complexity of my feelings for Emily clashed within me, a storm of conflicting loyalties and unspoken fears. Each thought of distancing myself from her, of stepping back to ensure her safety, was countered by an equally strong pull, a reluctance to leave her without the protection my presence afforded. The thought of the militia, with their hidden agendas and creeping influence, targeting her because of her investigative work was a scenario I couldn't bear.

As I paced the small, sparse room, the echoes of our past interactions, the warmth of our recent encounter, played over in my mind. Emily, with her relentless pursuit of the truth, her courage and resilience, deserved to carry out her work without the shadow of danger I inadvertently cast over her. Yet, the idea of stepping away, of severing our rekindled connection to safeguard her from a threat she was barely aware of, felt like a betrayal of a different sort.

My loyalty to my mission, to the values and duties ingrained in me as a SEAL, demanded a certain detachment, a focus that left little room for personal entanglements. But my heart, irrevocably entwined with the town and its people, refused to comply. Emily, more than just a symbol of my past, represented a tangible link to the very essence of what I was fighting to protect. Her passion for her work, her dedication to exposing the truth, mirrored the commitment I felt to my own mission. Yet, it was this shared dedication that placed us both at the heart of the danger.

In the quiet hours of the night, I wrestled with these torn loyalties, the dual aspects of my life that seemed increasingly irreconcilable. The notion of distancing myself from Emily, of adopting a colder, more calculated approach to protect her, battled against the deeper, more instinctual desire to stand by her, to confront the coming storm together. It was a tactical decision, viewed through the lens of mission parameters and operational security, but it was also a deeply personal dilemma.

The knowledge that my mission, my very identity in this town, could become a weapon used against her by the militia was a chilling realization. The stakes of my undercover work, already high, were magnified by the personal connections that anchored me to this place. My role as a protector, both as a SEAL and as someone who cared deeply for Emily, demanded a level of vigilance and sacrifice that left little room for the vulnerabilities of the heart.

In search of clarity, I reached out to an old comrade, Brian, someone who had walked the fine line between duty and personal life with a grace I envied. We met under the guise of catching up, but as the conversation progressed, the depth of my turmoil must have been evident, even as I danced around the specifics of my mission.

"Jake," Brian began, his voice tempered by experience, "we carry these burdens because we're capable, because we've been trained to handle what would break most. But we're also human. You can't forget that."

I nodded, the lump in my throat growing. It was one thing to understand the mission's importance intellectually, quite another to navigate the emotional minefield it laid in my personal life.

"You're talking in circles a bit, buddy," he observed, his gaze sharp. "If this is about more than just the mission—if it's about someone from your past, maybe—it doesn't diminish your commitment. It just means you've got more skin in the game."

The mention of someone from my past, so casually broached, hit closer to home than I expected. Emily's image flashed before my eyes, her determined pursuit of the truth, her unwitting entanglement in a web I had helped weave.

"It's... complicated," I admitted, the words feeling inadequate to describe the maelstrom of emotions I was wrestling with. "Let's just say there's someone who might get caught in the crossfire of this thing I'm working on. And I'm trying to figure out how to protect them without compromising the mission."

Brian leaned back, considering this. "Sounds like you've already decided what's important," he said after a moment. "The question is, how do you balance it? Our training teaches us to compartmentalize, to keep the mission front and center. But we're not robots. Our connections, the people who matter to us, they're why we fight. They're what we're protecting."

His words resonated deeply, offering a semblance of comfort in their acknowledgment of the duality of my situation. "So, what, I just follow my heart? Hope it doesn't lead me off course?"

"Not exactly," Brian chuckled, the sound warm in the cool evening air. "Following your heart is important, but so is discipline. You've got the skills, Jake. You know how to assess a situation, to make the hard calls. Just remember, those skills don't just apply to the battlefield. They're just as crucial when navigating personal waters."

The advice, simple yet profound, provided a new lens through which to view my predicament. It wasn't a matter of choosing duty over personal connection or vice versa. It was about integrating the two, leveraging the strengths and insights gained from each to inform my decisions.

As our conversation drew to a close, with promises to catch up again soon, I felt a renewed sense of purpose. Brian's words had offered a guiding light through the fog of uncertainty that had clouded my thoughts. Personal connections, like my relationship with Emily, weren't just vulnerabilities to be managed or obstacles to be navigated. They were reminders of what I was fighting for, beacons that could guide my actions and inform my choices.

Walking away from our meeting, the night seemed a little less oppressive, the weight on my shoulders a little lighter. The path ahead remained fraught with peril, the balance between duty and personal connection delicate and complex. But Brian's counsel had provided a crucial piece of the puzzle, a reminder that the heart and the mission weren't mutually exclusive. In the intricate dance of loyalty and love, each step was informed by the other, each decision a reflection of both the soldier and the man I was.

I walked to the bridge overlooking the town, my town. As I stood there, the weight of my mission pressing down on me, I couldn't help but think of Emily. Her presence in my life, once a source of pure joy, had become a complexity I hadn't anticipated. My feelings for her, as undiminished by time as they were unexpected, added a layer of personal stakes to the already high price of failure.

Yet, amid the swirling maelstrom of emotions, a resolve began to take shape. I had a duty to perform, a community to protect, and a threat to neutralize. These were non-negotiable, the core of the mission that had brought me back to this place I still called home.

But intertwined with that was something equally fundamental—the need to protect Emily, to ensure that the dangers I faced didn't spill over into her life.

As the night deepened, wrapping the town in shadows, my thoughts clarified. Yes, the mission was fraught with danger, and yes, my feelings for Emily complicated an already complex situation. But I was a SEAL, trained to face adversity, to make the hard decisions in the service of a greater good. My love for Emily, far from being a weakness, was a reminder of what was at stake, a source of strength that anchored me to the very essence of why I fought.

With a deep breath, I stepped away from the railing, my gaze lingering on the quiet streets below. The resolve that had solidified in the solitude of the night was more than just a commitment to the mission; it was a vow to protect the town and its people, Emily included, from the shadows encroaching upon it.

As I made my way off the bridge, the determination that filled me was a beacon as bright as the lights below. The path ahead was perilous, filled with unseen dangers and moral quandaries. But I was ready to face it, armed with the skills of a SEAL and the heart of a man who loved deeply. The mission would demand everything I had, and I was prepared to give it, for the sake of duty, for the sake of love.

The Story Builds

Emily

Sitting alone, the steady rhythm of my heartbeat seemed to echo through the quiet, dimly-lit office. The unexpected ping of my email jolted me, breaking the stillness like a stone cast into a calm pond. On my screen, an anonymous message blinked back at me, promising critical information about the Black Oak Militia, but with a catch—it demanded secrecy, a clandestine meeting shrouded in the shadows on the outskirts of town.

The weight of the decision pressed upon me, each word of the message threading through my thoughts with a mix of intrigue and apprehension. This could be the breakthrough I had been chasing, the key to exposing the militia's underbelly. Yet, the insistence on secrecy, the chosen isolation of the meeting place—it all whispered of the risks involved, of the danger that lurked just beyond the glow of my computer screen.

For a moment, I allowed myself to lean back, to look beyond the computer's glare and into the shadows of my office. My father's old desk, littered with notes and clippings from his own journalistic endeavors, stood as a silent testament to the legacy I carried forward. The risk of meeting with an unknown source, especially one so intimately tied to a group as volatile as the Black Oak Militia, was not lost on me. But then, neither was the importance of what this meeting could mean for my investigation.

With a deep, steadying breath, I considered the options. Ignoring the tip could mean missing out on vital information, a lead that could potentially dismantle the militia's plans and protect the town. Yet, accepting it, stepping into the unknown with little more than my recorder and my wits, was to walk a tightrope without a net, where the fall could be catastrophic.

The decision, heavy with the weight of potential consequences, hung in the air like a specter. Yet, as I stared into the dimness of my office, the answer became clear. The drive to uncover the truth, to shine a light into the darkest corners of our community, was too ingrained in me to ignore. It was more than a calling—it was a duty, one that came with risks, certainly, but also with the potential to safeguard the very fabric of our town.

Resolved, I typed a cautious reply, agreeing to the meeting but on my terms. I would take every precaution, inform a trusted colleague of my whereabouts, and ensure that my steps were tracked. The preparation for such a meeting was meticulous, a blend of journalistic rigor and the survival instincts that my career had honed over the years.

As I sent the email, the charged air around me seemed to pulse with the gravity of my choice. The silence of the office wrapped around me once more, but now it was a cloak of determination, a mantle I wore as I set forth to confront whatever secrets awaited in the shadows. The tip was more than a lead; it was a challenge, a test of my resolve, and I was ready to meet it head-on.

As I prepared to follow up on this lead, a heavy silence enveloped me, broken only by the soft ticking of the clock. It was in these quiet moments that doubt crept in, wrapping its fingers around my resolve. The ethical implications of my investigation loomed large, a constant weight on my shoulders.

I couldn't shake the feeling of standing on a precipice, about to step into the unknown. The information I sought had the power to expose, to alter lives and perceptions. But the thought of potentially misinterpreting someone's intentions, of unjustly casting them in a light that could change their life forever, was daunting. Journalism, I reminded myself, was a tool of truth, but wielded carelessly, it could also harm.

The people involved in my story were not mere characters; they were real, with lives and families that could be affected by my words. The responsibility of narrating their actions, of delving into the militia's shadowy existence, was immense. I pondered the fine line between public interest and personal privacy, between the right to know and the risk of harm.

Each step of my investigation felt like navigating a minefield, where a single misstep could have unforeseen consequences. The possibility of misinterpretation, of drawing conclusions from the shadows without seeing the full picture, was a concern that gnawed at me. How could I ensure that my pursuit of the story did not inadvertently become an act of injustice?

Yet, amid these swirling doubts, a core of steel formed within me. The purpose of my work, the reason I had chosen this path, was to bring light to the hidden corners of our world, to give voice to those who had none, and to hold those in power accountable. This mission, to expose the Black Oak Militia's plans and protect my community, was a testament to that purpose.

I thought of the silent battles fought in the name of truth, of the journalists who had stood where I now stood, wrestling with their own doubts but driven by the conviction that the story must be told. Their courage, their determination to press on despite the weight of responsibility, bolstered my resolve.

In the stillness of my office, I made my decision. The risks were real, and the ethical challenges daunting, but the importance of uncovering the truth outweighed the fear of potential consequences. My role as a journalist was not just to report the news but to navigate the complexities of human stories with integrity and compassion.

The journalist in me—the seeker of truths, the voice for the voiceless—refuses to be silenced by fear or ethical quandaries. It's a part of who I am, as much as the blood coursing through my veins or the breath filling my lungs. This isn't just about curiosity or the thrill of the chase; it's about something far more significant. It's about safeguarding the very essence of my community, about ensuring that the shadows creeping at its edges are brought into the relentless light of scrutiny.

I glance at the cryptic message on my screen once more, its words a silent challenge to my resolve. The source, whoever they are, holds a piece of the puzzle that I've been tirelessly searching for—a key that could unlock the hidden machinations of the Black Oak Militia. The risk is undeniable, a shadow that looms large and threatening. Yet, what's at stake—the safety of my town, the lives of its people—demands action.

With a deep, steadying breath, I close my laptop, the click of its shutting a definitive sound in the quiet of my office. I reach for my recorder, its familiar weight a tangible reminder of the countless stories it has captured, of the truths it has helped unveil. This is my weapon, my shield—my commitment to journalism embodied in technology and determination.

I gather my belongings, each movement imbued with a sense of purpose. The cool night air awaits me, a vast expanse of possibility and danger. But within me burns a fire that no shadow can extinguish—the fire of a journalist determined to seek the truth, no matter the cost.

As I lock my office behind me, stepping into the embrace of the night, I carry with me more than just the tools of my trade. I carry a commitment to my community, a vow to pursue the truth with every fiber of my being. The road ahead may be fraught with challenges, but my path is clear. I will meet this source, come what may, armed with questions and a determination that is unyielding.

***

The night embraces the outskirts of town with an uneasy silence, the kind that seems to hold its breath, waiting for a secret to be whispered into its vast, dark expanse. As I navigate the dimly-lit streets, the outline of the abandoned warehouse looms ahead, an ominous silhouette against the starless sky. My footsteps, though cautious, resound with a determination that echoes off the deserted buildings, a testament to the gravity of the path I've chosen.

The door creaks ominously as I push it open, stepping into the shadow-filled interior of the warehouse. The air is stale, heavy with the dust of neglect and the lingering scent of decay. My eyes take a moment to adjust to the darkness, every sense heightened, every nerve alight with the acute awareness of the unknown that lies ahead.

There, in the far corner, a figure emerges from the shadows, their movements deliberate, cloaked in the anonymity that darkness provides. My heart skips a beat, not out of fear, but out of the realization of the pivotal moment this meeting represents. This is it—the clandestine rendezvous that could unravel the mysteries of the Black Oak Militia, that could alter the course of my investigation, perhaps even the safety of my town.

I step forward, my recorder clutched tightly in my hand, its presence a small comfort in the vast uncertainty of this encounter. The informant, a silhouette against the faint light filtering through the broken windows, waits silently, an enigma wrapped in the night.

"Thank you for meeting me," I begin, my voice steady despite the adrenaline coursing through my veins. "I understand the risks you're taking by speaking out. Know that your identity will be protected."

The informant nods, a slight movement that carries the weight of his decision to come forward. "The militia... they're planning something big," he whispers, his voice barely more than a breath, yet laden with a urgency that cuts through the silence. "Something that could put the whole town in danger."

I lean in, my recorder poised to capture every word, every nuance of this revelation. "Can you tell me more? What kind of plans? How imminent?"

The informant's words hang in the air between us, each one heavier than the last, sketching a scenario so dire it threatens to eclipse the faint hope I've been clinging to. "They're planning an operation," he continues, his voice a mere whisper, yet every syllable is infused with an urgency that rivets my attention. "Something big... designed to send a message, not just to our town, but to the entire state."

The implications of his words send a chill down my spine. This isn't just a group of disgruntled citizens venting their frustrations in secret meetings; this is a coordinated effort, a threat that looms large and menacing over the community I hold dear.

"What kind of operation?" I ask, my voice steady despite the tumult of emotions roiling inside me. "Do you have any details? Dates, locations, anything that can help us prevent it?"

The informant shifts uncomfortably, the shadows playing across their face. "I don't know everything," they admit, "but it's clear they're not just talking anymore. They're moving, acquiring... things. Weapons. It's like they're preparing for war."

The word 'war' echoes ominously in the deserted warehouse, a stark reminder of the stakes at play. My mind races, piecing together the fragments of information into a chilling mosaic of intent and preparation.

I absorb this revelation, the gravity of his words settling into the very marrow of my bones. The militia, a shadowy presence I've been chasing through hints and whispers, now emerges into stark relief, their intentions laid bare in all their terrifying clarity.

"They've mentioned a date," the informant adds reluctantly, "but it's been kept vague, on purpose. All I know is that it's soon, within the next few weeks. They're serious, Emily. More serious than anyone outside realizes."

I scribble notes frantically, my recorder capturing every word, every nuance of this pivotal conversation. The implications of the informant's revelations are clear: the Black Oak Militia is no mere group of disgruntled protesters. They are a formidable, organized threat, one that poses a real and immediate danger to the safety and security of our community.

"Is there anything else? Any names, any specific targets?" I probe, aware that each piece of information could be the key to thwarting their plans.

The informant hesitates, a shadow of fear crossing his obscured features. "I... I can't say much more. Just... just be careful. They're watching, and they're not above silencing those who get too close."

As the meeting concludes, a profound sense of responsibility settles upon me. The details provided by the informant, though terrifying, arm me with the knowledge needed to expose the militia's plans. The thought of what could happen if I fail to act, if this operation goes ahead unchallenged, propels me forward with a renewed sense of urgency.

Stepping out into the night, the cool air does little to quell the fire that burns within me. The Black Oak Militia's plan for a large-scale operation is no longer a shadowy rumor; it's a clear and present danger that I must bring to light. The community I love, the people I've sworn to inform and protect, are counting on me, even if they don't know it yet.

As I drive back to town, the darkness seems less oppressive, not a veil for secrets and lies, but a canvas upon which the truth, once unveiled, will shine all the brighter. My resolve is ironclad; the story I'm about to tell could change everything. It's a daunting task, but I am undeterred. I am a journalist, and this is my duty. The plan unveiled by the informant is not just a story; it's a call to action—a call that I will answer.

Sitting alone in the dim glow of my desk lamp, the stillness of the night presses in around me, amplifying the solitude of my thoughts. The information given by the informant looms large in my mind, a tangled web of potential consequences and moral quandaries. How do I navigate the fine line between informing the public and potentially inciting panic? The weight of the decision before me is immense. On one hand, the public has a right to know, to be aware of the danger lurking in the shadows of their everyday lives. Knowledge is power, and in this case, it could very well be the key to preventing a catastrophe. On the other hand, there's the risk of causing undue alarm, of setting off a chain reaction that could escalate tensions and perhaps even play into the militia's hands.

I find myself wrestling with these thoughts, turning them over in my mind like puzzle pieces that refuse to fit together. The ethical implications of my next steps are daunting, a labyrinth of "what ifs" and potential fallout that I must navigate with care.

The decision to proceed with the story is not one I can make lightly. Each potential headline, each angle I consider, is weighed against the possible outcomes. How do I strike the balance between alerting the community and avoiding unnecessary alarm? How do I ensure that my reporting leads to awareness and preparation, rather than fear and division?

These questions haunt me as I pore over my notes, the informant's words echoing in my head. The burden of knowledge is a heavy one, made all the more challenging by the isolation of my position. I can't consult openly with colleagues or seek the reassurance of friends without risking the integrity of the information or exposing them to danger.

In the end, the decision rests squarely on my shoulders. I must tread carefully, crafting a narrative that informs without sensationalizing, that prompts action without panic. It's a delicate balancing act, one that requires all of my skill and judgment as a journalist.

As I finally begin to type, the words on the screen seem to take on a weight of their own, each sentence a testament to the gravity of the situation. My resolve solidifies with every paragraph; despite the risks, this story must be told. The community deserves to know, to be given the chance to understand and respond to the threat among them.

The burden of knowledge, though heavy, is ultimately a catalyst for action. In the face of danger, silence is not an option. I am a journalist, and my duty is clear. I will tell this story with integrity and caution, armed with the truth and the hope that it will make a difference.

With the early morning light casting long shadows across my cluttered desk, I pause, realizing I need perspective beyond my own. The voices of my father's old colleagues, seasoned journalists with decades of experience navigating ethical minefields, echo in my mind. It's time to seek their counsel, to gain clarity on how best to move forward with the explosive information now in my possession.

I reach out, setting up a series of phone calls that feel more like lifelines than consultations. The first is with Mr. Thompson, a grizzled reporter who had been a mentor to my father, known for his unwavering commitment to the truth and his ability to navigate the tightrope of journalistic ethics.

"Emily," he greets me, his voice carrying the weight of experience. "Your father would be proud of the journalist you've become, but remember, with great power comes great responsibility. Your story has the potential to shake the very foundations of your community. Proceed with caution, but don't let fear dictate your actions."

His words, firm yet encouraging, provide a semblance of comfort, a reminder of the legacy I carry forward. The next call is with Mrs. Patel, a former investigative journalist who had transitioned to teaching, imparting her wisdom to the next generation. Her advice is more pragmatic, focused on the mechanics of reporting on sensitive issues.

"Document everything, Emily. Verify your sources twice over. And before you go public, consider the ramifications. It's not just about breaking the story; it's about what happens after. How will you ensure that your reporting leads to positive change, rather than panic or backlash?"

Her questions, pointed and challenging, force me to confront the broader implications of my work. It's a sobering conversation, but one that reinforces the importance of thoroughness and responsibility in my reporting.

The final call is with an old friend of my father's, Mr. Allen, who had once told me that journalism was as much about what you choose not to report as what you do. His perspective is one of caution tempered by optimism.

"Emily, the truth is a powerful tool, but it's also a double-edged sword. Your duty is to inform, yes, but also to protect. How will your story serve the greater good? How will it help your community navigate the challenges it faces? These are the questions you must answer before you proceed."

Each conversation leaves me with much to ponder, a blend of encouragement, warning, and wisdom that guides my thoughts as I return to my investigation. Consulting with my father's colleagues, tapping into their vast reservoirs of experience, I find not just advice but a renewed sense of purpose.

Their collective wisdom, a beacon in the murky waters of my investigation, solidifies my resolve. I am reminded that integrity, caution, and a deep-seated commitment to the greater good must be the cornerstones of my reporting. Armed with their guidance, I am ready to face the challenges ahead, to tell the story that needs to be told with the responsibility and care it deserves.

The hum of my computer fills the silence of the early morning hours as I sit, poised and determined, in front of the glowing screen. The weight of the information I've gathered presses on me, a tangible reminder of the stakes at play. Now, it's time to weave the disparate threads of my investigation into a coherent narrative, one that will shed light on the shadows lurking within our community.

I start with an introduction that sets the stage, grounding the reader in the context of our seemingly tranquil town, a place where the undercurrent of unrest has simmered unnoticed by many. The cursor blinks steadily, a constant companion as I delve deeper into the heart of the story.

Each paragraph is crafted with precision, aiming to strike the perfect balance between informing the public and avoiding unnecessary alarm. The details of the militia's planned operations, drawn from the whispered confessions of disillusioned members and the ominous hints of impending action, are laid out with all the clarity and caution they demand.

I pause, reflecting on the conversations I've had with my father's colleagues, their advice echoing in my mind. Integrity. Responsibility. The need to tread carefully on this tightrope of truth-telling. These principles guide my hand as I navigate the complexities of reporting on such a sensitive issue.

The challenge is not just to expose the militia's intentions but to do so in a way that catalyzes constructive dialogue, that prompts action without panic. I strive to give voice to the concerns and fears of our community, to highlight the resilience and unity that have always been our strength in the face of adversity.

As the article takes shape, I find myself wrestling with the implications of my words. This isn't just a story; it's a call to awareness, a spotlight on the dark corners we've overlooked. It's an appeal to the better angels of our nature, a plea for vigilance, understanding, and collective action.

The final paragraphs are a testament to the courage of those who have come forward, the importance of staying informed, and the power of community solidarity. I conclude with a call to action, not just for the authorities but for every resident of our town. It's a declaration that, armed with knowledge, we can stand together against threats to our peace and security.

Pressing 'save', I lean back, the tension slowly ebbing from my shoulders. The draft of the article, now complete, represents more than just my work as a journalist; it's a beacon of hope, a promise that with transparency and determination, we can navigate the challenges ahead.

Yet, as I sit in the quiet of my office, surrounded by the glow of the screen, I'm acutely aware of the risks ahead. This article, once published, will mark me indelibly, drawing the militia's ire directly to me. But the decision to proceed feels not just right but necessary. The story of the Black Oak Militia, with all its implications and dangers, needs to be told. And I, armed with the truth and a steadfast commitment to my community, am ready to tell it.

Dangerous Liaisons

Jake

In the shadow-draped outskirts of the warehouse, our unexpected meeting unfolded with the tension and surprise of a clandestine drama. I was there, hidden in the darkness, my eyes trained on the comings and goings that whispered of militia activity. My mission was clear, yet fraught with complexities I had yet to fully navigate. The weight of my duty pressed heavily upon me, a constant reminder of the stakes at play.

And, I found myself once again in Emily's unexpected company. This wasn't our first encounter since my return; the Harvest Home Festival had already set the stage for this complex dance of rekindled feelings and unspoken tensions. Yet, here, against the backdrop of a mission that thrummed with covert dangers, our meeting felt charged with a different kind of intensity.

As I watched her, a silhouette against the faint glow of her camera screen, memories of the festival flickered through my mind—a mixture of joy and caution, of old flames whispering to life in the autumn air. Seeing her now, determined and fearless, reignited the warmth that had simmered beneath the surface since that night, stirring a whirlwind of emotions I had struggled to compartmentalize.

"Why are you here, Emily?" I found myself asking, my voice low, tinged with a mix of concern and incredulity. It wasn't just curiosity that drove my question but an undercurrent of fear. The dangers lurking in the shadows were not for the faint-hearted, and Emily, with her fierce determination and relentless pursuit of truth, had unknowingly stepped into a perilous web.

Her presence there, in the very heart of potential danger, was a testament to her courage and her commitment to unveiling the shadows that threatened our town. Yet, as she turned to face me, her camera a silent witness in her hands, I could see the resolve that framed her features—a resolve that both impressed and worried me.

"I received a tip about the militia," she answered, her voice steady, betraying none of the fear I felt for her. "There's a story here, one that needs to be told. And I'm going to be the one to tell it."

The conviction in her words struck a chord within me, echoing the very reasons that had driven me to accept this mission. Yet, whereas I was shrouded in secrecy and deception, Emily wielded her truth like a beacon, fearless in the face of the darkness we both sought to illuminate.

"What about you, Jake?" Her question, simple yet loaded with unspoken implications, hung between us. "Why are you here?"

The truth of my presence, cloaked in the guise of a disillusioned veteran, was a narrative spun from necessity, a cover that allowed me to move unseen. But standing there before Emily, the facade felt brittle, threatened by the genuine connection that had always existed between us.

"I... I'm looking for answers," I said, the truth bending under the weight of my deception. "Just like you."

In that moment, the distance between our worlds—hers, bathed in the light of her quest for truth, and mine, obscured by the shadows of covert duty—seemed insurmountable. Yet, the shared danger of our pursuits, the parallel paths we walked, albeit cloaked in different veils, drew us together in a silent acknowledgment of the risks we faced.

"Be careful, Emily," I urged again, the warning a feeble attempt to bridge the chasm that my secrets had erected between us. "This story... it's bigger than we thought."

The chill of the evening air did little to dampen the tension that hung between us, a palpable force that seemed to draw from the very danger we had stumbled upon. It was in the midst of surveilling a secluded clearing, rumored to be a militia rendezvous point, that Emily and I found ourselves thrust into a precarious alliance. It was there, in the pursuit of a hidden cache rumored to reveal the militia's dark intentions, that we found ourselves allied in purpose, if not in method. Finding the hidden weapons was a shock. They were well-hidden but clearly meant for something bad. This discovery showed us just how serious the situation with the militia was. Everything they had been planning and preparing was right there in front of us, in a quiet spot away from prying eyes. Seeing all this made it real – we were dealing with a big threat to our town. It wasn't just about chasing a story or following a mission anymore; it was about facing a danger that could hurt the place we grew up in.

"Looks like we're in this together now," I murmured, my gaze locked on the concealed trove of explosives and plans that lay sprawled before us. The revelation was a stark reminder of what was at stake, not just for us, but for the entire community. The threat was no longer abstract, hidden in shadows and whispers; it was real, tangible, and alarmingly close.

Emily's response was a nod, her usual resolve tempered with a hint of reluctance. The dynamics of our forced cooperation were complex, layered with the history and emotions we both carried. Yet, the urgency of the situation left no room for hesitation or doubt. We had to act, and we had to act together.

"We need to document this, get it to the authorities without tipping off the militia," I said, the soldier in me taking command, even as I remained acutely aware of Emily's presence by my side. Her skills as a journalist, her eye for detail, and her commitment to the truth were assets we could not afford to ignore.

As we set to work, our movements synchronized in a dance of necessity, I couldn't help but feel the weight of our shared past. Here we were, Jake Thompson and Emily Harris, drawn together not by the nostalgia of what we once had, but by the gravity of a threat that loomed over our hometown.

The task required precision and stealth. Emily, with her camera, captured the evidence that would be crucial in exposing the militia's plans, while I scouted the perimeter, ensuring we remained undetected. It was a delicate operation, fraught with risk, but underscored by a sense of purpose that transcended our personal entanglements.

As we wrapped up, ensuring no trace of our presence was left behind, I caught Emily's eye, a silent exchange that conveyed volumes. Despite the tension, there was a mutual respect, a recognition of each other's strengths and the critical role we each played in this impromptu mission.

"Thank you, Jake," she whispered, her voice barely audible over the rustle of the leaves. "For being here, for doing this."

The gratitude in her voice struck a chord, reminding me of the depth of our connection, of the shared history that, despite everything, still bound us together. "We're doing what needs to be done," I replied, my words a testament to the reluctant partnership that had formed in the face of danger.

In the tense silence that followed our discovery of the militia's cache, Emily and I made our cautious retreat through the underbrush, hearts pounding not just from the exertion but from the gravity of what we had uncovered. The night was eerily quiet, our whispered communications punctuated by the sounds of our careful steps. It was a high-stakes game of hide and seek, played out under the cover of darkness, with stakes far higher than either of us had anticipated when the evening began.

Suddenly, the brittle snap of a branch underfoot sounded like a gunshot in the silence, halting our escape. We froze, listening, as the subtle rustle of movement reached our ears—someone, or several someones, were approaching.

Without a word, Emily acted. Pulling me towards her, her lips found mine in a desperate kiss, a ruse born of quick thinking and sheer necessity. As the footsteps neared, the implications of our situation crystallized between us—this was our disguise, our cover story made manifest in the most primal of acts. We were not intruders or spies in that moment, but lovers seeking the seclusion of the woods for a stolen moment of intimacy.

The militia members emerged from the shadows and Emily and I quickly parted, our breaths mingling in the cool night air, pretending to be startled lovers. They paused, their figures outlined by the faint moonlight, as if unsure of what they had stumbled upon. The leader, a figure of authority even in the dim light, eyed us warily, his suspicion evident even as it warred with the scenario before him.

"We didn't mean to intrude," Emily said, her voice steady despite the adrenaline undoubtedly coursing through her veins. "We'll just be on our way." Her words were a gamble, a bet placed on the militia's willingness to overlook our presence in favor of the more benign, albeit unexpected, narrative we presented.

For a moment, everything hung in balance, the night holding its breath along with us. Then, with a grunt that might have been acknowledgment, the leader gestured for his men to back off. They retreated into the darkness from which they had come, leaving us alone once more.

As their footsteps faded, the tension that had held us in its grip began to dissipate, replaced by a new, different tension born of the ruse we had employed. The drive to my grandfather's house was filled with an electric silence, each of us lost in our thoughts about the danger we'd narrowly avoided and the unexpected intimacy that had sprung from necessity.

The kiss, a tactic in the moment, had reignited something between us, a spark that had not been fully extinguished. Now, as we navigated the dark roads back to safety, that spark threatened to catch fire, fueled by the night's adrenaline and the unresolved tension of our past. The sexual tension that filled the car was palpable, a current that charged the air between us, drawing us into a dance as old as time, yet as new and fraught with meaning as our current predicament.

As we settled into the car for the drive back, a silence fell between us, dense and charged with the echoes of our hasty escape and the unexpected kiss that had been both a cover and a revelation. The air between us felt electric, buzzing with the words we hadn't yet found the courage to say and the emotions that swirled around us like the autumn leaves outside.

The car's interior felt smaller than ever, the space between us charged with a tension that was almost tangible. Every shift of the gears brought our hands perilously close, the brief brushes of skin sending jolts of awareness through me. It was a dance of near touches and quick withdrawals, a silent conversation played out through the language of accidental contact.

Occasionally, I caught Emily looking at me, her gaze lingering just a moment too long before she turned away, her cheeks tinged with a color that the car's dim light couldn't hide. Each glance was like a match struck in the darkness, illuminating the growing attraction that neither of us seemed fully prepared to acknowledge.

The road stretched before us, winding through the dark like the complicated path of our relationship. Every turn seemed to draw us closer, the confines of the car a bubble away from the rest of the world. It was in these moments, caught between the safety of silence and the risk of revelation, that the full weight of our situation pressed down upon us.

Yet, amidst the tension, there was also a thrill—an anticipation of what might come next. The close calls of the evening, the shared danger, had stripped away some of the barriers between us, leaving a raw, undeniable connection. It was as if the events of the night had peeled back the layers of time and distance that had settled between us since I left, revealing the raw, unfinished story of us.

The drive was a journey through the landscape of our past and the uncertain terrain of our present, each mile a step towards a destination unknown. With every fleeting touch and stolen glance, the line between duty and desire blurred, leaving me to wonder where one ended and the other began. It was a precarious edge to walk, yet for the moment, trapped in the charged silence of the car, it was a risk I found myself increasingly willing to take.

When we finally arrived at my grandfather's house, it was under the guise of it being the closest place of safety. The old house, with its familiar contours bathed in the soft glow of the porch light, felt like a haven from the chaos we'd left behind. As we stepped inside, the weight of the night's events seemed to lift slightly, replaced by a sense of intimacy fostered by the solitude and memories the house held.

The rooms were filled with echoes of the past, each corner a testament to the life my grandfather had lived and the childhood I had spent here. This backdrop of nostalgia and memory seemed to deepen the connection between Emily and me, casting our current predicament in a starkly different light. The danger that had been ever-present just moments before now felt distant, as if we had stepped into a different world where the rules of engagement were altered.

The quiet of the house enveloped us, a stark contrast to the adrenaline-fueled escape from the militia. Here, in the safety and seclusion of my childhood home, the tension that had been building between us found a new edge. It was as if the walls themselves were urging us to explore the connection that had been reignited, to give in to the emotions that the day's perilous events had only served to amplify.

As I showed Emily around, each room we entered seemed to add another layer to our burgeoning relationship. The intimacy of the space, combined with the shared experiences of the night, created an atmosphere charged with anticipation. The house, with its memories and sense of continuity, acted as a catalyst, transforming the sexual tension into something palpable, a force that neither of us could easily ignore.

Inside the house, the air felt different, charged with a tension that made every movement significant. Offering Emily a drink, our hands brushed, and it was like a spark jumped between us. Such a simple touch, but it lingered, heavy with meaning. Sitting together on the old couch, the space between us felt charged, every inch a statement of restraint and temptation. The act of simply being near each other, sharing the same air, became an exercise in self-control.

As the night deepened, our conversation flowed more freely, diving into territories we hadn't ventured into before. We spoke of fears, of dreams that had kept us awake at night, and of the surreal intensity of the moment. Each word shared was like peeling back a layer, revealing parts of ourselves that we had kept hidden. This verbal intimacy wove seamlessly with the physical tension that hummed between us, thickening the air with the promise of what could be.

In the quiet, private space of the house, every glance and every word seemed magnified, loaded with an intensity that was hard to navigate. The proximity, once comforting, now felt like a test of willpower. It was a dance of closeness and restraint, where the mundane act of sitting side by side became a testament to the complexity of our feelings.

This deep, meaningful conversation marked a turning point. It wasn't just about the danger we had escaped or the mission that lay ahead; it was about us, about the undeniable connection that refused to be ignored. The emotional and physical tension wove a tight web around us, making the air thick with unspoken possibilities and promises.

The room fell into a charged silence, the kind that speaks louder than words. It was during one of these pauses, a moment suspended in time, that our eyes locked, and everything else seemed to fade away. The lingering touch of our hands, a connection neither of us withdrew from, spoke volumes. It was an acknowledgment of the desire that simmered just beneath the surface, a force we had both been trying to deny.

The intensity of our gaze broke only to acknowledge the undeniable attraction between us, a pull as natural as gravity yet fraught with implications. "Emily," I found myself saying, my voice barely above a whisper, "we both know what's happening here." It was a confession, an admission of the danger not just outside, but in the vulnerability we posed to each other.

In that moment, suspended between desire and duty, our resolve crumbled under the weight of our longing. Closing the distance between us, we found ourselves drawn into a tender, passionate embrace. My arms wrapped around her, pulling her closer, as if trying to bridge every inch of distance that had ever separated us. Our lips met in a kiss that was both a revelation and a homecoming, a confluence of all the emotions we'd tried so hard to restrain.

The kiss deepened, fueled by the pent-up longing and the sharp tang of danger that our proximity evoked. It was as if, in that embrace, we sought to communicate everything that words had failed to convey. The warmth of her against me, the taste of her lips, the way she responded so eagerly—it all felt like finding an oasis in the midst of a desert.

As the intensity of our kiss deepened, a silent conversation passed between us in the mere meeting of our eyes—a question on my part, seeking permission, an affirmation on hers, granting it. With a sense of resolve and an unspoken understanding, I gently lifted her, our lips never parting.

The world beyond the walls of the old house faded into insignificance as we moved, locked in a dance as old as time. Each step was a beat in the rhythm of our desire, each breath a note in a melody that spoke of longing, of memories, and of the uncharted future that lay ahead.

I took my time unbuttoning her blouse, then removing her bra. Exploring every inch of her flesh with my eyes and hands. She bent to remove her pants, then mine. It was the dance of love.

Gently, I traced the line of her blouse with my fingers, each button undone with deliberate care, revealing the softness beneath. Her bra followed, a whispered descent of lace and fabric. My gaze and touch roamed, adoring every curve and contour of her unveiled skin. Together, we shed the remainder of our barriers, her hands working to release me from my clothing as I assisted in removing hers. It was a dance as ancient as desire itself, a silent symphony of longing and connection.

I gently cupped her soft breasts, marveling at how perfectly they fit in my hands. I brushed my thumbs over her nipples, feeling them pebble and stiffen at my touch. She arched into my palms with a breathy sigh. Encouraged, I began kneading the pliant mounds, reveling in their warm weight.

Unable to resist, I dipped my head and captured one rosy peak between my lips. She gasped as I swirled my tongue around the sensitive bud before drawing it into my mouth and suckling. Her hands flew to my hair, holding me to her as I lavished attention on first one breast, then the other.

Kissing a trail down her stomach, I settled between her parted thighs. Her scent was intoxicating, her arousal glistening on her delicate folds. Slowly, I ran a finger along her slit, marveling at the slick heat I found there. She shivered and her hips lifted, silently begging for more. I was more than happy to oblige.

I circled her entrance before gently pushing one finger inside. Her needy moan spurred me on as I began thrusting, curling to stroke her inner walls. I added a second digit, stretching her, as my thumb found her sweet spot. I caressed the sensitive nub until she was rocking against my hand, her soft cries filling the air.

Replacing my thumb with my tongue, I licked and suckled the swollen bundle of nerves as my fingers continued their steady strokes. Her thighs began to tremble, her breathy moans raising in pitch. I could feel her walls starting to flutter around my fingers as I drove her towards her peak.

With a cry, she shattered, fingers clenching in my hair as her climax crashed over her. I continued, drawing out her pleasure as long as I could before gently withdrawing.

Moving to cover her body with my own, I let my rigid length glide through her slick folds, coating myself in her essence. Then, with a smooth surge of my hips, I entered her welcoming heat, groaning at the feeling of her walls gripping me tight. I paused briefly when I was buried to the hilt, savoring the sense of intimate connection.

My heart raced as I moved inside her, our bodies joined as one. She arched her back, tilting her hips to take me deeper with each thrust. I could feel her muscles fluttering and gripping me tight.

A gasp escaped her lips and her fingernails dug into my shoulders. The sharp sting only spurred on my desire. I wanted to make her lose control, to feel her quivering and pulsing around me as she surrendered to bliss.

Our rhythm grew faster, more urgent, chasing the climax we both craved. Sweat beaded on my skin from the exertion but I was relentless, pouring all my passion and need into each snap of my hips. She moved with me perfectly, our bodies in sync, electric friction building between us.

I could tell she was close by the way she tensed and shivered beneath me, her moans pitching higher. Knowing I was the cause of her pleasure was intoxicating. I angled myself to hit that sensitive spot inside her over and over. She cried out my name and it pushed me to the edge.

We climbed together, our movements growing frantic and desperate, until finally the coil of tension snapped. Her release triggered my own and I lost myself in the intense, blinding waves of shared ecstasy washing over us both. In that perfect moment, nothing existed but her and I and the erotic bliss consuming us utterly.

***

In the dimly lit room, the only sounds were our synchronized breathing and the distant chirping of crickets outside, weaving a serene tapestry of peace around us. Emily's head rested on my chest, her hair tickling my skin with every breath she took, a tangible reminder of the intimacy we'd shared. My fingers traced idle patterns on her back, each touch a silent conversation.

The air, still warm from our closeness, carried the faint scent of the jasmine from the window sill, mingling with the deeper, muskier notes that spoke of our recent connection. I watched a strand of moonlight dance across Emily's shoulder, highlighting the soft curve of her skin, a landscape I'd come to know with a reverence that bordered on sacred.

There was a weightlessness to this moment, a sense of being untethered from the world's gravity, where the complexities of our lives and the shadows that chased us seemed momentarily irrelevant. Here, in this quiet after, the whispers of doubt and the clamor of duty faded into the background, leaving a clarity of emotion that felt both exhilarating and terrifying in its intensity.

Every so often, Emily's fingers would find mine, a gentle squeeze conveying volumes of unspoken thoughts and shared vulnerabilities. This simple act, a mingling of warmth and tenderness, became a testament to the depth of our connection, a promise made without words.

As the night deepened, so did the silence between us, a rich, comfortable quiet that felt full of meanings yet to be discovered. In the embrace of that silence, I found a solace I hadn't known I was seeking, a sense of belonging that went beyond the physical space we shared.

The world outside, with all its turbulence and uncertainty, had not vanished, but within the sanctuary of my grandfather's house, with Emily by my side, it felt distant, manageable. Lying there, I realized that the strength we needed, the courage to face the coming challenges, lay not just in our actions but in the rare, unguarded moments of connection that fortified the soul.

This tranquility, this profound sense of being understood and accepted, was a balm to the weariness that had shadowed me. And as I held Emily close, feeling her steady presence, I knew that whatever tomorrow brought, we had found an anchor in each other, a quiet resilience that spoke of hope, defiance, and an unbreakable bond.

Uncovered Secrets

Emily

The glow of my laptop screen pierced the dimness of my makeshift home office, casting long shadows across walls lined with notes and clippings. My eyes, strained from hours of scrutiny, flicked across the digital labyrinth of online forums and encrypted messages. The hunt for the truth about the Black Oak Militia had become my world, each lead a potential breakthrough, each dead end a bitter pill.

It was well past midnight when it happened. A series of clicks through a particularly obscure forum led me to a post buried beneath layers of coded language and bravado. At first glance, it seemed like another dead end, a mix of conspiracy theories and grandstanding so common in these parts of the internet. But a pattern in the phrasing caught my eye, a repetition that seemed too deliberate to be coincidental.

With a growing sense of anticipation, I began decoding the message, piecing together the fragments hidden within. The process was painstaking, a test of wills between the author's intention to conceal and my determination to reveal. And then, clarity emerged from the chaos of cryptic sentences and coded references.

The message outlined a plan, audacious and terrifying in its scope. The Black Oak Militia was planning an event they called "The Awakening," a show of force intended to rally their cause and intimidate their perceived enemies. The details were sparse, but the target was unmistakably clear: the town's annual Founder's Day celebration, a day when the community came together in a spirit of unity and celebration, now marked for chaos.

My heart raced as the implications of this discovery sank in. The Founder's Day celebration was only days away, a public event that drew crowds from across the county, including families with children, unaware of the danger that might descend upon them. The thought of what could happen—a peaceful gathering turned into a scene of fear and violence—sent a shiver down my spine.

I knew then what I had to do. This information couldn't stay buried in the shadows of the internet. The community needed to be warned, the authorities alerted. But I also knew the risks. Exposing the militia's plan would paint a target on my back, thrusting me into the eye of a storm I'd been observing from a distance.

With a deep breath, I began compiling the evidence, organizing my findings into a coherent narrative that would be impossible to ignore. My fingers flew over the keyboard, driven by a mix of adrenaline and a sense of duty to the town that had shaped me. The story I was writing was more than an exposé; it was a call to action, a plea to stand against the darkness threatening to engulf our community.

As I worked, the first rays of dawn began to seep through the blinds, casting a pale light over the chaos of my office. The night had passed in a blur of activity, but as I prepared to send my findings to my editor and the local authorities, I felt a moment of calm. The road ahead would be difficult, fraught with danger and uncertainty, but I was no longer just a bystander. I was a defender of the truth, armed with nothing but my words and my resolve.

For a fleeting moment, the glow of accomplishment—of having unearthed a truth so pivotal—had warmed me against the chill of the early morning. But as the adrenaline waned, replaced by the stillness of dawn, the enormity of what I'd done began to crystalize, cold and sharp, within my chest.

The evidence I'd compiled wasn't just another story; it was a revelation that carried with it the power to ignite a conflagration. The words "ticking time bomb" echoed in my mind, not as a metaphor but as a literal forewarning of the potential havoc the militia's plans could wreak upon our unsuspecting town. With each tick of my apartment's old clock, the imagined sounds of chaos and fear at the Founder's Day celebration grew louder, more vivid, as if my action had set the hands of fate in motion, accelerating toward an inevitable collision.

My breaths came shallow, caught in the tightness of a chest constricted by the gravity of my newfound responsibility. The secret I had uncovered and now shared bore the weight of potential consequences I had only begun to comprehend. It was a Pandora's box of truths, once opened, that could not be closed or unseen, its contents poised to alter lives and shatter the peace of the community I held dear.

The silence of the room seemed to thicken, heavy with unspoken threats and the shadow of danger now cast over my own life. The realization that my pursuit of truth had perhaps naively overlooked the personal risks involved sent a tremor of fear through me. The militia, with its veiled presence and now exposed intentions, was not an adversary to be underestimated. My role as the revealer of their plans marked me, isolating me in a spotlight I hadn't fully anticipated stepping into.

In the solitude of my apartment, surrounded by the evidence of nights spent chasing shadows, I felt a profound loneliness, a disconnect from the normalcy of life outside my door. The people I had sought to protect—neighbors, friends, strangers united by the geography of a town—seemed suddenly distant, their routines and concerns a world apart from the storm I had summoned.

The burden of knowledge, of holding a secret, weighed heavily on my shoulders. It was a mantle I had assumed with the intent to inform and protect, but in the clarity of dawn's light, it felt more like a shroud, cloaked in the potential for backlash and violence. The line between journalist and activist, observer and participant, had blurred, leaving me in a limbo of uncertainty and apprehension.

In that moment of realization, the danger I had unleashed became palpable, a specter lurking just beyond the reach of the morning light. The ticking time bomb I had identified was not just the militia's plan but the story itself—a narrative that, once set in motion, had the power to reshape the fabric of our town and my life within it.

With a deep, steadying breath, I rose from my chair, the movement a physical attempt to shake off the paralysis of fear. The day ahead loomed large, filled with unknowns and the inevitable confrontation with the consequences of my actions. Yet, as I stood there, facing the first light of dawn, a resolve began to take shape amid the turmoil—a determination not just to confront the coming storm but to weather it, armed with the truth and the hope that, in the end, it would be enough to safeguard the town I called home.

As I meticulously copied the evidence, a ritual of preservation against threats veiled in the unknown, each flash drive felt like a fragment of hope—tiny sentinels standing guard over the integrity of my mission. They were hidden in nooks only I knew of, entrusted to the silent protection of the mundane corners of my life, while others were secreted away in the anonymity of a bank's security. This act of concealment was not just about the preservation of data; it was a testament to my resolve to see this story told, come what may.

Yet, amidst the practicalities of safeguarding the evidence, a deeper realization dawned—a recognition of the precariousness of my stance, standing alone against the shadow that loomed over our town. It was a vulnerability that beckoned for reinforcement, for a connection that went beyond the mere exchange of information or strategies.

Jake.

The mere thought of reaching out to him sent a ripple through the calm I had fought so hard to maintain. It wasn't just his expertise or his understanding of danger that I sought; it was the echo of a connection we had shared, a bond formed in the simplicity of our shared past and present; and tested by the complexities of our divergent paths.

Picking up the phone, dialing, he answers. "Emily?" His voice was a blend of surprise and an inexplicable warmth, a tone that spoke of late-night conversations under starlit skies and whispered dreams that only we knew.

"Jake, I've found something... It's about the militia," I started, the words a tightrope walk between caution and the need to share this burden. The impulse to protect the integrity of my discovery warred with a longing for the understanding and support I knew he alone could offer.

"I can't divulge much over the phone. But I need you, Jake. Your advice, your presence... it might make all the difference," I confessed, the admission uncovering layers of unspoken trust and a flicker of something deeper, a yearning for the solace found in shared strength.

There was a pause, a breath held between the reality of danger and the intangible promise of reunion. "Emily, are you okay?" Concern laced his words, a tangible thread pulling at the fabric of my resolve.

"I've taken precautions," I assured him, my voice a mere whisper against the magnitude of what loomed ahead. "Copies of the evidence are secured, hidden away from prying eyes. But if they uncover what I know, the consequences..."

"We'll navigate this together," he interjected, his voice a bastion against the tide of uncertainty. "Let's meet, somewhere safe. We need to talk, to plan."

The simplicity of his acceptance, devoid of hesitation, was a beacon in the fog of my fears. "Yes," I agreed, the word a testament to the trust that time had not eroded.

As we outlined the contours of our meeting, a plan sketched in the shadows of caution and the unknown, a warmth blossomed within me. It was more than the relief of no longer facing the darkness alone; it was knowing that Jake would be there.

Hanging up, the silence of my apartment enveloped me once more, but the isolation I had felt was shattered, replaced by a flicker of hope and a burgeoning sense of something more—a strength not just borne of shared purpose, but of our reawakened intimacy that promised not just solace, but perhaps, the resurgence of feelings long thought stilled by time's passage.

The phone call with Jake, while a balm to the soul, had also laid bare the gravity of the crossroads at which I now stood. In the quiet aftermath, a tumult of thoughts and fears waged a silent war, each vying for dominance in the landscape of my conscience.

At the heart of this internal maelstrom was a choice, deceptively simple yet fraught with complexity: to bring my findings into the glaring light of public scrutiny or to retreat into the shadows, safeguarding my own safety but at the cost of silence. This dilemma, a tightrope stretched over an abyss of moral and ethical quandaries, encapsulated the essence of my struggle.

To go public with the story of the militia's plans for "The Awakening" was to stand by the ideals that had driven me to journalism—the pursuit of truth, the defense of the community, the unyielding belief that information was a beacon in the fight against darkness. This path, while noble, shimmered with the sharp edges of risk, each potential consequence a shard capable of shattering the precarious balance of my existence.

Conversely, the choice to stay silent, to hold the truth close like a guarded secret, promised a veneer of safety, a retreat from the direct line of fire. Yet, this option bore its own weight, a burden of guilt and complicity in whatever outcomes might unfold from the militia's unchecked actions. The specter of "what if" loomed large, casting long shadows of doubt and regret that threatened to eclipse the sanctuary of silence.

As I sat alone, the silence of the room punctuated only by the distant sounds of the waking town, I felt the keen edge of this dilemma slicing through the fabric of my resolve. The ideals that had always guided me—the commitment to shine a light on injustice, to give voice to the voiceless—now seemed both my compass and my curse.

With a deep, steadying breath, I embraced the path laid out by my convictions, acknowledging the fears but refusing to be swayed by them. The story of the militia's plans, of "The Awakening," was not just another article; it was a clarion call to action, a rallying cry for the community to stand vigilant against the encroaching darkness.

***

The café was nondescript, a deliberate choice, its windows fogged from the early morning chill, obscuring the world outside. It was here, amidst the aroma of brewing coffee and the low murmur of early risers, that I awaited Jake, the tumult of my decision to go public still echoing in the recesses of my mind. The choice made in the solitude of dawn now felt all the more real, its weight a constant presence as I watched the door with an anxious anticipation.

When Jake entered, the world seemed to momentarily pause, the years and distance that had stretched between us folding into the background. He carried himself with an assurance honed by service, yet as his gaze met mine, I saw a flicker of the same concern that mirrored my own.

"Emily," he greeted, his voice a low blend of warmth and caution as he took the seat across from me. The familiarity of his presence was both comforting and disconcerting, a reminder of what we shared and what was now at stake.

"Jake," I returned, forcing a smile that felt brittle against the gravity of our meeting. "Thank you for coming."

He nodded, his eyes never leaving mine, searching, always searching. "You said it was important. What's going on?"

The question, direct and laden with unspoken anxiety, was the gateway to the flood of fears and doubts I had wrestled with alone. Yet, in the shared space between us, those fears found voice, tumbling out in a rush of words that sketched the outline of the militia's plans and the perilous path I had chosen.

Jake listened in silence, his expression a mask of concentration, absorbing every detail. When I had finished, the café around us seemed to recede, leaving only the palpable tension that hummed like a live wire.

"Emily, do you understand the risk you're taking?" His voice was soft, not in question, but in concern, the weight of his experience lending gravity to his words.

I nodded, the lump in my throat a testament to the enormity of it all. "I do, Jake. But if I don't do this, if I stay silent, I'm not sure I could live with myself."

The admission hung between us, a stark truth laid bare. Jake's hand reached across the table, an anchor in the swirling sea of uncertainty. His touch was grounding, a tangible reminder of the shared strength that bound us together.

"We need to be smart about this. You're not just a journalist in this, Emily; you're a target and I don't want anything to happen to you," he said firmly, his resolve a mirror to my own.

His words, though laced with a hard edge of reality, were not a deterrent but a bolster to my resolve. The strategy we discussed was meticulous, a blend of caution and boldness that would shield me as much as possible from the backlash that was sure to come.

As the meeting drew to a close, the unspoken connection that had drawn taut in the space between us remained, a silent acknowledgment of the journey ahead. Jake's concern, his unwavering support, was the unseen anchor that steadied me against the storm I had summoned.

Walking out into the cool embrace of the morning, the café and its cocoon of safety a memory, I carried with me not just the burden of my mission, but the reassurance of an ally. Jake's presence, both a reminder of the past and a bridge to the future, was a beacon of hope in the shadowed path I had chosen.

The road ahead was fraught with danger, the outcome uncertain, but in the reflection of Jake's support, I found a newfound strength. Together, we had faced the specter of fear, not with denial, but with the determination to confront whatever lay ahead, side by side, united in the pursuit of truth and the defense of all we held dear.

The rhythmic tap of keys under my fingers was a stark contrast to the turmoil that brewed within me. Each word that flowed onto the screen was a piece of myself, a testament to the resolve that had crystallized in the dim light of dawn and been fortified in the presence of Jake. The café, with its transient bubble of safety, felt worlds away now, replaced by the solitude of my workspace where the weight of my decision pressed close, a constant companion.

The article before me was more than a collection of facts and evidence; it was a beacon, a clarion call that I was about to send into the heart of our community. With every sentence crafted, I felt the dual pull of duty and apprehension, a dance of conviction with the shadow of consequence. The militia's plans, the impending threat they posed to the Founder's Day celebration, had to be brought to light, yet the path to doing so was fraught with pitfalls, each step forward a delicate balance between revelation and the protection of those who had trusted me with their stories.

As I pieced together the narrative, the responsibility of my role as a journalist weighed heavily upon me. To expose without exposing, to illuminate without endangering, was a tightrope walk of ethical journalism I had pledged myself to navigate. The anonymity of my sources, the veiled hints and covert meetings that had led me to this juncture, were sacrosanct. Their safety was a mantle I bore with solemnity, weaving through the fabric of my writing a shield of obfuscation that protected even as it revealed.

With each paragraph, I found myself pausing, second-guessing not the necessity of the revelation, but the phrasing, the tone. Was I being clear enough in the urgency of the threat? Was I safeguarding my sources with enough diligence? The questions were relentless, a chorus of doubt that sought to undermine my resolve.

Yet, for every moment of hesitation, there was a counterpoint of clarity, a flash of determination that cut through the uncertainty. This article, this unveiling of the shadows that had crept into our midst, was a duty I could not turn away from. The knowledge I had garnered, the evidence amassed, was not just information; it was a charge to act, a responsibility to my community that I could not—would not—shirk.

The final review of the piece was a marathon of meticulous scrutiny, each word weighed, each sentence measured for its impact and integrity. The balance I sought between alarm and information, between caution and action, felt like a razor's edge, a precarious path that I tread with the utmost care.

When at last the article stood complete, a comprehensive exposé poised on the brink of public consciousness, the enormity of the step I was about to take settled around me with a palpable intensity. The click of the 'submit' button was a simple act, a mere flicker of movement, yet it carried the weight of irrevocable change. With it, I was not just sending an article into the editorial process; I was sounding the alarm, a herald of truths that could no longer remain hidden.

The quiet that enveloped me in the aftermath of my decision was a stark, unforgiving landscape, marked by the shadows of isolation and the weighty presence of consequence. It was a silence borne not of peace, but of the tumultuous undercurrent of anticipation, the quiet before the storm whose arrival was imminent, its impact yet unknown.

In this solitude, my thoughts turned, unbidden but not unwelcome, to Jake. The memory of our recent meeting, the shared understanding and silent promises exchanged, became a beacon in the swirling uncertainty that threatened to engulf me. It wasn't just the strategy or the advice he offered that lingered in my mind; it was the echo of a connection rekindled, a bond forged in the fires of shared passion, purpose and mutual concern.

The isolation of my secret, the burden of the truth I carried, weighed heavily upon me, a constant companion in the hours that stretched into infinity as I awaited the dawn of revelation. Yet, in the quiet reflection of those solitary moments, I found solace not in the silence, but in the memory of moments spent with Jake—of whispered confidences under the veil of night, of laughter shared in the face of adversity, of silent looks that spoke volumes.

These memories, these echoes of a past intertwined with the present, served as a wellspring of strength, a reminder that though the path I walked was fraught with peril, I did not walk it alone. The commitment we shared, to protect the town that had shaped us, to stand in defense of its people and its peace, was a thread that bound us, invisible but unbreakable.

It was this shared commitment, this unspoken alliance, that fortified me as I faced the precipice of my decision. The act of publishing the exposé, of bringing to light the shadows that lurked within our midst, was no longer a solitary burden but a testament to the courage found in the collective strength of those who stood with me, seen and unseen.

Torn Between Two Worlds

Jake

Under the cloak of night, nestled within the dense underbrush that skirts the edge of the Black Oak Militia's encampment, I found myself a silent witness to a conversation that would alter the course of our already precarious situation. My heart seemed to pause as the gravity of their words sank in. The militia, emboldened by shadows and secrecy, was planning something far beyond the scope of anything we had anticipated. Their next move, cloaked in the innocuous guise of the upcoming Founder's Day celebration, promised chaos and destruction on a scale that sent a chill down my spine.

As the details of their plan unfolded—a calculated strike designed to sow discord and incite fear among the unsuspecting townsfolk—my resolve hardened into something cold and sharp. Yet, even as determination took root within me, a deep-seated fear for Emily's safety blossomed alongside it. Emily, with her unwavering commitment to truth and justice, had become entangled in this web of danger, her recent findings about the militia's movements drawing her ever closer to the heart of the storm.

Her voice echoed in my mind, recounting her discoveries with a mix of excitement and concern. I remembered the flicker of apprehension in her eyes, a reflection of the peril we both knew her investigations invited. That fear, once a whisper in the back of my mind, now roared to the forefront, amplified by the critical information I had just uncovered. The militia's plans, coupled with what Emily had already unearthed, painted a target on her back far larger than either of us had feared.

The weight of my duty, both to my country and to the woman I loved, pressed down on me with a newfound intensity. My role as an undercover operative had always been fraught with danger, a constant balancing act between gathering intelligence and maintaining my cover. Yet, the thought of Emily, so fiercely dedicated to shedding light on the darkness we faced, becoming a casualty of this war against tyranny, was unbearable.

As I slipped away from the encampment, the night's darkness enveloping me once more, my mind raced with plans and contingencies. The need to protect Emily, to ensure her safety without curtailing the passion that drove her, became my guiding principle. The information I had gathered tonight was a weapon—one that could potentially dismantle the militia's plans if wielded correctly. But it was also a beacon, illuminating the depth of the danger we faced, a danger Emily was marching towards with open eyes and a resolute heart.

My training as a SEAL had instilled in me a code—a commitment to protect and serve, to defend my country against its enemies, both foreign and domestic. This code had been my compass, guiding me through the moral complexities of my duties with a clarity that seemed unshakeable. Until now. Now, the lines that had once seemed so clear were blurred, mired in shades of gray that clouded my judgment and tugged at my conscience.

The plan uncovered—the militia's "The Awakening"—was not just a threat to the physical safety of my hometown; it was an assault on the very principles that I had sworn to uphold. The people I had pledged to protect were not abstract entities, figures in a report or faces in a crowd. They were my neighbors, my friends, my family. And among them was Emily, a beacon of integrity and courage, whose determination to expose the truth had placed her squarely in the crosshairs of danger.

The responsibility to act, to use the information I had obtained to thwart the militia's plans, was clear. Yet, it was the personal stakes involved, the risk to Emily and others like her, that imbued my mission with a sense of urgency and complexity that went beyond the parameters of my training. It was no longer enough to simply execute my duties from the shadows; I found myself drawn into the light, forced to navigate a path that required not just tactical acumen but moral courage.

In the solitude of the morning, as I prepared for the day ahead, I reflected on the oath I had taken as a SEAL. It was a vow not just to fight against visible enemies but to stand as a guardian against all threats to freedom and justice, even those that lurked within the boundaries of my own country. The fight against "The Awakening" was a manifestation of that vow, a test of my allegiance not just to the flag, but to the people it represented.

The realization that my duty extended beyond the battlefield, that it encompassed the protection of the very fabric of our society, was both a revelation and a challenge. It demanded of me a level of bravery and resolve that went beyond physical courage, asking instead for a sacrifice of the heart and soul.

The encampment was alive with the mundane routines of the day, the stark contrast to the turmoil brewing within its confines lost on most. Amidst the orchestrated chaos, my secure line vibrated discreetly, a silent herald of news from the world beyond these secluded woods. The message, encrypted and terse, bore the weight of a nightmare turned reality: Emily's exposé had not just ruffled feathers; it had placed her squarely in the crosshairs of those who lurked in the shadows, waiting for a moment to strike.

The screen blurred before my eyes as the words sank in, each letter a hammer blow to the fortress I had built around my emotions. Emily, whose only crime was a relentless pursuit of the truth, had become a target.

The haunting realization that Emily's life was at stake because of her bravery transformed my mission. No longer was it solely about gathering intelligence or thwarting the militia's plans; it was about protecting one of our own, about ensuring that the light Emily had brought into the darkness was not extinguished.

With a resolve sharpened by urgency and a heart heavy with concern, I made a silent vow. I would use every resource at my disposal, every skill I had honed over years of service, to safeguard Emily. The fight against "The Awakening" had become personal, a battle not just for the soul of our town, but for the life of someone who embodied the very best of what we were fighting for.

In that moment, as I prepared to reach out to my contacts, to marshal the forces necessary to protect Emily, I understood the true weight of duty. It was not just a commitment to a cause or a country, but to the people who made those ideals worth defending. And I would move heaven and earth to keep her safe, to ensure that the courage and integrity she had shown would not be her undoing.

***

As I extricated myself from the dense underbrush that skirted the Black Oak Militia's encampment, the cacophony of the night enveloped me, a symphony of natural sounds that seemed oblivious to the human machinations brewing in its midst. The information I had just intercepted weighed heavily on my mind, a burden that seemed to grow with each step I took away from the heart of potential chaos and towards a place of personal sanctity.

The journey from the encampment to our sacred spot, a hidden clearing known only to Emily and me, was a journey back in time. Each step felt like a retreat from the soldier I had become, back to the person I was when those dreams and secrets were first shared under the canopy of ancient oaks. The path, illuminated only by the faint glow of the moon filtering through the dense foliage, was as familiar to me as my own heartbeat, a constant in a world that had become unrecognizably complex.

As I navigated the familiar terrain, the stark contrast between the present and those long-gone days of innocence and promise became painfully clear. Back then, the biggest fears we faced were of the unknown future, of paths yet untrodden. Now, the future loomed like a storm cloud, dark and ominous, filled with the very real threats of violence and loss.

The deeper into the woods I ventured, the more palpable the transition became. The sounds of the night grew softer, more reflective, as if the natural world itself recognized the sanctity of the place I was headed. My footsteps slowed, my breath evened, and the tightness that had coiled within me since overhearing the militia's plans began to loosen, thread by thread.

Finally, as the trees parted like curtains drawn back to reveal a stage, I stepped into our clearing. The moonlight here was unhindered, bathing the small open space in a silver glow that lent an ethereal quality to the surroundings. This place, our place, was untouched by the world's chaos, a timeless sanctuary where the memories of our shared dreams and whispered secrets hung in the air like motes of dust in a sunbeam.

I took a deep breath, allowing the peace of this sacred spot to seep into my bones. The fears for Emily's safety, the weight of my duty, the uncertainty of our future—they all remained, but here, they felt distant, manageable. This was where we had planned a future bright with possibilities, where we had laughed and loved with the reckless abandon of youth.

Sitting at the base of the large oak that had been our confidant and witness to so many of our hopes and fears, I found myself speaking into the silence, recounting the events of the evening as if Emily were seated beside me. I spoke of my fears, my resolve, and my unwavering commitment to protect her and our town from the impending storm.

In the quiet that followed, a profound sense of clarity enveloped me. The sacred spot where Emily and I had shared our deepest dreams and darkest fears was not just a place of past memories; it was a beacon, guiding me towards the future we hoped to build—one of truth, justice, and love, undeterred by the shadows that threatened to engulf us.

The knowledge that Emily was being targeted, that her life was at stake because of her unwavering pursuit of justice, ignited within me a fire that no fear could extinguish. It was a call to arms, a reminder of the oath I had taken not just as a SEAL but as a protector of those who dared to stand against tyranny in all its forms.

As I stood to leave, casting one last glance at the clearing that had seen the best and worst of us, I felt a sense of clarity cut through the fog of my doubts. The path ahead was fraught with danger, yes, but it was a path I would walk with the strength of my convictions and the memories of what had once been and was again, to guide me.

In this place of shared history, of laughter and promises whispered on the wind, I had found not just solace but a renewed purpose. The fight against "The Awakening," against the forces that sought to tear us apart, was not just a mission; it was a testament to the love and loyalty that had been forged in the heart of these woods.

With a heart both heavy and determined, I stepped back onto the path, the shadows of the forest enveloping me once more. The moment of vulnerability had passed, leaving in its wake a resolve as steadfast as the ancient oaks that stood sentinel over our memories. The battle ahead would be fought not just in the name of duty, but in defense of the light that Emily and I had once found in each other, a light that, despite the gathering darkness, refused to be extinguished.

***

Under the stark fluorescence of the makeshift command center, tucked away in a nondescript building that bore no sign of the critical operations conducted within, I stood before a table strewn with maps and intelligence reports. The air was charged with a palpable tension, the kind that precedes the storm, as eyes, trained to assess and act with ruthless efficiency, turned towards me.

The men and women in this room were not just colleagues; they were brothers and sisters in arms, allies in a war that often blurred the lines between the just and the necessary. Our bond was forged in the crucible of shared danger, a bond that went beyond mere duty to touch the very essence of our shared humanity.

Yet, as their questions began—a barrage seeking clarity, intent, and information—a chasm opened within me, a divide between the loyalty I owed these allies and the commitment I had made to protect Emily. They were unaware of the personal stakes involved, of the haunting realization that had driven me to seek solace among the memories of a time less complicated, less fraught with peril.

"Jake, we need to know everything. Any detail could be the key to preempting whatever these bastards are planning," the lead analyst, a woman whose acumen for strategy had saved countless lives, pressed with an intensity that brooked no evasion.

I found myself navigating the precarious line between transparency and obfuscation, weighing each word before it left my lips. To reveal too much could compromise not just the mission but Emily's safety. Yet, to withhold information was to betray the trust that was the bedrock of our operation.

"My intel suggests the militia's planning something big for the Founder's Day celebration. It's not just a display of force; it's meant to be a statement," I began, choosing my words with care, omitting the personal dimension of my concern. "They've got the means and, it seems, the will to escalate their operations beyond mere propaganda or intimidation."

Questions flew, sharp and unrelenting, as my allies sought to dissect the information, to build a strategy that could counter the looming threat. With each query, the line I walked grew thinner, a tightrope suspended over a chasm of potential disaster.

I could see the frustration, the need for actionable intelligence reflected in their faces, and it mirrored my own internal turmoil. Yet, within this maelstrom of strategy and speculation, I remained acutely aware of the silent vow I had made in the quiet of the forest—to protect Emily, to shield her from the consequences of her courage.

The confrontation with my allies, though devoid of hostility, was a test of my loyalties, a challenge to my ability to serve the greater good while safeguarding those precious few who had become my personal charge. It was a delicate balance, one that required not just tactical acumen but a deep understanding of the human heart.

As the meeting drew to a close, plans laid and roles assigned, I felt the weight of my dual responsibilities more keenly than ever. My colleagues, sensing perhaps the depth of my concern, offered nods of solidarity and understanding, unaware of the full scope of my burden.

Stepping out into the chill of the early evening, I was acutely aware of the solitary path I had chosen. The battle against the militia, against the darkness they sought to spread, was not just a matter of national security; it was a deeply personal crusade, a fight for the soul of our community and for the safety of one who had dared to stand in the light.

***

The world outside was shrouded in darkness, the kind that seemed to press against the windows with a tangible weight, as if trying to seep through the glass and extinguish the light within. Inside, the stark contrast of my dimly lit room served as a sanctuary, a place where the cacophony of the day's demands faded into a silence that was both comforting and suffocating.

In the solitude of that room, a plan began to take shape in my mind, a notion so radical, so divergent from the path I had walked thus far, that it seemed to belong to someone else's story. Yet, as I turned it over, examining its contours and implications, the idea of running away with Emily, of leaving everything behind to protect her, felt like the only clear note in an otherwise discordant symphony.

This was not a decision born of fear, though fear was a constant companion in these turbulent times. It was a decision forged in the fires of love and duty, a paradox that had defined much of my existence. Emily's safety was paramount, a beacon that guided me through the storm of my responsibilities and the shadows of my profession.

As I contemplated the proposal, the thought of broaching this plan with Emily filled me with a tumult of emotions. How would she react to the suggestion that we abandon everything—the town that had shaped us, the causes that had called us to action, the lives we had built—in pursuit of safety? Would she see it as an admission of defeat, a retreat from the principles that had drawn us together in the first place?

Yet, as I weighed the possibilities, the memories of our shared past, of moments of laughter and dreams whispered beneath the canopy of Black Oak woods, reminded me of the strength of our bond. Emily and I had always found solace in each other, a respite from the chaos that surrounded us. This plan, this escape, could be the ultimate expression of that solace, a chance to forge a new path free from the threats that loomed over us.

The practicalities of the proposal were daunting. Leaving everything behind meant not just physical relocation but a severing of ties with our past, with the identities that had defined us. It meant living in the shadows, away from the light of truth and justice that Emily had fought so hard to uphold.

But in the depth of night, as the plan crystallized into a tangible course of action, these considerations paled in comparison to the singular, overriding imperative to protect the woman I loved. The thought of a life without Emily, of a future dimmed by the loss of her light, was unthinkable. If running away together offered even a chance of safety, of happiness, then it was a path worth pursuing, a gamble worth taking.

The resolve to propose this plan to Emily, to lay before her a path fraught with uncertainty but alive with the possibility of peace, settled over me with a weight that felt both terrifying and exhilarating. It was a decision that would change the course of our lives, a pivot away from the darkness and towards a future we would carve out together, against all odds.

As dawn began to paint the sky with the first light of morning, the proposal took on the sheen of inevitability. It was a leap into the unknown, but one I was willing to take, for Emily, for us. In the clarity of that early light, I understood that the greatest act of protection, of love, was not to shield her from the world, but to build a new one with her, far from the dangers that stalked our every step.

With a heart heavy with anticipation and hope, I prepared to face Emily, to offer her not just a plan, but a promise—a vow to forge a future together, beyond the reach of shadows, in a place where the only weight we would bear would be that of our shared dreams and the love that bound us together, unbreakable and true.

The first light of dawn cast a soft glow through the windows, illuminating the contours of my room with a gentle luminescence that seemed at odds with the turmoil churning within me. As the world outside slowly awakened, I found myself ensnared in a moment of profound introspection, the weight of the decision before me more palpable with each passing second.

The plan to leave everything behind, to ask Emily to forsake her life, her career, and the fiery passion for journalism that burned at the core of her being, was a proposal fraught with complexity and contradiction. It was a path that offered sanctuary, yet it demanded sacrifice—a sacrifice so profound that it threatened to alter the very essence of who we were.

The thought of presenting this plan to Emily filled me with an indescribable mixture of hope and dread. Hope, for the possibility of a life beyond the reach of the dangers that now shadowed our every step; dread, for the possibility that in making this offer, I was betraying the principles that had drawn us together, the shared commitment to truth and justice that had been the bedrock of our connection.

To ask Emily to abandon her pursuit of truth, to turn away from the calling that had defined so much of her life, seemed a selfish act, a request that placed my need to protect her above her own dreams and aspirations. Yet, as I grappled with the implications of my plan, I couldn't escape the visceral fear that clung to my heart—the fear of losing her to the very dangers we were fighting against.

The internal battle that raged within me was a microcosm of the larger war we faced, a struggle between duty and desire, between the call of the heart and the demands of conscience. The prospect of a life in shadow, hidden from the threats that sought to tear us apart, was a tempting vision, yet it was one that came at a cost I was unsure we were prepared to pay.

As I stood at the precipice of this heart-wrenching decision, the clarity I sought remained elusive, shrouded in the mists of uncertainty and fear. Yet, in the depth of my contemplation, a truth emerged, stark and undeniable—the love I bore for Emily, the bond that united us, was a force more powerful than any threat we faced.

With a heavy heart and a resolve tempered by love, I knew that the path I would choose, the proposal I would make to Emily, would be one that honored not just our desire for safety, but our commitment to the ideals and passions that had defined our lives.

It was a decision that would carve the course of our future, a future forged in the crucible of love, sacrifice, and the unyielding hope for a dawn beyond the darkness.

The day had unfolded with the relentless pace of a ticking clock, each second a reminder of the decision that lay heavy on my heart. My resolve, though steadfast, was a ship navigating the stormy seas of doubt and fear, searching for a beacon of light to guide its way. It was in this tumult of thought and emotion that I received Emily's message, a digital whisper across the ether that cut through the chaos with the precision of a knife.

Her words, though brief, were a testament to the strength of her spirit, a declaration of her unwavering commitment to publish her exposé, regardless of the looming shadows of personal risk. Reading her message, I was struck by the profound courage it embodied, a courage that seemed to transcend the confines of our precarious situation. Emily's determination to stand in the face of danger, to speak truth to power even as the specter of retribution loomed large, was a clarion call that resonated deep within my soul.

In that moment, the plan I had contemplated, the proposal to flee and leave everything behind, seemed not just inadequate but fundamentally at odds with the essence of who Emily was—and, by extension, who I was. Her bravery, her refusal to be silenced, was a mirror reflecting my own values, a reminder of the oath I had taken not just as a SEAL but as a protector of the ideals that defined us.

The realization dawned on me with the clarity of a sunrise dispelling the night's shadows. The best way to protect Emily, to safeguard the future we both envisioned, was not to run from the threat but to confront it head-on, together. Her courage, so vividly displayed in the simple act of sending that message, ignited within me a renewed sense of purpose, a determination to stand by her side, not as a guardian shadowing her steps, but as an equal partner in the fight for truth and justice.

This decision marked a pivotal moment in our shared journey. It solidified my resolve to support Emily, to lend my strength to her cause, and to face the darkness together, as a united front. The path ahead would undoubtedly be fraught with danger, but in the strength of our combined resolve, I found a hope that was both invigorating and profound.

Inspired by Emily's bravery, I reached out to her, not with words of caution or proposals for escape, but with a message of solidarity and support. I offered her not just the protection of my skills and training but the partnership of my heart and soul, a commitment to stand beside her as we navigated the treacherous waters that lay ahead.

As I sent my message, the weight of the decision lifted, replaced by a sense of rightness, a conviction that our path, though perilous, was the only one true to the love and respect that bound us. This moment of choice, of choosing courage in love, was a testament to the power of unity in the face of adversity, a pledge to fight for a future where Emily's pursuit of truth and my duty to protect could coexist in harmony.

The battle that awaited us was more than a conflict with external forces; it was a fight for the very soul of our community, a stand against the tide of darkness with the light of truth as our guide. Together, Emily and I were more than just two people bound by affection; we were allies in the struggle for a better world, partners in the quest for justice and peace. And in that unity, I found not just the courage to face the challenges ahead but the belief that, together, we could overcome them, forging a future defined by love, truth, and the unwavering courage to stand for what is right.

Love and Duty

Emily

The world seemed to hold its breath as twilight merged into the deep blues of evening, casting long shadows across the small, cramped space I'd come to call my makeshift office. Here, amidst the clutter of papers, the glow of my laptop screen served as a beacon in the growing darkness, a solitary light in the pursuit of truth that had consumed my every waking moment.

But tonight, my focus was fractured, splintered by a growing unease that had nothing to do with the threats looming over our town or the shadows that danced just beyond the reach of the light. No, this disquiet was far more personal, rooted in the subtle shift I'd observed in Jake—shifts that were becoming harder to ignore with each passing day.

Jake's behavior had always been a cipher, a puzzle I'd gradually learned to decipher over the years. But recently, a new layer of secrecy had enveloped him, a barrier that seemed to widen the gap between us with every evasive answer and sidestepped question. His reticence, once an occasional shadow in his otherwise open demeanor, had grown into a constant presence, casting a pall over our interactions.

I couldn't shake the feeling of frustration that bubbled up each time I tried to breach the subject, only to be met with half-truths or diversions. It was as if he was holding himself back, walling off a part of his world from me, and I couldn't understand why. Didn't he realize that whatever burdens he was shouldering, we could face them better together?

The concern for his well-being intertwined with my frustration, creating a maelstrom of emotions that left me feeling both helpless and irritated. It wasn't just the secrets he kept; it was the distance those secrets created between us, a chasm that seemed to grow wider with each passing day.

As I sat there, the cursor on my screen blinking in a steady rhythm that mirrored the beat of my troubled thoughts, I made a decision. This couldn't continue. The uncertainty, the secrecy—it was eroding the foundation of trust we'd built, a foundation that was crucial not just to our relationship, but to the very fight we were embroiled in.

Determined, I closed my laptop, the click of the lid a resolute sound in the quiet room. I would confront Jake, demand the honesty and transparency that had always been the bedrock of our partnership. It wasn't just about my need to understand; it was about preserving the trust that was essential to both our survival and the success of our endeavors.

The resolve that filled me as I stood was a welcome relief from the helplessness that had plagued me. Yes, the conversation ahead would be difficult, perhaps even painful, but it was necessary. The secrets, the evasions—they were barriers we could ill afford, not when so much was at stake.

With a deep breath, I stepped out of my office, the resolve in my heart a guiding light as I went to seek Jake, ready to face whatever truths lay hidden in the shadows of his reticence. Tonight, I decided, would be a turning point, one way or another. The tension, the unspoken fears and frustrations, would find their voice, and together, we would navigate the stormy waters of uncertainty, anchored by the hope of understanding and the strength of our connection.

The air felt thick as I made my way to Jake, each step fueled by a blend of resolve and trepidation. The shadows cast by the evening light seemed to stretch endlessly before me, mirroring the uncertainty that lay ahead. Finding Jake was easy; he was where I expected, lost in a sea of maps and notes that spoke of dangers unseen but deeply felt.

He looked up, his expression shifting from concentration to concern at the sight of me. It was a look I knew well, one that had offered comfort in moments of despair. But tonight, it only served to steel my resolve.

"Jake, we need to talk," I began, my voice firmer than I felt. The room suddenly seemed too small, the walls closing in as the gravity of our impending conversation pressed down upon us.

He nodded, a silent acknowledgment, as he cleared a space for me to sit. But I remained standing, the need for action, for confrontation, keeping me on my feet.

"It's about the secrets, Jake. The things you're not telling me." My words hung in the air between us, a challenge laid bare. "I can't help feeling like you're shutting me out, and I don't understand why. If we're going to get through this, I need you to trust me."

Jake's gaze held mine, a tumult of emotions flickering in the depths of his eyes. "Emily, it's not that I don't trust you. It's just... complicated. There are things about my mission, about what I'm doing, that are... difficult to explain."

The frustration that had been simmering within me bubbled to the surface. "Difficult or not, Jake, I deserve to know. How can we stand together if you're keeping me in the dark? How can I fight alongside you if I don't even know what we're fighting against?"

The intensity of our gaze locked, an unspoken battle of wills. The air crackled with the raw energy of our confrontation, charged with the weight of unspoken fears and the desperation to bridge the gap that had formed between us.

"Emily, it's not about deserving to know. It's about keeping you safe," Jake finally said, his voice laced with a raw edge of emotion. "Every piece of information I keep from you, it's a bullet I'm trying to put back in the gun. I can't bear the thought of you getting hurt because of what I've shared."

His words, though spoken from a place of protection, only fueled my determination. "But don't you see, Jake? By keeping me out, you're putting me at greater risk. Knowledge is power, and right now, I feel powerless."

The silence that followed was heavy, filled with the weight of unspoken truths and the ache of our shared fears. It was a standoff, not of adversaries, but of two hearts struggling to find their way back to each other through the fog of war that surrounded us.

Finally, Jake sighed, a sound that seemed to carry the weight of the world. "Okay," he whispered, his resistance crumbling. "Okay, I'll tell you everything. But you have to understand, some of these things... once you know them, there's no going back."

I nodded, my heart aching for the burden he carried, for the shadows that had crept into his soul. "I understand. And whatever it is, we'll face it together. Like we always have."

The conversation that followed was a deluge, a floodgate of secrets and truths that had been held back for too long. It was raw, painful, and liberating all at once. And as Jake shared the depths of his mission, the dangers he faced, and the fears that haunted him, I felt the chasm between us begin to close, bridged by the strength of our shared vulnerability.

As Jake's revelations unfolded, the danger and duty that he had borne in solitude, the initial relief of his honesty gave way to a deeper, more turbulent sea of conflict between us. His justifications, woven from a sincere desire to protect me, clashed violently with the very principles that defined who I was, both as a journalist and as a person.

"Jake, I understand you're trying to protect me, but don't you see? By keeping me in the dark, you're undermining everything I stand for," I said, my voice steady despite the storm of emotions raging within. "I've dedicated my life to uncovering the truth, to shining a light on the shadows. How can I do that if I'm being kept in one?"

Jake's frustration was palpable, a tangible force that seemed to fill the room. "Emily, this isn't about principles or ethics. It's about survival. The things I'm dealing with—they're not just stories to be published. They're real threats, with real consequences. I can't risk your safety for the sake of transparency."

The divide between us felt insurmountable in that moment, a chasm widened by our conflicting ideals. "But that's exactly why the truth matters, Jake. Yes, these threats are real, but how we choose to face them defines us. Hiding from the truth, keeping it locked away—it only gives more power to those who wish to harm us."

My mind raced back to my upbringing, to the lessons learned at the knee of my journalist parents. They had instilled in me a belief in the sanctity of truth, in the fundamental right of every individual to be informed, to make decisions based on knowledge rather than fear. "My parents taught me that the truth is the only weapon we have against tyranny and oppression. If we abandon that, what are we left with? How can we claim to fight for justice if we're willing to compromise on the very thing that lays its foundation?"

Jake looked torn, a man caught between the duty of his role and the love he bore for me. "I'm not asking you to abandon your principles, Em. I'm just asking you to trust me, to believe that when I say I'm doing this to protect you, it's because there's no other choice."

The intensity of our exchange, the clash of our principles, laid bare the core of our struggle. It was a battle not of right and wrong, but of how to navigate the treacherous waters where duty and love intersected, where the personal became profoundly political.

"I do trust you, Jake. More than anyone. But trust goes both ways. If we're going to make it through this, we need to be on the same page, sharing the same truths, no matter how hard they may be to face."

As our argument reached its crescendo, the air between us charged with the passion of our convictions, it became clear that this clash was not a barrier but a bridge. In voicing our fears, our frustrations, and our deepest beliefs, we were forging a deeper understanding, a recognition of the complex tapestry of love and duty that bound us together.

The conversation that followed, though fraught with emotional landmines, was a testament to the strength of our bond. With each word, each shared secret and revealed fear, we navigated the delicate balance between protecting one another and honoring the values that defined us. It was a dance of love and principle, a journey through the shadows with the promise of light guiding our way.

As our argument escalated, the space between us became charged with the raw energy of our emotions, a tumultuous landscape where fears and vulnerabilities were laid bare. The words we exchanged were like flares, illuminating the darkest corners of our hearts, revealing the depth of our feelings and the internal conflicts that waged within us.

"Jake, I'm scared," I admitted, the confession tearing from me with a force that left me breathless. "Not just of what might happen to me, but of losing you—to this mission, to the secrets that seem to consume you. I need you to see that my fight for the truth isn't just about my career; it's about fighting for us, for a future where we don't have to hide in the shadows."

Jake's response was a mirror to my own vulnerability. "And I'm terrified of failing you, of not being able to protect you from the things I know are coming. Every decision I make, every secret I keep, it's with the weight of that fear pressing down on me."

The intensity of our exchange, the emotional exposure, was both painful and cathartic. For the first time, we were truly seeing each other, not just as allies in a shared cause, but as individuals grappling with the weight of our responsibilities and the fears that accompany them.

"Our love, this connection we have—it's the one thing I'm sure of in all this chaos," Jake said, his voice breaking with emotion. "But how do we hold onto that when the world around us seems determined to pull us apart?"

His words echoed my own thoughts, a reflection of the internal battle I faced every day. "By choosing each other, Jake. Every day, no matter what comes. We anchor ourselves to that choice, to the love that binds us, even when everything else is uncertain."

The vulnerability we shared in those moments, the raw honesty of our fears and desires, drew us closer than any physical embrace could. It was a profound connection, forged in the fires of our shared trials, a testament to the strength that lies in openness and emotional exposure.

As the fervor of our argument softened, replaced by a quiet understanding, we were left with a sense of unity that felt unbreakable. We had exposed the depths of our hearts to each other, revealing the scars and fears that marked us, and in doing so, we found a new strength, a new resolve to face the challenges ahead together.

This moment of emotional exposure, as difficult as it was, served as a crucial turning point for us. It underscored the complexity of navigating love and duty, of balancing our personal desires with our professional responsibilities. But more than that, it reminded us of the power of vulnerability, of the strength that comes from laying bare our fears and standing together in the face of them.

In the charged silence that followed our raw exposure of fears and vulnerabilities, a palpable shift occurred between Jake and me. The air, once thick with tension and unspoken grievances, began to clear, as if our honest confrontation had purged something toxic from our midst.

Then, Jake did something unexpected. He reached across the void that our argument had carved between us, bridging it with words that were both a balm and a revelation. "Emily, I see you," he said, his voice laced with a newfound understanding. "I see your strength, your commitment to truth. And it terrifies me, not because I doubt you, but because I know the dangers you're willing to face head-on, without hesitation."

This admission, so stark in its honesty, marked a turning point not just in our argument but in our relationship. Jake's acknowledgment of my perspective, his admission of his own fears concerning my safety, acted as a key, unlocking a door to a deeper level of understanding between us.

The nature of our conversation transformed in that moment, shifting from confrontational to conciliatory. It was as if Jake's words had disarmed us both, stripping away the defenses we had erected in the name of protection and revealing the simple, unvarnished truth of our shared vulnerability.

"I'm scared too, Jake," I confessed, feeling the weight of my own defenses crumbling. "Scared of what we're up against, scared of losing you. But hiding from the truth, from each other—that's not who we are. It's not who I want us to be."

Jake nodded, a gesture heavy with meaning. "I know," he said, his hand finding mine across the space that no longer felt insurmountable. "I don't want that either. I guess I've been so caught up in trying to shield you from the darkness that I've lost sight of the light that you bring into this fight. Your courage, your passion—it's what drew me to you in the first place. I don't want to be the reason that dims your light, even if it's for the sake of keeping you safe."

The simplicity of his words, the sincerity shining in his eyes, stirred something profound within me. Here, in the aftermath of our most heated argument, we found a common ground, a mutual acknowledgment of the fears that drove us and the love that bound us.

This turning point in our relationship illuminated a path forward, one where honesty and vulnerability were not liabilities but the very foundation upon which we could build our future. It was a realization that, despite the external pressures and the internal conflicts, our connection was a source of strength, a testament to the resilience of love in the face of adversity.

As we sat together, hand in hand, the remnants of our argument dissolving into the quiet of the evening, I felt a sense of peace settle over me. The breakthrough we had achieved, born of confrontation and tempered by understanding, had not only resolved the immediate tensions but had deepened our connection in ways I had not anticipated.

As the space between us filled with a charged, yet tender silence, Jake leaned forward, his forehead resting gently against mine. This simple act of closeness felt like a balm to the raw edges of our souls, a silent communication of understanding and forgiveness that words could scarcely convey.

"I'm sorry, Emily," he whispered, the warmth of his breath mingling with mine, a tactile reminder of the depth of our connection. "For all the walls I've put up, for every moment of doubt I've cast on us. I was so focused on protecting you from the world that I forgot to trust in the strength of what we have together."

His apology, sincere and heartfelt, unlocked something within me—a wellspring of emotion that I had held back in the name of resilience. "And I'm sorry for pushing so hard," I admitted, my voice barely above a murmur. "I should have realized the weight you're carrying, the battles you face even when you're standing still. I forgot that sometimes, courage means admitting we're scared and leaning on each other to find our way through the darkness."

In the shared silence that followed, a profound sense of mutual forgiveness enveloped us, weaving the frayed threads of our argument into a tapestry of deeper understanding. The tension that had once threatened to unravel us now served as the catalyst for a more profound connection, a testament to the resilience of love when tempered by the fires of conflict.

Gradually, the distance that had separated us vanished, our bodies drawing closer in a dance as old as time itself. As Jake's lips met mine, the kiss was a confluence of all the passion and tenderness that had always simmered beneath the surface of our relationship, now set ablaze by the trials we had overcome. It was a moment of exquisite vulnerability, where the walls we had built crumbled under the weight of our desire for one another.

This tender reconciliation was more than just a physical union; it was the rekindling of a bond that had been tested by fire and emerged stronger, more resilient. In the sanctity of that embrace, we found solace and strength, a reminder that together, we were more than the sum of our parts. Our love, forged in the crucible of duty and tempered by the honesty of our vulnerabilities, was a beacon that would guide us through whatever storms lay ahead.

As we surrendered to the moment, to the profound connection that bound us, I realized that this reconciliation was a reaffirmation of our commitment to each other. It was a promise, made in the language of touch and whispered vows, that no matter the challenges we faced, our love would remain unwavering, a source of light in the darkest of times.

In the quiet of Jake's embrace, I found not just forgiveness but a renewal of our shared destiny. We were two souls, intertwined by love and duty, ready to face the future together, fortified by the understanding that our vulnerabilities were not weaknesses but the very foundation of our strength.

In the aftermath of our reconciliation, the world around us seemed to hold its breath, granting us a moment of tranquility amidst the storms that raged beyond the confines of our sanctuary. Jake and I remained entwined, the echo of our intimacy lingering like a gentle caress, a testament to the depth of the connection we had rediscovered.

"I've always believed in the power of truth," I began, my voice a soft reflection of the myriad thoughts swirling within me. "Even as a child, watching my parents dedicate their lives to journalism, to uncovering stories that needed to be told, I understood that knowledge wasn't just power—it was justice. It was their legacy, and it's become my calling."

Jake listened, his gaze steady and supportive, encouraging me to peel back the layers of my motivations, to share the core of my dedication to my work. "But it's not just about following in their footsteps," I continued, my heart buoyed by the safety of his understanding. "It's about believing that, in the face of injustice, silence is complicity. My writing, my investigations—they're my way of speaking out, of making a difference."

The silence that followed was not empty but full, charged with the weight of shared ideals and the recognition of shared struggles. Jake's hand found mine, a tangible symbol of his presence, of his support.

"Emily, knowing you, seeing your courage and your commitment—it's inspired me, challenged me," Jake said, his voice tinged with a vulnerability that tugged at my heart. "In the field, in the face of danger, it's easy to feel like what I'm doing is making a difference. But it's also easy to lose sight of the bigger picture, to get lost in the darkness. You've been my light, reminding me of why we fight, of what's at stake."

His confession, a mirror to my own revelations, deepened the connection that pulsed between us, weaving our separate journeys into a single tapestry of purpose and passion. "But I'm scared too," he admitted, his gaze dropping to our intertwined hands. "Scared of what this fight might cost us, of the possibility of losing you to the very darkness we're trying to dispel."

Hearing Jake voice his fears, fears that mirrored my own, was both a balm and a catalyst, driving home the realization that our battles, though fought on different fronts, were intrinsically linked by the bonds of love and duty.

"Jake, I won't pretend I'm not afraid," I replied, squeezing his hand as if to anchor him to me. "But knowing you're with me, that we're in this together, it makes all the difference. Your strength, your dedication—it gives me hope, even in the darkest of times."

Our conversation, quiet and reflective, was a journey through the landscape of our souls, a mutual exploration of the fears and aspirations that defined us. It was a reaffirmation of our commitment not just to our individual causes, but to each other, to the belief that together, we could face whatever the future held.

As the night deepened around us, our shared confidences became the foundation of a renewed resolve, a resolve to stand together against the tides of darkness, fortified by the knowledge that our deepened connection was a source of unparalleled strength. In the sanctity of our shared vulnerability, we found not just understanding but a profound sense of purpose, a beacon to guide us through the uncertainty of the battles ahead.

"It's strange," I mused, breaking the comfortable silence that had settled between us, "how love and duty, two forces that seemed at odds, have become the very source of our strength. I used to think I had to choose between them, but with you, I've found a way to embrace both."

Jake's smile, warm and reassuring in the dim light, was a reflection of my own thoughts. "I feel the same, Emily. You've shown me that the heart doesn't divide; it multiplies. What we share, it doesn't detract from our duties—it enhances them. Together, we're more than just lovers or allies; we're a force to be reckoned with."

As we spoke, a sense of renewal enveloped us, a feeling of being reborn into a world where the trials we had faced had only served to deepen our connection, forging it into something unbreakable. We recognized that the road ahead would not be without its challenges, that the darkness we fought against was a relentless adversary. Yet, in acknowledging this, we found not despair but a fierce determination, a shared resolve to stand against whatever storms may come, anchored by the love and trust that bound us.

"We've been through so much, faced down fears and uncertainties that would have torn lesser bonds asunder," I said, my voice steady with conviction. "But here we are, stronger for it, more united than ever. Our love, our duty—they're not just aspects of who we are; they're the very essence of our strength."

Jake took my hand, his grip firm and filled with promise. "Together, we'll face the future, whatever it may bring. We'll stand as a testament to what can be achieved when love and duty walk hand in hand. No challenge is too great, no darkness too deep, that our light can't pierce through."

In that moment, as we made our vows not with words but with the silent language of hearts in perfect sync, I felt a profound sense of peace settle over me. The challenges ahead were many, the path fraught with danger and uncertainty. But we would walk it together, our bond a beacon of hope in a troubled world.

The Infiltration

Jake

Each morning I find myself straddling the razor-thin line between breakthrough and disaster. The Black Oak Militia's encampment, a sprawling nest of tents and makeshift structures hidden away in the dense forest, has become both my hunting ground and my cage. Here, amidst the murmurs of dissent and the clatter of preparations, I move like a shadow, my identity cloaked in the guise of allegiance to a cause that stands in stark opposition to everything I hold dear.

My days are a carefully choreographed dance of subterfuge and surveillance, every interaction laden with the potential to either propel my mission forward or unravel it completely. The deeper I delve into the heart of the militia's web, the more palpable the danger becomes. Conversations pause as I approach, sidelong glances follow me like specters, and the weight of suspicion grows heavier with each passing moment.

The militia, a volatile mix of discontent and radical ideology, is a ticking time bomb, and I am both the fuse and the potential extinguisher. The articles that Emily has courageously published have stirred a hornet's nest, igniting a fury within the ranks that has expedited their plans. I hear my name whispered in the shadows, a question mark hanging over my loyalty, and I know that my every move is scrutinized, my every word dissected for signs of betrayal.

Yet, it is in these moments of heightened danger that the critical pieces of their scheme come to light. Huddled around flickering campfires or buried in hasty meetings in the dead of night, the leaders of the militia lay bare their intentions, unaware that their confidences fall upon the ears of their nemesis. The imminent attack, a dark specter looming over the town, is now a clear and present danger, its outlines sharp and defined in the intelligence I've gathered.

But with this clarity comes a crippling fear for Emily's safety. Her name, too, has become a whispered specter in the camp, a symbol of the resistance that they aim to crush. The knowledge that her pursuit of truth has painted a target on her back is a constant ache, a reminder of the personal stakes that lie beneath the surface of my mission.

Each night, as I lay in the cold embrace of my tent, the dilemmas of my deep cover mission weigh heavily on my soul. The balance I must strike between gathering the intelligence needed to thwart their plans and maintaining the façade that keeps me embedded within their ranks is a precarious one. Too much caution, and I risk missing the vital information that could save lives; too much zeal, and I might expose not only myself but Emily to mortal danger.

In the shadowy depths of the militia's encampment, my mission teeters on the edge of a knife, every decision, every action fraught with consequence. Yet, despite the ever-present danger of exposure and the growing threat to the woman I love, my resolve has never been firmer. The sacrifices demanded by this mission, the toll it takes on heart and soul, are prices I am willing to pay.

For in the heart of this darkness, I am not alone. The light of Emily's courage, the bond that ties us together, shines brightly, guiding me through the perilous path I tread. It is for her, for our shared future, and for the community that has shaped us, that I press on, determined to dismantle the threat that looms over us all, no matter the cost.

In the wake of Emily's articles, the atmosphere within the Black Oak Militia's encampment shifted palpably. Whispers swirled like leaves caught in a tempest, each passing comment laced with a venom directed not just at the world outside but at the perceived betrayal from within. It was during one such clandestine gathering, under the guise of night and secrecy, that I found myself a silent observer to the tempest that was about to unfold.

Mark Dalton, the militia's leader and a man whose charisma was only matched by his capacity for ruthlessness, stood at the heart of the gathering. His silhouette, illuminated by the flickering light of a solitary lantern, cast long shadows on the faces of those assembled, each one hanging on his every word.

"Emily's articles have exposed our plans to the world," Dalton spat, his voice a serrated blade cutting through the hushed murmurs of the crowd. "She's painted us as villains in the eyes of the public, twisting our cause to fit her narrative. But we will not let this stand. We will not be deterred by the machinations of the media or the corrupt institutions they protect."

Beside him, a man I knew only as Cutter, Dalton's second-in-command and a fervent believer in the cause, nodded in agreement. "We've been too cautious, waiting for the perfect moment. Emily's interference has shown us that time is a luxury we no longer have. It's time to act, to show the world the strength of our resolve."

The crowd murmured their assent, a dangerous energy brewing in the space between words. I remained silent, an observer cloaked in the semblance of loyalty, even as my heart raced with the realization of what their accelerated plan could mean for Emily, for the town, and for the fragile thread on which my cover balanced.

"It's decided, then," Dalton declared, his gaze sweeping over the crowd, igniting sparks of fervor in his wake. "We move forward with the operation. This Founder's Day will be remembered as the dawn of a new era, the moment when we took back control from those who seek to oppress us. Let them write about that."

The meeting dispersed as quickly as it had convened, the conspirators melting back into the shadows from which they had emerged. Left alone with my thoughts, I wrestled with the weight of the intelligence I had just gathered. Dalton and his lieutenants, driven by rage and a perverse sense of righteousness, were willing to sacrifice innocents in their quest for visibility, their plans now set on a collision course with disaster.

As I made my way back to my own quarters, the darkness around me felt suffocating, laden with the ghosts of futures that might never come to pass. The knowledge I held was a damning indictment of the path the militia had chosen, a path marked by violence and zealotry. Yet, it was also a beacon, a call to action that I could not ignore.

Emily's bravery, her refusal to back down in the face of intimidation, had inadvertently accelerated the militia's timeline, but it had also provided a critical advantage. We now knew the stakes, the timeline, and the resolve of our adversaries. The battle lines were drawn, not just in the sand of ideological conflict, but in the very real world where actions had consequences, where the pen and the sword were both mightier than ever.

With each passing day, as the Black Oak Militia's accelerated agenda took on a life of its own, my role within their ranks became a precarious balancing act. The very thing that gave me an edge—my deep integration into their operations, my access to their darkest plans—also painted a bullseye on my back, a constant reminder that my cover could be blown with a single misstep.

Mark Dalton's fervor, once a smoldering ember, had ignited into a wildfire, spreading through the ranks with a zeal that brooked no dissent. Meetings became more frequent, plans more detailed, and the air within the encampment crackled with a sense of impending action. To maintain my cover, I had to mirror their enthusiasm, to nod along to diatribes about "the cause" and "the corrupt" while every fiber of my being screamed in opposition.

The dual identity I navigated was a labyrinth of moral and ethical quandaries. By day, I was one of them, a brother-in-arms to men and women who believed they were fighting for freedom, for liberation from a system they viewed as fundamentally broken. But by night, in the solitude of my own quarters, I was a man tormented by the knowledge of the destruction they sought to unleash, a man whose every action was a calculated move to undermine the very group he pretended to support.

Rumors and suspicions swirled like vultures, drawn to the scent of potential betrayal. Whispers of a mole within the ranks began to surface, whispered conversations that halted abruptly as I approached, suspicious glances that lingered too long. The atmosphere of paranoia that Mark Dalton cultivated as a means of control now worked against me, turning every interaction into a minefield.

Amidst this tightening noose of suspicion, my thoughts invariably turned to Emily. Her articles, the spark that had ignited this accelerated timeline, also served as a beacon of truth in a sea of deceit. The irony was not lost on me; the very person I sought to protect through my infiltration was the catalyst for the increased danger we both faced.

My loyalty, torn between my duty to my country and my commitment to Emily, became a weight that threatened to drag me under. I wrestled with the fear that my actions, however well-intentioned, might inadvertently expose her to greater danger. The thought of her coming to harm because of my role in this twisted game was a specter that haunted my every moment, a possibility more terrifying than any personal risk I faced.

As the militia's plans crystallized, as D-Day loomed ever closer on the horizon, I found myself at a crossroads. The knowledge I had gained, the secrets I had unearthed, were weapons in their own right, tools that could be used to dismantle the militia's plans and save countless lives. Yet, wielding these weapons meant exposing myself, stepping out of the shadows at the risk of everything I held dear.

In this tangled web of loyalty and betrayal, love and duty, I found a resolve I didn't know I possessed. With each step I took, each piece of intelligence I gathered, I reaffirmed my commitment to the cause of justice, to the promise of a future free from the tyranny of fear. The road ahead was uncertain, the risks immense, but my purpose had never been clearer. For Emily, for the community that had shaped us both, I would navigate the complexities of my role, ready to sacrifice my cover, my safety, for the greater good.

The tension within the Black Oak Militia's encampment had reached a palpable crescendo, a simmering pot threatening to boil over at any moment. My days were filled with a constant vigilance, my nights with plotting and planning, all under the guise of loyalty to a cause that stood in direct opposition to everything I believed in. It was during one of these fraught nights, under the cover of darkness, that I stumbled upon the final piece of the puzzle—a detail that would prove to be both the key to thwarting the militia's plans and potentially my undoing.

Hunched over a table littered with maps and makeshift plans, illuminated only by the dim glow of a lantern, Mark Dalton and his closest advisors spoke in hushed, urgent tones. Their words, fragments of sentences laced with the venom of their intent, were like whispers of a storm on the horizon. I lingered in the shadows, a ghost among them, my presence unnoticed yet intensely focused on their conversation.

"It's all set for dawn on Founder's Day," Dalton was saying, his voice a low growl of anticipation. "The explosives are in place, the routes secured. By the time they realize what's happening, it'll be too late."

The mention of explosives sent a jolt of adrenaline coursing through me. This was no mere demonstration of power, no symbolic act of defiance. They were planning an attack that would endanger countless lives, an act of terror masked as a call to arms.

The risk of staying any longer was immense, but the need for information was paramount. I forced myself to remain, to commit every detail to memory, even as the weight of my discovery bore down on me.

"We'll make a statement that can't be ignored," another voice added, one I recognized as Cutter's. "After this, they'll have to listen. They'll have to see that we're not to be trifled with."

As they continued to outline their plan, a cold resolve settled over me. I had what I needed, the crucial detail that could unravel their schemes, but at what cost? The moment I acted on this information, the moment I stepped out of the shadows to warn the authorities, my cover would be irrevocably blown. Mark Dalton, a man known for his cruelty as much as his charisma, would not hesitate to retaliate, and Emily—my heart clenched at the thought—Emily would be at the top of his list.

With a final glance at the conspirators, I slipped away into the night, the weight of my mission heavier than ever. The information I had gathered was a double-edged sword, offering a chance to save lives but exposing me to a danger I had long feared.

The plot I had uncovered was a ticking time bomb, set to detonate on Founder's Day, and I was the only one who could defuse it. The path ahead was fraught with danger, the shadows that I had navigated for so long now poised to envelop me. But my resolve was unshaken. For the sake of the community, for the love I bore Emily, I was prepared to step into the light, to expose the darkness I had found, and to face whatever consequences that act might bring.

In the days that followed, I watched as Mark Dalton's ire towards Emily grew, fueled by her articles that cast a glaring spotlight on the militia's activities. Conversations once centered on strategies and plans shifted towards retribution, with Emily's name often whispered with a venom that left no doubt as to the depth of their animosity.

I knew I had to act, to put measures in place to ensure Emily's safety, all while navigating the treacherous waters of my undercover role. Each step I took was calculated to avoid detection, from encrypted messages sent through channels I had painstakingly secured, to discreet inquiries into potential threats, all executed with the utmost care to shield her from the militia's growing wrath.

Despite the meticulous nature of my efforts, the fear that my actions might inadvertently cast a brighter spotlight on Emily was a constant companion. The delicate balance I had maintained between my role within the militia and my mission to protect her felt more precarious with each passing moment. The irony that my attempts to safeguard her could potentially expose her to greater danger was a cruel twist, one that kept me awake through the long, restless nights.

I enlisted the help of trusted contacts outside the militia, individuals whose dedication to justice mirrored my own, to keep a watchful eye on Emily without drawing undue attention. I provided them with information on potential threats, descriptions of key militia members, and routes Emily might take, all while emphasizing the need for discretion.

As the day of the militia's planned attack drew nearer, my resolve to protect Emily hardened into something fierce and unyielding. I knew that the path I had chosen was fraught with danger, that the steps I took to safeguard her might well lead to my own undoing. But there was no other choice. Emily's safety, her freedom to speak the truth, was a beacon that guided me, a cause worth any risk, any sacrifice.

I steeled myself for what was to come. My actions to protect Emily, cloaked in secrecy and executed with precision, were but the opening salvos in a battle for our future—a battle I was determined to win, no matter the cost.

* * *

Under the cloak of night, with the world around me wrapped in silence, I found myself drawn to the local veterans' memorial, a place I had visited many times before, but never with a heart as heavy as it was tonight. The cool night air brushed against my skin as I walked, a solitary figure moving through the darkness, driven by a need for clarity and courage that seemed just out of reach.

The memorial stood solemn and majestic in the moonlight, its stones etched with the names of those who had served, who had sacrificed for the ideals and freedoms we hold dear. Among those names was my grandfather, a man whose legacy of bravery and duty had been a guiding light throughout my life. Tonight, more than ever, I sought the wisdom that his memory might impart, a beacon to guide me through the storm that loomed on the horizon.

As I approached, the silence of the memorial enveloped me, a sacred hush that seemed to transcend time and space. The names inscribed on the stone, each a testament to courage and sacrifice, stood as silent sentinels, their legacy a weighty reminder of the cost of freedom, of the duty that runs like a current through the blood of those who serve.

I traced the letters of my grandfather's name with my fingertips, the cool stone a tangible connection to the past, to the lineage of service and sacrifice that defined my family. In that moment, the challenges I faced, the fears that haunted me, seemed both monumental and yet surmountable, viewed through the lens of the sacrifices made by those who had come before me.

"My grandfather stood where I stand now, faced with the darkness of his own times," I whispered into the night, my voice a low murmur that seemed to blend with the whispers of the past. "He fought for what he believed in, for the future he wanted to secure for his family, for his country. Can I do any less?"

The veterans' memorial, with its rows of names and its aura of solemn dignity, was more than just a monument to the past; it was a mirror reflecting the choices that lay before me. Each name was a reminder that the fight for justice, for freedom, is never without cost, but it is always worth the sacrifice.

Standing there, under the gaze of the moon and the silent watch of my grandfather's memory, a sense of clarity began to take shape within me. The fears that had threatened to paralyze me, the doubts that had clouded my judgment, were dispelled by the simple, unyielding truth that duty and love were not mutually exclusive but were, in fact, two sides of the same coin.

The legacy of those who served, who laid down their lives in the pursuit of a better world, was a legacy of hope, a promise that the darkness could be overcome, that the future was worth fighting for. My mission, my role in this unfolding drama, was a continuation of that legacy, a testament to the belief that the sacrifices we make in the name of duty, in the name of love, are what define us, what make us truly human.

My grandfather's name, etched among the many, served as a stark reminder of the cost of freedom, of the duty that had been passed down through the bloodlines to rest upon my shoulders. It was a legacy that I had always carried with pride, but in the shadow of the impending conflict with the Black Oak Militia, it took on a new, profound significance.

As I reflected on the mission that lay before me, on the choices and sacrifices it entailed, I couldn't help but consider the broader impact of my actions. The militia's plans, if brought to fruition, would not only endanger lives but would tear at the very fabric of our community, sowing fear and division where there should be solidarity and peace. The stakes were higher than my own safety, my own well-being; they encompassed the welfare of every person who called this town home.

The visit to the memorial, a pilgrimage of sorts, solidified my resolve. It bridged the gap between the motivations that had driven me to serve in the first place and the actions I must undertake now. The legacy of sacrifice embodied by the names around me was a clarion call to action, a reminder that true courage often lies in the willingness to face the darkness, not for glory or recognition, but for the sake of others.

As I left the memorial, the first light of dawn breaking on the horizon, I carried with me not just the weight of my mission but the strength of generations who had fought their own battles, who had faced their own darkness. The reflection on sacrifice, on the cost of the fight for freedom, was no longer a burden but a beacon, guiding me forward.

The decision to proceed, to push through with my mission despite the risks, was not made lightly. Every step I had taken, every piece of intelligence I had gathered, had led me to this moment, where the path forward was fraught with danger, but the consequences of inaction were far worse. The Black Oak Militia, emboldened by secrecy and driven by a misguided zeal, was on the brink of unleashing chaos on the community I had sworn to protect. The knowledge I held was a key that could unlock their downfall, but wielding it meant stepping into the light, exposing myself to the wrath of those I had deceived.

As the memorial had reminded me, the legacy of those who served before me was one of sacrifice and duty. My grandfather, whose name I had traced in the stone, had faced his own battles, his own moments of decision where the cost was measured in more than just personal safety. He, like countless others memorialized alongside him, had made the choice to stand for something greater than himself, to protect the ideals and freedoms that define us.

Embodying the spirit of those who served before me, I knew that my commitment to safeguarding my community was a torch passed down through generations, a duty that transcended personal risk. The decision to continue with my mission, to expose the militia's plans and prevent the impending attack, was a continuation of that legacy. It was a pledge to stand against the darkness, to fight for the light that the names at the memorial had died defending.

The harrowing decision to proceed was thus made with a heavy heart but a steadfast spirit. I was acutely aware of the potential cost—my cover could be blown, my life put in immediate danger, and the future I envisioned with Emily thrown into jeopardy. Yet, the alternative, to stand by while harm came to those I loved and the community I called home, was unthinkable.

As the first light of dawn broke over the town, casting long shadows and promising the start of a new day, I felt a solemn peace settle over me. The decision had been made, the course set. The challenges ahead would test me in ways I could scarcely imagine, but I would face them head-on, fortified by the courage and sacrifice of those who had come before me.

The mission ahead was not just a tactical operation; it was a stand for justice, for peace, for the future. In making the decision to proceed, I was not just an operative working in the shadows; I was a guardian of the light, a defender of the community that had shaped me. The path forward was uncertain, the risks immense, but my resolve had never been stronger. For the sake of all we held dear, I would see this mission through to the end, embodying the spirit of sacrifice and duty that the veterans' memorial had so poignantly reminded me of.

Breaking Point

Emily

The cursor hovered over the 'publish' button, a digital precipice that felt as daunting as any physical cliff I had ever stood before. The early morning light filtered through the curtains, casting a soft glow over my workspace, a stark contrast to the storm of emotions raging within me. My finger paused, suspended in a moment of heightened anticipation, the culmination of months of investigation, of digging through layers of secrecy and deception, distilled into a single, decisive action.

The fear was palpable, a cold thread winding its way through my veins. It wasn't just the fear of backlash, of the vitriol and threats that would inevitably flood in from the shadows. It was the fear of the unknown, of the potential consequences my actions could unleash, not just on me but on those I cared about. Jake, who was out there in the thick of it, his own life a web of danger and duplicity, weighed heavily on my mind.

But alongside the fear, there was excitement—a pulsing, vibrant thread that thrummed with the promise of impact, of change. This article, a deep dive into the heart of the Black Oak Militia's operations, was more than just an exposé; it was a call to arms, a beacon for those who had suffered in silence, too afraid or too powerless to speak out.

And underpinning it all was a deep, unwavering resolve. The pursuit of justice, the commitment to truth—these were not just ideals I held dear; they were the very core of who I was, the compass that guided every decision I made, every story I chased. The potential consequences, while terrifying, paled in comparison to the weight of silence, of the complicity in inaction.

With a deep breath, a silent prayer for courage and strength, I clicked the button. The article, my painstakingly gathered evidence and carefully crafted narrative, was now out in the world, a ripple in the pond that I hoped would grow into a wave of awareness and action.

The immediate aftermath was a strange blend of relief and tension, a release paired with the tightening anticipation of the fallout to come. The digital silence of the early morning hours felt like the calm before the storm, a temporary reprieve before the onslaught of reactions that would surely follow.

As I sat back, the glow of the screen the only light in the dim room, I felt a profound sense of vulnerability. Putting my work out there, especially something as potentially explosive as this investigation, was akin to baring my soul to the world, inviting scrutiny, criticism, and danger.

But more than that, I felt a fierce pride in what I had accomplished. Despite the fear, despite the risks, I had chosen to stand in the light, to use my voice and my skills to shine a spotlight on the darkness. This article, this moment of anticipation and release, was a testament to that choice, to the belief that one voice, however small, could make a difference.

Sitting alone in the dim light of early morning, I watched, heart lodged firmly in my throat, as the comments section beneath my article transformed into a battlefield. Each new notification was a pulse in the rapid heartbeat of public opinion, a vivid illustration of the dichotomy of support and vitriol that my work had ignited.

Supportive comments flowed in, a torrent of gratitude and solidarity from those who saw my article as a beacon of truth in a landscape often shrouded in shadow. "Thank you for shedding light on this," one comment read, its simple sincerity a balm to the gnawing anxiety that had taken root within me. "Your courage gives us hope," said another, a reminder of why I had chosen this path, why the risk felt necessary.

Yet, for every message of support, there was an equal measure of backlash. Vitriol spilled from the screen, harsh words and threats from those who saw my exposé as an affront, a betrayal of ideals they held dear. "You've gone too far this time," one commenter warned, their anonymity doing nothing to lessen the chill their words sent down my spine. "Watch your back," another sneered, a stark reminder of the tangible dangers that my journalism invited.

"You're playing with fire, and you're going to get burned," another warned, the implication clear and chilling. My breath caught in my throat as I continued to scroll, the litany of threats weaving a tapestry of danger that felt all too real. The courage that had buoyed me as I hit 'publish' seemed a distant memory, replaced by a visceral understanding of the personal cost of standing in the truth.

One email, in particular, stopped me cold, its words a vivid echo of the darkest fears that had haunted me since embarking on this path. "Watch your back, because we are," it promised, a sinister assurance that my actions had not gone unnoticed, that the spotlight I had turned on the Black Oak Militia had, in turn, cast me into their shadow.

The room around me felt oppressively quiet, the only sound the relentless buzz of my phone as more notifications poured in. With each new message, each new threat, the walls seemed to close in, a physical manifestation of the pressure that threatened to suffocate me. The vulnerability I felt was overwhelming, a stark contrast to the resolve that had driven me to this moment.

The comments section, a microcosm of the broader societal divide, was a tangible manifestation of my deepest fears and highest hopes. With every supportive message, I felt a surge of validation, a sense of camaraderie with those who shared my vision for a world unburdened by secrets and lies. But each hostile comment was a shadow, a dark reflection of the risks I had taken by standing in the truth.

As the article went viral, spreading across social media platforms and news outlets, the intensity of the public's reaction grew. My phone buzzed incessantly with notifications, each one a reminder of the weight of what I had done. The impact of my words stretched far beyond the confines of my small town, igniting debates, discussions, and, in some cases, outright hostility.

Watching the fallout unfold, I was torn between a profound sense of accomplishment and a gnawing apprehension. The article, a culmination of months of investigation and countless hours of work, was my attempt to peel back the layers of secrecy that had allowed the Black Oak Militia to thrive. Yet, in exposing their darkness to the light, I had also stepped into the crosshairs, a target for those who thrived in the shadows.

In the whirlwind of reactions, my thoughts inevitably drifted to Jake, to the dangers he faced in the heart of the storm. The knowledge that my work could inadvertently increase the peril he faced was a heavy burden, one that mingled with my fear for his safety.

As the day wore on and the reactions continued to pour in, I was buoyed by the support, strengthened by the knowledge that my work had touched a chord with so many. Yet, the vitriol served as a constant reminder of the battles still to be fought, both in the digital world and beyond.

I forced myself to take a deep breath, to try and stem the rising tide of panic that threatened to overwhelm me. The knowledge that Jake was out there, potentially in even greater danger because of my actions, was a constant, gnawing presence at the back of my mind. The personal attacks, while terrifying, paled in comparison to the thought of him coming to harm.

As I sat there, my notifications a relentless stream of hatred and menace, I realized that this was the price of my conviction, the cost of shedding light on the darkness. My resolve, so firm in the light of day, was tested now in the shadow of these personal attacks.

Yet, even in the midst of this storm, a defiant spark of courage flickered to life within me. The threats, intended to intimidate and silence, instead served as a grim reminder of the importance of my work, of the need to stand against those who would use fear as a weapon. I was vulnerable, yes, but not defeated.

The personal cost of my courage, laid bare in the hateful words that filled my screen, was a burden I was willing to bear. For in the end, the truth was a light that not even the deepest shadows could extinguish, and I, its humble bearer, would not be deterred.

Amid the tempest of hostility, a haven of support began to manifest, a counterbalance to the darkness that threatened to engulf me. The constant barrage of my notifications, a source of dread mere moments ago, became interspersed with beacons of solidarity and encouragement. It was in this tumult of fear and support that my phone rang, cutting through the cacophony of digital noise. The name that lit up my screen was a balm to my frayed nerves—Marianne, my mentor, my guide through the labyrinth of journalism, whose wisdom had always served as a north star in my darkest moments.

"Emily, I saw your piece," Marianne's voice came through, a sturdy thread of warmth in the cold tapestry of my current reality. Her words were not just a salve but a reinforcement of the bond that we shared, a reminder that I was not alone in this fight.

"I won't pretend I'm not worried about you," she continued, her concern palpable even through the digital divide. "But I need you to know how proud I am—how important what you've done is. You've shone a light on shadows that many didn't even dare to acknowledge.

That's the essence of what we do, Emily. You're embodying the best of journalism."

Her words, imbued with years of experience and the battles she herself had faced, were a reminder of the lineage of truth-seekers I was a part of. In the face of threats and hostility, Marianne's support was a testament to the enduring power of truth, to the collective endeavor of those who strive to illuminate the darker corners of our world.

As we spoke, Marianne offered not just support but wisdom, a strategic counsel on navigating the backlash, on safeguarding myself without retreating from the mission at hand. "Remember, Emily, bravery isn't the absence of fear. It's the decision to keep moving forward despite it," she advised, her words echoing the resolve that had driven me to publish my article in the first place.

The call, though brief, was a poignant scene in the unfolding drama of my life, a moment of connection that bolstered my spirits and reaffirmed my decision. Marianne, with her unwavering support and sage advice, was a pillar of strength in a world that seemed determined to sway me from my path.

In the hours and days that followed, the support system that rallied around me became my lifeline. Close friends, allies in the journalistic community, and even strangers who had been moved by my work reached out with messages of encouragement, offers of assistance, and affirmations of solidarity. This network of support, this circle of light amidst the gathering darkness, was a tangible manifestation of the impact of my work and the shared commitment to justice and truth that bound us together.

Their support, their willingness to stand with me against the tide of hostility, was a powerful reminder of the strength that comes from unity, from the collective resolve of those who refuse to be silenced. It was a reinforcement of my belief that, despite the fear and the risks involved, my decision to expose the Black Oak Militia's plans was not just justified but necessary.

As I navigated the aftermath of my publication, bolstered by the support of my friends and mentors, I felt a renewed sense of purpose. The hostility I faced, while daunting, was overshadowed by the solidarity of my support system, by the knowledge that I was part of a larger struggle for truth and justice. Their support was not just a comfort but a call to arms, a reminder that, together, we were stronger than the forces that sought to intimidate us, a collective embodiment of the courage and resolve needed to change the world.

In the swirl of emotions following the publication of my article and the subsequent wave of support and hostility, a singular fear began to crystallize, sharpening into a point that pierced the heart of my resolve. Jake, deep undercover within the Black Oak Militia, was in a maelstrom of danger that my actions had only intensified. The thought of him, surrounded by those who would see harm come to me—and by extension, to him—was a constant thrum of anxiety, a shadow that no amount of support could fully dispel.

It was with a trembling hand and a heavy heart that I dialed Jake's number, the familiar digits a lifeline in the chaos that had become my reality. The phone rang, each tone echoing the rapid beat of my heart, until finally, his voice came through, a balm and a torment all at once.

"Emily, I saw the article," he began, his voice a mix of pride and concern that mirrored my own tumultuous emotions. "You did what you had to do. It's important work, but you've painted a target on your back. We need to talk about what this means—for both of us."

The conversation that unfolded was tense, laden with the emotional undercurrents of our shared fears and the unspoken realities of our respective battles. Jake's concern for my safety was palpable, his protective instincts warring with the knowledge that my work, like his, was driven by a deeper sense of duty.

"I'm worried about you, Jake," I admitted, the words barely a whisper, yet heavy with the weight of my fear. "The militia's reaction, the threats... I can't bear the thought of something happening to you because of my work."

Jake's response was immediate, a testament to the depth of our connection and the complexity of our situation. "I knew the risks going in, Emily. And so did you. We're in this fight together, even if we're on different fronts. I'll do everything in my power to stay safe, but I need you to do the same. We can't let fear dictate our actions."

His words, though meant to reassure, served as a stark reminder of the precariousness of our positions. Jake's protective stance was not dismissive but rooted in a shared understanding of the stakes involved. His support of my work, despite the dangers it posed, added another layer to the fabric of our relationship, a complex weaving of love, duty, and shared resolve.

"We need to be smart about this, Emily. Increase your security, be aware of your surroundings. We both know the risks, but we can't let them stop us. What we're doing—it matters. It's bigger than us," Jake continued, his voice firm, a rock amidst the roiling seas of fear and uncertainty.

In facing the potential dangers together, discussing them openly and without reservation, Jake and I had fortified our relationship, acknowledging the risks while refusing to be cowed by them. This tense, emotional exchange was not just a moment of vulnerability; it was a reaffirmation of our partnership, a pledge to face whatever the future held, united in purpose and unwavering in our support for one another.

In the aftermath of our conversation, the comforting glow of the screen dimmed, leaving me alone in the quiet of my room, the shadows of doubt creeping in with the fading light. The support of my friends and the resolve in Jake's voice were buoys in a sea of uncertainty, yet they couldn't fully dispel the storm of questions that raged within me.

Sitting there, the echo of Jake's assurances lingering like a half-remembered dream, I found myself ensnared in a web of doubt. My article, born of a relentless pursuit of truth and justice, had taken on a life of its own, sparking fires of both support and condemnation. But in illuminating the dark corners of the Black Oak Militia's plans, had I inadvertently cast the people I cared about most into danger?

The question was a weight, pressing down with the heaviness of potential consequences. Jake, whose undercover work was a tightrope walk over an abyss, now faced an even greater peril due to the spotlight I had shone. The thought of him, surrounded by danger, his every move fraught with the risk of discovery, sent a shiver of fear through me, a cold reminder of the stakes at play.

Was the story worth it? The question echoed in the silence, a haunting refrain that offered no easy answers. My commitment to my work, to the ideals of journalism and the responsibility to speak truth to power, was a core part of who I was. Yet, faced with the tangible risks that commitment had wrought, I couldn't help but wonder if my determination had been a folly, a reckless gamble with stakes higher than I'd fully comprehended.

The internal conflict was a storm of emotion, a tumultuous clash between my professional convictions and the personal cost of those convictions. Each article I had written, each truth I had uncovered, had been a step on a path I believed in, a path paved with the necessity of shining a light on injustice. But now, in the quiet aftermath of my latest publication, the path seemed fraught with shadows of doubt, each step a potential misstep that could lead to harm for those I loved.

Alone with my thoughts, I wrestled with the weight of my choices, the burden of potential consequences a heavy cloak around my shoulders. The fear for Jake's safety, the knowledge that my actions could have placed him in even greater danger, was a bitter pill, one that threatened to overshadow the pride and purpose that had driven me to this point.

This moment of doubt, this internal conflict, was not just a crisis of conscience; it was a crucible, testing the strength of my convictions and the depth of my courage. The choices I had made, the risks I had taken, were reflections of a commitment to a cause greater than myself. And though the path ahead was uncertain, fraught with danger and the potential for loss, it was a path I had chosen with eyes wide open, driven by a deep-seated belief in the power of truth.

In the solitude of that moment, questioning the cost of my pursuit, I found not weakness but humanity. The doubts, the fears, were part of the journey, a reminder of the stakes for which we fight. And though the road ahead might be shadowed by uncertainty, my resolve to continue, to stand for what I believed in, remained unshaken, a beacon of light in the gathering darkness.

The shadows of the evening stretched long across the room, a visual echo of the doubts that had clouded my mind. Yet, it was in the heart of this darkness that a spark of clarity began to ignite, fueled by a phone call that would serve as the catalyst for a profound shift within me.

The voice on the other end of the line was that of Claudia, a fellow journalist and a beacon of integrity in the often murky waters of our profession. Claudia, who had faced her own battles against the giants of corruption and deceit, carried in her words the weight of experience and the fire of an undimmed passion for justice.

"Emily, I've read your piece," she began, her tone a mixture of admiration and concern. "I know the road you're on, the weight of the burden you carry. It's easy to get lost in the storm, to forget why we started on this path in the first place."

Her words, simple yet profound, echoed in the silence that followed, a mirror reflecting the turmoil within me. But it was what she said next that would become the beacon I needed to find my way through the darkness.

"We do this because we must, because if not us, then who? We stand on the shoulders of those who came before us, those who believed that the pen could be mightier than the sword. It's not just about exposing the wrongs of the world, Emily. It's about lighting a path to a better one."

Claudia's reminder of our shared mission, of the legacy we carried forward with every story we told, was a lifeline thrown across the chasm of my doubts. The conversation shifted something fundamental within me, stirring the embers of conviction that had been dampened by fear and uncertainty.

As we spoke, memories of why I had embarked on this journey in the first place began to resurface. The stories that had moved me, the injustices that had called out for exposure, the voices that had been silenced—these were the reasons I had become a journalist. My desire for justice, for truth, was not just a professional obligation; it was a calling, a fundamental part of who I was.

The moment of reflection, sparked by Claudia's words, became a turning point. The doubts that had clouded my vision began to dissipate, revealing the path I had chosen with renewed clarity. The risks, the fears, the potential for loss—these were all part of the fight, the struggle to bring light to the darkest corners of our world.

With a deep, steadying breath, my resolve hardened, tempered by the trials I had faced and the support of those who stood with me. The story I had told, the truths I had uncovered, were more than just my work; they were contributions to a larger battle, one that required courage, resilience, and, above all, determination.

As I hung up the phone, a sense of purpose filled me, a resolve that was both a shield and a sword. The desire for justice and truth, the very reasons I had taken on this story in the first place, were now the bedrock of my renewed determination. This was not just my battle; it was ours, a shared endeavor to fight against the forces of darkness with the only weapons we had: our words, our integrity, and our unwavering belief in the possibility of a better world.

The renewed determination that Claudia's call had ignited within me transformed into action as the day unfolded. The shadows of doubt that had once threatened to paralyze me now receded, replaced by a clear sense of purpose. I was under no illusion about the road ahead; the backlash from my article, coupled with the militia's known hostility, painted a target not just on my back but on those I held dear. The need to protect them, to safeguard the life we had built together, was paramount.

The first step was a meeting with Angela, a lawyer whose expertise in First Amendment rights and personal security had been invaluable to journalists facing threats in the past. We sat across from each other in the quiet of my living room, the seriousness of the situation reflected in the lines of her face.

"Emily, we need to consider every angle here," Angela began, her voice steady and reassuring. "The threats you've received are not to be taken lightly. We'll issue a statement, making it clear that any harm coming your way will have legal consequences. But beyond that, we need to think about your immediate safety."

We discussed a variety of measures, from enhanced digital security to protect against hacking and surveillance, to physical safeguards for my home. Angela suggested reaching out to local law enforcement to make them aware of the situation, a suggestion I took to heart. The notion of living under such scrutiny, of turning my home into a fortress, was daunting, but necessary.

As Angela left, her words lingered, a reminder of the tangible steps I needed to take in the face of the storm that was brewing. The next call was to a security firm, setting up an appointment to install surveillance cameras and bolster the locks on my doors and windows. Each action was a testament to my resolve, a refusal to be cowed by the threats that loomed.

But it wasn't just my physical safety that concerned me; it was Jake's. His undercover work placed him in a far more precarious position, and the thought of my actions exacerbating his danger was a constant ache. I drafted a careful message to him, outlining the steps I was taking and urging him to be extra cautious. The digital divide that separated us felt vast, yet it was crucial that he knew I was doing everything in my power to mitigate the risks.

In the quiet that followed, with plans set in motion and precautions taken, I allowed myself a moment to breathe. The fear and uncertainty were still present, shadows at the edge of my consciousness, but they were tempered by the knowledge that I was not passive in the face of them. I was taking control, doing everything within my power to protect myself and those I loved.

In the face of adversity, I found strength, a resilience born of the belief that what I was doing mattered. The path ahead was uncertain, fraught with challenges and dangers, but I was ready. Ready to face whatever came, fortified by the knowledge that I was not alone, that the fight for justice was a collective one, and that together, we were a force to be reckoned with.

Clash of Loyalties

Jake

Within the dense canopy of loyalty and secrecy that defined the Black Oak Militia, the winds of suspicion had begun to shift, subtle yet unmistakable in their direction. My integration into the group, once seamless, now felt like navigating a minefield blindfolded. The acceleration of their plans, driven by a mixture of fervor and desperation, had heightened the stakes, and with it, the scrutiny on every member—including me.

The signs were small at first, almost imperceptible. A conversation that fell silent as I approached, the quick exchange of glances that were too loaded, too fleeting to be innocent. I could feel the fabric of trust, woven over months of careful interaction and shared endeavors, beginning to fray at the edges, pulled apart by threads of doubt and paranoia.

Mark Dalton, the charismatic yet ruthless leader of the militia, had always possessed an uncanny ability to read people, to sense disloyalty like a shark senses blood in the water. It was this quality, perhaps, that first led him to cast a more discerning eye in my direction. A misplaced comment I made, intended to blend in but slightly off mark, caught his attention during one of our planning sessions. The momentary flicker of suspicion in his eyes was a clear signal that my facade was under scrutiny.

In the days that followed, I noticed an increase in the instances where I was left out of key discussions, only to be briefed afterward with information that felt deliberately curated, sanitized of the more sensitive details. The exclusion was subtle, designed not to alarm but to isolate, a tactic that left me grappling with the challenge of maintaining my cover while being increasingly boxed out of the inner circle.

The atmosphere within the camp, once thick with camaraderie and shared purpose, now carried an undercurrent of tension when I was present. Conversations were more guarded, plans discussed with a new level of opacity that seemed designed to test my reactions, to probe for signs of dissent or discomfort.

I recall a specific moment, a casual exchange by the fireside that turned into an impromptu interrogation. A few of the militia members, emboldened by the group's shifting dynamics, began to question the depth of my commitment, their words laced with an edge that was hard to ignore. My responses, carefully measured to deflect and reassure, felt hollow even to my own ears, a performance under the spotlight of suspicion.

Each interaction, each glance that lingered too long, was a reminder of the precariousness of my position. The trust I had worked so hard to build was evaporating, replaced by a fog of doubt that clouded every interaction. The sense of belonging I had once fabricated so convincingly was now a gossamer thread, ready to snap at the slightest misstep.

Navigating this landscape of suspicion, I was acutely aware of the dual dangers that faced me. Exposure would not only mean the end of my mission but could potentially put Emily and others at risk. The information I had gathered, the insights into the militia's accelerated plans, were of critical importance, yet their value was overshadowed by the growing risk of discovery.

As I lay in my bunk each night, the sounds of the encampment around me, I found myself wrestling with the reality of my situation. The rising suspicion within the militia was a clear signal that the time for action was drawing near, that my role as an undercover operative was reaching its inevitable climax. The trust I had once navigated with confidence was now a tightrope, each step forward a calculation of risk and necessity, played out under the watchful eyes of those I sought to deceive.

***

The air in the makeshift command tent was thick, charged with a tension that made every breath feel heavy, every moment stretched taut with anticipation. I stood at the center, the focus of every eye in the room, each gaze a weight upon my shoulders. Mark Dalton, flanked by his inner circle, regarded me with a look that was both calculating and cold, his instincts for detecting deceit honed to a razor's edge over years of leading the militia.

"Jake," Dalton began, his voice deceptively calm, "in light of recent... developments, we've found ourselves reassessing the loyalty of everyone in this camp. Your contributions have been noted, but so have certain... inconsistencies."

The word hung in the air between us, a silent accusation that threatened to unravel everything I had worked for. My heart pounded, a drumbeat of fear and adrenaline as I prepared to navigate the minefield of his questions. This was it—the moment of truth, where every word could either cement my place or spell my downfall.

"Of course, Mark," I replied, striving to keep my voice steady. "I understand the need for caution. I'm committed to our cause."

Dalton's eyes narrowed slightly, as if trying to peer into my soul. "Then perhaps you can explain why you were seen talking to an unknown contact outside of our operations zone last week?"

The question was a curveball, a reference to a brief, unavoidable encounter I had had while trying to maintain my cover. I had known it was risky, but the necessity of the moment had outweighed the danger. Now, it seemed, the danger had caught up with me.

"I was gathering information," I said, the lie slipping out smoothly, practiced in the countless hours of preparation for just such a moment. "You know as well as I do that we can't operate in a vacuum. My contact was someone I trusted from my time before joining the militia—someone who could provide us with valuable intel."

Dalton listened, his expression unreadable, as I wove a tale of espionage and counterintelligence, all fabricated but grounded in enough truth to be plausible. The room was silent, the tension a living thing that wrapped around us, tightening with every word I spoke.

"And what about the discrepancies in your reports?" Dalton pressed, his gaze unwavering. "Some of the intel hasn't matched up with our own sources. Care to explain that?"

This was the more dangerous territory, the discrepancies he mentioned a result of my careful manipulation to steer the militia away from innocent targets. "Intel can be tricky," I responded, forcing a confident smile. "Sources have their own agendas, misinformation is rife. I've done my best to verify everything, but in this line of work, some discrepancies are inevitable. My priority has always been the safety and success of our operations."

Dalton watched me for a long moment, his scrutiny intense. Around him, the inner circle waited, their loyalty to him absolute, their suspicion of me a shared bond. The atmosphere in the tent was a crucible, my every answer forging the next link in the chain of trust or betrayal.

Finally, Dalton nodded, the barest tilt of his head that offered no insight into his thoughts. "Your explanations seem... reasonable, Jake. But understand this: in our fight, there can be no half measures. Loyalty is everything. Any hint of betrayal, any deviation from our path, and the consequences will be severe."

The warning was clear, the threat implicit in his words a stark reminder of the perilous game I was playing. As the meeting adjourned, and I was left to gather my thoughts, the relief of having navigated Dalton's interrogation was tempered by the knowledge that I was walking a razor's edge. My loyalty had been challenged, my answers scrutinized, but for the moment, I had managed to maintain my cover.

The aftermath of the interrogation left a lingering chill, a harbinger of the storm that was yet to come. It wasn't long before Dalton called me aside, his demeanor one of cold calculation, the prelude to a challenge that would test the very fibers of my being. The mission he laid out was a gauntlet thrown at my feet, a test of loyalty designed to ensnare me in the moral quagmire that the militia called justice.

"Jake, we have a situation that requires a... delicate touch," Dalton began, his eyes locked on mine, searching for any hint of hesitation. "There's a local who's been a little too curious about our activities, someone who could pose a problem if left unchecked."

The implications of his words were clear, a veiled directive that danced on the edge of legality and morality. The task was a direct assault on the principles I held dear, an act that would not only bind me closer to the militia's cause but also mark me with the stain of their extremism.

My mind raced, searching for a way to navigate the treacherous waters Dalton had set before me. The mission was abhorrent, a line I could not cross, yet outright refusal would cast irrevocable doubt on my loyalty, potentially blowing my cover and endangering everything I had worked for.

"I understand the concern, Mark," I replied, my voice steady despite the turmoil within. "You can count on me to handle it."

Dalton's nod was one of approval, but the weight of his gaze was a clear reminder of the stakes. As I left his presence, the mission weighed heavily on my soul, a burden that threatened to drag me into the depths of despair.

The target was a local journalist, someone whose only crime was a pursuit of the truth, a pursuit that mirrored my own and that of Emily's. The irony was a bitter pill, a twisted reflection of the very ideals I was fighting to protect. My mind churned with possibilities, each more desperate than the last, as I sought a way out of the moral quagmire Dalton had crafted.

In the solitude of the night, as I wrestled with the implications of the task before me, I realized that compliance was not an option. To carry out Dalton's orders would be to betray everything I stood for, to cross a line from which there could be no return. Yet, defiance carried its own risks, a direct challenge to Dalton's authority that could end my mission—or my life—in an instant.

The decision, when it came, was born of necessity and conviction. I would not become the instrument of Dalton's malice, would not lend my hands to an act that would haunt me for the rest of my days. The resolve that filled me was a cold fire, a determination to undermine the militia's plans without exposing my true allegiance.

As dawn broke over the encampment, the plan took shape, a daring gambit that would require all my skills in deception and stealth. I would use my position within the militia to redirect the focus of their suspicion, to protect the innocent while sowing the seeds of doubt among Dalton's ranks. It was a risk, a high-stakes play that could unravel at the slightest misstep, but it was a risk I was willing to take.

The test Dalton had devised was meant to bind me to the militia's cause, but instead, it became the catalyst for my rebellion, a line drawn in the sand that marked the true battle I was fighting. In the clash of loyalties that defined my existence, I chose the path of righteousness, a path that led through the heart of darkness but aimed for the light on the other side. The moral quagmire that threatened to drown me became the ground on which I would take my stand, a declaration of my allegiance not to the militia's twisted cause but to the ideals of justice and truth that had guided me from the start.

In the midst of my internal turmoil, as I plotted a course through the dangerous waters of defiance and duty, a beacon of light pierced the darkness—the soft, insistent buzz of my phone, signaling a message from Emily. The world around me, with its looming threats and shadowy figures, momentarily receded, giving way to a profound sense of longing and connection.

Opening the message, I found myself transported beyond the confines of the militia's camp, beyond the relentless pressure and the ever-present danger, to the essence of what truly mattered. Emily's words flowed through the screen, a lifeline thrown across the vast divide that separated us.

"Jake, in the midst of all this chaos, I just wanted to remind you that I'm here, thinking of you. Stay safe, and remember what we're fighting for—not just the stories we chase, but the world we want to create. A world built on truth, on justice. I believe in us, in our future. Love, Emily."

Her message was a balm to my weary soul, a poignant reminder of the stakes of my mission, of the personal cost of the choices I faced. Each word was infused with love, with hope, and with an unwavering belief in the ideals that had drawn us together. It was a testament to the strength of our bond, to the shared vision that sustained us even as we navigated our separate battles.

The escalating tension within the militia, the suspicion and danger that surrounded me, were realities I could not escape. But Emily's message, her unwavering support and belief in our cause, was a reminder of the enduring power of hope and love. Amidst the darkness, it was a light that I clung to, a promise of what lay beyond the struggle—a world of truth and justice that we were fighting to create, together.

In the stillness of the night, with only the flicker of a single lamp for company, I found myself standing at a precipice, my soul teetering on the edge of an abyss. Dalton's task was clear, a mission that promised to solidify my standing within the militia, to quell the murmurs of doubt that had clung to me like a second skin since my arrival. Yet, as straightforward as the task appeared, it was fraught with a moral complexity that left me grappling with a storm of conscience and duty.

To carry out this mission would mean crossing a line from which I feared there could be no return. It was not merely a matter of obeying orders or securing my place within the group; it was about the lives that would be caught in the crossfire, innocent lives that could be irrevocably shattered by my actions. The weight of this decision bore down on me with an intensity that was both personal and profound.

As I sat alone, wrestling with my thoughts, I realized that this was more than just a critical juncture in my mission; it was a defining moment of my character. The choice between my cover and my conscience presented a dilemma that cut to the very core of who I am. On one hand, completing the mission would alleviate the suspicions around me, drawing me closer into the militia's inner circle. On the other, it would mean betraying the very essence of my moral compass.

Taking a deep breath, I summoned the depths of my resolve, preparing to make a choice that would not only determine my path forward but also define the legacy I wished to leave behind. In the end, my decision was guided not by strategy or allegiance to a cause, but by the unwavering voice of my conscience. It was a choice made in the light of my own moral integrity, a stand against crossing a line that I believed should never be breached, no matter the personal cost.

As I acted on that decision, I did so with the knowledge that true bravery is not found in the absence of fear, but in the courage to face it head-on, to stand steadfast in the face of adversity, guided by the compass of one's own convictions. In that defining moment, I chose to walk a path aligned with my values, understanding that some costs are too great to bear, even in the shadowy world of espionage and undercover work. This choice, though fraught with danger and uncertainty, was mine to make—and I made it with my eyes wide open to the consequences, ready to face whatever storms may come.

The act itself was simple in execution but monumental in its implications. With every step I took in opposition to the directive, I felt the ground shift beneath me. I was acutely aware of the immediate risk my actions posed—not just to my standing within the militia, but to my very life. The choice to defy Dalton, to go against the grain of his command, was akin to drawing a line in the sand, a clear demarcation that identified me as an adversary to his cause.

As the reality of my defiance settled in, a profound sense of isolation enveloped me. I was no longer just an undercover agent; I was a marked man within the ranks of those I sought to dismantle. The gravity of my decision weighed heavily on my shoulders, a burden I carried with a mix of fear and resolve. I understood that my actions would not go unnoticed, that my betrayal of the militia's directive would be met with swift and severe retaliation. Yet, in the face of such dire consequences, I found a strange sense of peace, a clarity that came from acting in alignment with my deepest values.

The consequences of my act of defiance unfolded with a speed and ferocity that took even me by surprise. In the days following my deliberate choice to go against Dalton's orders, the atmosphere around me grew increasingly charged, a tangible sense of foreboding hanging in the air. My once covert presence within the militia, shrouded in the guise of loyalty, was now under intense scrutiny. Dalton's suspicion, which had once lingered on the edge of his perception, sharpened into a focused beam of certainty. I could feel the eyes of the militia on me, their gaze heavy with accusation and distrust.

The precarious position I found myself in was not just a matter of damaged relationships or lost trust; it was a matter of life and death. My true identity, the one fact I had guarded with every fiber of my being, teetered on the brink of exposure. Each interaction felt like a dance with danger, every word weighed and measured for its potential to betray my secrets. The tension was palpable, a constant companion that followed me through the corridors of our makeshift headquarters and into the restless nights that offered little reprieve.

Dalton's approach to dealing with perceived betrayal was as methodical as it was ruthless. His network of loyalty within the militia was extensive, leaving me isolated and vulnerable. The steps he took to verify his suspicions were invisible but unmistakable, a tightening noose around the truth of my identity. The sense of impending doom was inescapable, a dark cloud looming on the horizon, signaling the storm that was about to break.

The retaliation from the militia was not immediate, but the threat of it hung over me like a sword of Damocles. It was a strategic silence, a calculated calm before the inevitable storm. This was their territory, their rules, and I was now an enemy within their ranks. The knowledge that my actions had not only endangered my mission but also my life, was a heavy burden. The paths I had walked so carefully, the relationships I had cultivated, were now avenues of vulnerability, each interaction a potential trap.

As the reality of my situation set in, I prepared for the onslaught. My training had taught me how to survive in hostile environments, how to think on my feet and stay one step ahead of my enemies. Yet, no amount of training could have fully prepared me for the emotional and psychological toll of my predicament. The knowledge that I had brought this upon myself, through my actions and choices, was both a source of strength and a point of despair.

The isolation was the hardest part. Cut off from any real support, I had to rely solely on my own resources, my wits, and my resolve.

The connections I had made, once sources of potential support, now represented risks. Every friendly face was a potential informant, every conversation a possible interrogation. The strain of constant vigilance, of living in a state of heightened alert, was exhausting, both mentally and physically.

Yet, amidst the fear and the uncertainty, there was a flicker of hope, a stubborn belief in the righteousness of my cause. I had made my choice with my eyes wide open, fully aware of the consequences. My act of defiance was not just a rejection of a single directive; it was a stand against the entire ideology that the militia represented. In facing the storm, I was not just fighting for my own survival but for something much larger than myself.

Caught between the world of shadows in which I operated and the normalcy that Emily represented, I found myself torn asunder by conflicting loyalties. My duty to the mission, to bring down the militia from within, was a burden I had borne willingly, a cause I believed in with every fiber of my being. Yet, as the stakes had risen, so too had the cost. My love for Emily, pure and untainted by the duplicity of my double life, stood in stark contrast to the murky ethical waters in which I found myself. And amidst it all, my moral code, the compass that had guided me through the darkest of nights, now seemed to pull me in directions that threatened to tear me apart.

The isolation that ensued was not just physical, a matter of evading those who sought to do me harm. It was an isolation of the soul, a rift between the man I was and the roles I was forced to play. The knowledge that my actions had endangered Emily, that the fallout from my decisions could harm her, was a source of constant agony. Each moment spent away from her, each decision made in the line of duty, felt like a betrayal of the trust and love we shared.

Confronted with the possibility of losing everything I held dear, I was forced to reckon with the consequences of my choices. The path I had chosen, a path walked in the shadows, was one fraught with danger and moral ambiguity. Yet, in choosing to stand against the militia, to defy Dalton and all he represented, I had also chosen to stand for something greater—a principle, a belief in right and wrong that transcended the immediate concerns of my mission.

As I navigated the treacherous terrain that lay before me, the thought of Emily served as both a salve and a wound. She was the reason I fought, the vision of a life that could be, untainted by the violence and betrayal that had become my constant companions. Yet, in fighting for that future, I had exposed her to the very dangers I sought to shield her from. The clash of loyalties, of duty and love, left me adrift, caught in a maelstrom of emotion that offered no easy answers.

In those moments of reflection, I came to understand that the battle I waged was not just against the militia or even for my own survival. It was a battle for the very essence of who I was, for the chance to build a future free from the shadows that currently enveloped me. The realization that I might lose everything, that the cost of my defiance might be more than I was prepared to pay, was a sobering thought. Yet, it was also a clarion call to action, a reminder that some things were worth fighting for, regardless of the odds.

In the end, the love I held for Emily, and the duty I felt towards my mission, were not opposing forces but rather two sides of the same coin—a commitment to fight for a world where innocence was protected, where love could flourish free from the threat of violence. As I faced the uncertain days ahead, I did so with a resolve tempered by the trials I had endured, fortified by the knowledge that, no matter what the future held, I had remained true to myself, to Emily, and to the values that defined me.

The Fallout

Emily

The nature of the threats had evolved. They became more specific, more personal, and far more chilling. Addresses not publicly linked to me, thinly veiled references to my daily routines, and photos that could only have been taken without my knowledge began to surface. The dismissive bravado I had armed myself with crumbled, leaving me exposed to a fear I had never known.

The realization that these weren't just empty threats struck me with the force of a physical blow. Someone out there wasn't just angry about my exposé; they were angry enough to potentially act on it. The world I had navigated so confidently suddenly felt hostile, every shadow a potential threat, every unknown caller a possible adversary.

The steady hum of anxiety that had taken up residence in my chest crescendoed into a deafening roar by the time I decided to call Jake. My fingers hovered over his contact name, trembling slightly. Jake had always been my rock, the one person who could navigate the murky waters of fear and uncertainty with unwavering confidence. But this was different; this was personal, and the stakes were frighteningly high.

When he answered, his voice was a balm to the chaos that raged within me. "Emily, talk to me," he said, and just like that, the floodgates opened. I poured out my fears, the threats, the photos, the unnerving specificity of it all. There was a brief silence on his end, a pause that felt like an eternity. When he finally spoke, his words were measured, but the underlying urgency was palpable.

"Emily, you need to listen to me very carefully," he began, his tone grave. "These threats... they could be credible. We can't afford to take any chances." His confirmation of my worst fears was a gut punch, a stark validation of the danger I was in. The room seemed to tilt, reality shifting in a way that left me feeling untethered, adrift in a sea of uncertainty.

Jake continued, outlining a plan with a precision that was both comforting and terrifying. He talked about safe houses, secure lines of communication, protocols for moving around unseen. It was a language foreign to me, a stark reminder of the chasm between Jake's world and the one I had inhabited until now.

The gravity of the situation truly hit me then, a visceral realization that my life as I knew it was over. "But my work, my life... I can't just disappear," I protested, a desperate attempt to cling to the remnants of normalcy.

"Emily, your safety is the only thing that matters right now," Jake countered, his voice a mix of sternness and concern. "We'll figure out the rest later. Trust me." The finality in his voice brooked no argument, a clear signal that this was not a situation that could be bargained with or wished away.

As we discussed the next steps, a plan slowly began to take shape, a lifeline amidst the tumult of my fears. Jake's insistence on caution, on the need to take immediate action, was a wake-up call. The person I was just a few days ago, the life I led, seemed like a distant memory, a chapter abruptly closed by forces beyond my control.

Hanging up the phone, I felt a profound sense of isolation, but also a flicker of resolve. Jake's willingness to risk his own cover, to step into the line of fire for my sake, was a testament to the depth of his commitment. It was a turning point, the moment the reality of my situation crystallized into a sharp focus. My world had changed, irrevocably and terrifyingly, but I wasn't facing it alone. Jake's plan, daunting as it was, offered a path forward, a glimmer of hope in the encroaching darkness.

The decision to go into hiding, made in the shadow of an impending threat, felt both unreal and inevitable. Standing in the midst of my apartment, I looked around at the life I had built, a life now punctuated by the necessity of disappearance. Jake's instructions were clear: "Pack light, only the essentials and anything you can't bear to part with." His voice was a steady presence in my mind as I moved almost mechanically, selecting items with a deliberateness that belied my inner turmoil.

I reached for a small duffel bag, laying it open on the bed. The essentials were easy enough—a change of clothes, toiletries, my laptop. It was the personal keepsakes that gave me pause, each item a tangible link to a life that felt increasingly distant. A photo of my parents, smiling in the sunshine of a forgotten holiday; a necklace given to me by my grandmother, its metal cool against my fingers; a small, well-worn journal filled with fragments of thoughts and dreams. These items, so inconsequential to anyone else, were the anchors of my identity, reminders of the person I was beyond the headlines and exposés.

The act of choosing what to take felt like a cruel exercise in prioritization, a tangible representation of the loss I was experiencing. Each item left behind was a piece of myself, abandoned in the rush to safety. The weight of what I was doing settled heavily on me as I zipped the bag closed, the finality of the action echoing in the empty room.

Stepping out of my apartment, I couldn't shake the feeling of stepping into a nightmare. The familiar hallway, once a path to comfort and security, now felt like a tunnel leading into the unknown. The sensation of leaving my life behind was palpable, a physical ache that resonated with each step I took away from the safety of my home. The realization that I might never return, that the life I had known was being left behind, was heart-wrenching.

The journey to the safe house passed in a haze, the world outside the window blending into a mosaic of indistinct shapes and colors. Jake's voice played over in my mind, reminding me how to spot signs of being followed. So, my eyes darted frequently to the rearview mirror, searching for any hint of pursuit, even though Jake couldn't be there beside me. His absence was palpable, a void filled with the silent strength of his last instructions and the weighty gravity of our situation. We spoke little during our previous conversation, yet the space between his words was filled with unasked questions and unspoken assurances, resonating within me as I navigated the path he had laid out, alone yet guided by his unseen presence.

Arriving at the safe house, reality seemed to shift, leaving me feeling as though I was observing someone else's life from the outside. The place was stark, purely functional, nothing like the warmth and personality of my own apartment. Jake's voice echoed in my mind, his instructions from our earlier phone call guiding me through the necessary security measures and safety protocols. I mechanically nodded to his imagined presence, a part of me still grappling with the surreal notion that this nondescript space was now my reality.

That night, as I lay in a bed not my own, surrounded by the starkness of my temporary sanctuary, the full impact of my decision washed over me. I was in hiding, cut off from the world I knew, all because I had dared to speak the truth. The sense of loss was overwhelming, a grief for the life I had been forced to leave behind. But amidst the sorrow, there was also a flicker of resolve. I had made this choice not out of naivety, but out of a belief in the power of truth, a belief that, even now, in the darkness of my current circumstances, offered a glimmer of light.

In the safe house, my new reality feels like a tight-fitting garment, uncomfortable and foreign against my skin. The walls seem to lean in too close, and the silence is a constant, oppressive force, pressing down on me with an intensity that makes it hard to breathe. It's a stark contrast to the chaos of the past few days, and in the quiet, my emotions begin to spiral uncontrollably.

Anger surges through me first, a fiery, pulsating force that demands an outlet. I'm angry at the situation, at the people who forced me into hiding, at the world for allowing such darkness to thrive. Then comes fear, a cold, slippery thing that coils around my heart. It's not just the fear for my own safety anymore; it's a deeper, more pervasive dread of what the future holds, of how unrecognizable my life has become.

Disbelief is my constant companion, whispering in my ear that this can't be happening, that any moment now, I'll wake up from this nightmare. But the cold, hard surface under my fingertips and the unyielding walls around me serve as constant reminders that this is all too real.

The isolation is perhaps the hardest part to bear. Cut off from the world, from my friends, my family, and my work, I feel like a ghost haunting the edges of my own life. The lack of human connection, the absence of familiar faces and places, weighs heavily on me, a tangible reminder of everything I've lost. I find myself longing for even the most mundane aspects of my old life—the morning rush to get to work, the casual chats with my neighbors, the simple freedom of walking down the street without fear.

As I cycle through these emotions, I try to find footing in this new reality, to make sense of the upheaval that has upturned everything I once knew. The safe house, with its bare walls and utilitarian furnishings, becomes a blank canvas on which my fears, hopes, and uncertainties play out in vivid detail.

In moments of quiet introspection, I realize that this experience, however harrowing, is reshaping me in ways I can't yet fully understand. The resilience it takes to face each day, the strength required to hold onto hope in the face of despair, is forging a new version of myself. Yet, as I navigate this strange, liminal space between the life I knew and the unknown future that awaits, I can't help but mourn for the person I used to be, for the life that was irrevocably altered the moment I stepped into the shadows to speak the truth.

The question haunts me, looping endlessly in the silence: Was it worth it? The cost seems immeasurable now, a price paid not just in the currency of personal safety but in the peace of mind, relationships, and the simple joys of everyday life. Doubt creeps in, insidious and persuasive, whispering that perhaps my pursuit of truth was misguided, a quixotic venture that has led me to this point of isolation and fear.

In this moment of reflection, I find a measure of peace in the chaos that has enveloped my life. The guilt, while not entirely dispelled, is tempered by the reaffirmation of my purpose. The path I chose was fraught with danger, yes, but it was also a path paved with integrity and the unshakeable conviction that exposing the truth is not just important—it's essential, no matter the personal cost.

This realization steadies me, grounding me in the midst of the storm. It's a reminder that, despite the fear, the isolation, and the uncertainty of what lies ahead, I stand by my actions. The exposé, for all the turmoil it has caused, remains a testament to the power of truth, a beacon that, even in the darkest of times, guides me forward. With this renewed sense of purpose, I face the unknown future not with regret, but with the resolve to continue fighting for transparency, for justice, and for the belief that, in the end, the truth will prevail.

In the cocoon of isolation that the safe house has become, my tether to the outside world is as slender as it is vital—a secure phone Jake entrusted to me before we parted ways. Each time it rings, a jolt of anticipation shoots through me, slicing through the monotonous silence of my days. Jake's voice, when it comes through, is both a balm and a stark reminder of the reality I'm temporarily shielded from.

Our conversations are brief, often whispered, always tense. He provides updates on the situation outside—how my exposé continues to ripple through public consciousness, the ongoing investigations, and, more worryingly, the persistent threats that linger like shadows, just beyond reach. Jake's updates are my only glimpses into a world that feels increasingly distant, a lifeline that keeps me connected to a life I can barely recall.

Yet, with every call, the semblance of normalcy these conversations provide is tinged with the gravity of my circumstances. Jake's voice often carries a weight, a seriousness that belies the calm he tries to project. He reminds me, time and again, of the need for caution, for vigilance. "You're not out of the woods yet, Em," he says, his words a gentle but firm reminder of the dangers that still lurk. It's a sobering thought, one that grounds me in the reality of my situation, even as I cling to the normalcy his calls provide.

With each call, I am reminded of the strength required to navigate this new reality. The brief glimpses into the world outside, offered through Jake's voice on the other end of the line, become my anchor, a reminder that I am not forgotten, that the fight for truth and justice continues even as I stand still. And in the silence that follows each conversation, I find a renewed resolve to face the days ahead, buoyed by the connection to the outside world and the solemn reminders of the need for continued caution.

With each day that passes in the monochrome existence of the safe house, snippets of information filter through, painting a picture of a world in flux, a society grappling with the revelations of my exposé. The secure phone becomes a window to the outside, through which I glimpse the tumult my work has unleashed. Jake's updates, supplemented by my cautious forays into the digital realm, reveal a landscape altered by the truths I unearthed.

I learn of debates ignited in the halls of power, of policy discussions that mention my findings as a catalyst for change. Legal actions unfold, some directly tied to the evidence I presented, others inspired by the broader themes of accountability and transparency my work advocated. It's both surreal and humbling to hear my name whispered in the context of these monumental shifts, to realize the ripples caused by my actions have turned into waves crashing against the established order.

The impact is not confined to the legal or political arenas. On forums, social media, and in the comments of the articles that continue to dissect my exposé, a societal reckoning is taking place. Individuals and groups, previously unaware or indifferent to the issues I highlighted, now engage in passionate discussion about reform, ethics, and the role of journalism in uncovering uncomfortable truths.

This broader impact of my work brings with it a complex mix of emotions. Pride, certainly, at having sparked such significant discourse and potential change. Yet, there's also a profound sense of responsibility that settles in the pit of my stomach—a recognition of the power of words and the duty of those who wield them to do so with care and integrity.

As the days bleed into each other, marked only by the rise and fall of the sun, a transformation unfolds within the confines of this nondescript safe house. The initial shock of my new reality, with its cloak of fear and mantle of uncertainty, begins to give way to a burgeoning resolve. The very forces that sought to silence me, to bury the truths I uncovered, have instead ignited a fiercer determination to continue my work, to speak louder against the shadows.

In this solitude, I find strength I hadn't known I possessed. The secure phone, my solitary link to the world beyond these walls, becomes more than just a lifeline—it's a conduit for defiance. Inspired by the resilience of those who continue to fight outside, I start to document my experiences in hiding. Each word I write is a testament to the endurance of the human spirit, an act of rebellion against those who wish to see me silenced.

The pages of my journal begin to fill with reflections, analyses, and plans. The quiet that once felt oppressive now provides the clarity to think, to strategize. I explore avenues to continue my work, to leverage my situation rather than be hindered by it. Ideas that once seemed unfeasible within the limitations of my hiding now take shape as potential pathways to impact. The digital realm offers a world of possibility, a way to reach out, to connect, to influence without revealing my location. The challenge lies in navigating this space with caution, ensuring my safety while amplifying the call for transparency and accountability.

As I chart my next steps, the uncertainty of the future looms large. Yet, it's an uncertainty I'm ready to face, armed with a renewed sense of purpose and a determination that hardens with each passing day. The path ahead may be fraught with challenges, but I stand ready to meet them head-on. The fight for truth and justice is far from over, and I, despite the odds, remain a steadfast soldier in its ranks. This transformation, from a reporter to a symbol of defiance, sets the stage for the battles to come, battles I am now more prepared to fight than ever before.

With each day that passes in the monochrome existence of the safe house, snippets of information filter through, painting a picture of a world in flux, a society grappling with the revelations of my exposé. The secure phone becomes a window to the outside, through which I glimpse the tumult my work has unleashed. Jake's updates, supplemented by my cautious forays into the digital realm, reveal a landscape altered by the truths I unearthed.

As I sit in the quiet of the safe house, reflecting on these developments, a renewed sense of purpose solidifies within me. The isolation, the fear, the threats—while daunting, they pale in comparison to the tangible impact of my work. The realization that my efforts have not only shed light on hidden injustices but have also catalyzed debate and action is a potent reminder of why I embarked on this journey.

This understanding reaffirms my belief in the actions I took, in the necessity of bringing the truth to light, regardless of personal cost. It's a reminder that journalism, at its core, is about more than just reporting facts; it's about challenging the status quo, prompting reflection, and, ultimately, inspiring action.

Armed with this knowledge, my resolve to continue my work, to remain a voice for transparency and accountability, is stronger than ever. The path ahead may be uncertain, fraught with challenges both known and unforeseen, but the impact of my exposé—a testament to the power of journalism to effect change—serves as a beacon, guiding me forward. In the silent battles fought from the shadows of anonymity, I am reminded that the pen, guided by truth and courage, remains mightier than the sword.

The Final Stand

Jake

The confrontation at the militia's outer defenses was a calculated risk, one I knew was necessary to create a diversion and buy us the time needed to enact the final phase of our plan. Nestled in the dense forest that bordered the town, the militia had established a series of outposts designed to serve as an early warning system against any form of attack. Penetrating this perimeter undetected was essential to maintaining the element of surprise for the main assault.

Utilizing the cover of night and the dense foliage, I moved with the stealth my SEAL training had ingrained in me. The darkness was both ally and adversary, concealing my movements while hiding potential threats. Each step was measured, each breath controlled as I navigated through the treacherous terrain, mindful of the traps and patrols that were part of the militia's defense.

The outermost post was manned by a small team, likely expecting nothing more than the quiet of the night. I used a combination of distraction and non-lethal incapacitation techniques to neutralize the threat they posed. A carefully thrown rock to misdirect, followed by a swift, silent approach to ensure they would wake with nothing more than headaches and confusion. It was imperative to avoid unnecessary casualties, to remember that many of those I faced had been led astray, seduced by ideologies they barely understood.

With the first obstacle overcome, I continued my journey, dodging sporadic patrols and employing every trick at my disposal to remain unseen. The tension was a living thing, a constant companion that kept my senses honed to a razor's edge. Every shadow could conceal a watchful eye, every rustle in the underbrush might herald an impending confrontation.

As I made my way through the militia's defenses, I couldn't help but reflect on the gravity of what was at stake. The town, Emily, our future—all hung in the balance, dependent not just on the success of my mission but on my ability to return to the safe house, to bring back the intelligence we needed to strike the final blow.

The journey back to the safe house feels endless, each step fueled by a mix of adrenaline and anxiety. The confrontation with the militia's outer defenses had been more intense than I'd anticipated, a stark reminder of the high stakes of our final stand. My mind races with the possibilities of what I might find upon my return, the fear of loss a constant companion.

As the safe house comes into view, my pace quickens, driven by an urgency that's as much about seeing Emily safe as it is about confirming the success of our plan. The weight of my weapons, the grime and sweat of the battle—they all seem trivial in comparison to the need to see her, to know she's alright.

I reach the door, my hand pausing on the handle for a moment, gathering my thoughts, steeling myself for what lies beyond. Then, with a breath to steady my racing heart, I push it open.

The sight that greets me is one I've played over in my mind a thousand times, yet the reality of it strikes me with a force that's both shocking and profoundly reassuring. Emily stands there, her figure bathed in the soft light of early dawn, her face reflecting the turmoil of the night but untouched by physical harm. The relief that washes over me is visceral, a tide of emotion so powerful it feels as though it might sweep me away.

Our eyes meet, and in that moment, everything else fades into insignificance. Time seems to stand still, suspended in the intensity of our gaze.

A surge of profound affection swells within me, mingling with the relief that courses through my veins. It's an emotion that's been building for months, forged in the fires of adversity and the shared experience of our fight. Seeing her there, knowing the risks she's faced, the courage she's shown—it's as if all my fears, all my doubts, dissolve in the face of this undeniable truth: that what lies between us is more than just a bond forged by circumstance. It's something deeper, more elemental.

Without a word, I cross the room, my steps unhesitant. When I reach her, our embrace is a collision of relief, love, and a myriad of unspoken emotions. It's fierce and gentle all at once, a physical manifestation of our journey, of the trials we've endured and the strength we've found. In her arms, I find not just solace but a sense of belonging, a certainty that no matter what lies ahead, we'll face it together.

The warmth of the embrace lingers as we pull slightly back, still within the sanctuary of each other's arms, and the magnitude of the moment settles upon us. The air around us is charged with an intensity that words could never capture. It's as though the very fabric of our beings recognizes the gravity of what we've just endured, the razor's edge upon which our fates teetered.

In the silence that stretches between us, a language beyond words unfolds. Our eyes lock, conveying volumes of fear, relief, and an unshakable resolve. It's a connection that goes beyond the physical—a fusion of souls, you might say. In this moment, the world outside, with all its chaos and uncertainty, could well be a million miles away. Here, in the eye of the storm, is a profound sense of peace, a reaffirmation of a bond that has been tested and has emerged stronger, more vital than ever.

As we stand in the quiet of the safe house, the chaos of the outside world held at bay, it's clear that what we have is something extraordinary. This isn't just about the thrill of adrenaline, the desperation of a fight for survival. It's about something much deeper, much more enduring. It's about a love that has become our anchor, our north star, guiding us through the tempest and back into each other's arms.

In the depths of Emily's eyes, I see not just my own reflection but the future—a future that, despite the uncertainty that surrounds us, seems suddenly full of possibility. Our embrace tightens, a silent pledge of solidarity, of a shared journey that stretches out before us, uncharted but undaunted.

As we come together, it's with a fervor that transcends the physical, a joining that speaks to the depths of our connection. Every touch, every kiss, is imbued with the intensity of our emotions, a tangible expression of a bond forged in the crucible of adversity. This encounter is profound, not merely a moment of physical union but a soul-deep communion that reaffirms everything we mean to each other.

In the safety of our embrace, the world's demands fall away, leaving only the immediacy of our connection. It's a testament to our love's resilience, to its ability to not just survive but to flourish in the face of challenges that would have sundered anything less strong. This moment, this passionate encounter, is both a celebration of the obstacles we've overcome and a vow—a vow that no matter what the future holds, we will face it as one.

As we eventually part, the echo of our connection lingers, a tangible reminder of the love that binds us. It's a love marked by resilience, by a depth of feeling that has been tested and has emerged all the stronger. This moment of passion, of profound connection, is more than just a point of solace—it's a declaration of our enduring bond, a symbol of hope that no matter what dangers we face, our love will remain, steadfast and unbreakable.

As we stand in this quiet sanctuary, the chaos of the world held at bay, there's a profound sense of peace that settles over me. It's a peace born not from ignorance of the challenges that lie ahead but from the certainty that together, there's nothing we can't face. The love we share is more than just a refuge from the storm; it's a beacon, guiding us forward, a source of strength and courage in the face of the unknown.

Looking into Emily's eyes, I see not just the reflection of my own feelings but the future—a future that, despite its uncertainty, I no longer fear. Because I know that whatever it holds, we'll face it together. Our love, tested and tempered by the trials of our past, is our greatest weapon, our shield against whatever the world might throw our way.

***

I survey the assembly, my mind racing through the final details of the plan we've laid out. It's a strategy born of countless hours of preparation, of reconnaissance and careful calculation, shaped by the intelligence I've gathered and the insights I've gleaned from my time within the militia's ranks. My SEAL training is the backbone of our approach, offering a tactical advantage we're banking on to tilt the odds in our favor. The operation is high-risk, a direct assault on the militia's stronghold, but it's our best shot at dismantling their operation and neutralizing the threat they pose.

As the moment to move out draws near, I pull Emily aside, my gaze locking with hers. The intensity of the situation, the danger we're about to face, hangs between us, unspoken but deeply felt. "Stay safe," I tell her, my voice low, imbued with every ounce of concern and care I hold for her. Her nod, the slight press of her hand against mine, conveys her understanding, her own resolve mirroring mine.

We move out at dawn, the world around us awash in the soft light of early morning. The militia's stronghold looms on the horizon, a bastion of shadows and secrets that we're determined to bring into the light. The approach is stealthy, every movement calculated to maintain the element of surprise for as long as possible.

My heart beats a steady rhythm, a cadence of focus and readiness that has been the hallmark of my training.

The initial engagement is swift, the element of surprise giving us the upper hand as we breach the outer defenses. The sound of gunfire shatters the morning quiet, a stark declaration of our intent. We press forward, moving with precision and coordination, the plan unfolding with every step we take towards the heart of the stronghold.

Resistance is fierce, the militia fighters dogged in their defense, but we've come prepared. Our advance is relentless, driven by the knowledge of what's at stake. I find myself at the forefront, navigating the chaos with a clarity born of years of combat experience. Every decision, every action, is guided by the singular goal of ending this threat once and for all.

The climax of the confrontation is intense, a final showdown that tests the limits of our resolve and our training. It's here, in the heat of battle, that the true strength of our unity, of our commitment to protect our town, is proven. The fight is hard-won, but in the end, the stronghold falls, the militia's plans unraveling under the weight of our assault.

As the dust settles, the reality of our victory begins to sink in. The stronghold, once a symbol of the militia's power, now stands as a testament to our resilience, to our refusal to be cowed by tyranny or terror. The cost has been high, the battle leaving its scars on both the land and our souls, but the outcome is clear: we've secured a future for our town, for ourselves.

The relief that washes over me is tinged with exhaustion, with the weight of what we've endured. Yet, amidst the fatigue, there's a profound sense of accomplishment, of a mission fulfilled. As I look around at the faces of my comrades, my friends, and finally, into the eyes of Emily, there's an unspoken acknowledgment of what we've achieved together. We've confronted the darkness, and in doing so, we've ensured the dawn of a new day for our town, a day filled with hope and the promise of peace.

This hard-won peace, though purchased at a high price, brings with it a profound sense of accomplishment. As I walk through the cleared stronghold, past the weary but resolute faces of my fellow fighters, there's a shared understanding that what we've achieved here today will echo through the lives of every town resident. We've not just reclaimed a physical space from the clutches of violence—we've restored hope to hearts that had known too much fear.

The bond between Emily and me, reinforced through shared adversity and common cause, has grown deeper, more integral to my being than ever before. As we gather with the others, our hands find each other's, a silent communication of love and mutual respect. This connection, this profound partnership, has been our stronghold amidst the chaos, a sanctuary of trust and understanding that no strife could breach.

In the days to come, as we begin the process of rebuilding and healing, the memory of this victory—and the sacrifices it entailed—will serve as a guiding light. It is a reminder that peace is sometimes forged in the fires of sacrifice, and that true strength often arises from the bonds we forge with others.

Today, as the dust settles and we look towards a horizon now free of the shadow that once darkened it, I feel a deep, abiding pride not only in what we have accomplished but in the knowledge that I had Emily by my side through it all. Our victory is a testament to the resilience of the human spirit, a declaration that even in the face of overwhelming darkness, together, we can bring forth light.

As the smoke clears and the adrenaline subsides, Emily and I stand together amid the remnants of what was once a fierce battleground. The dawn breaks softly over us, washing the torn landscape in hues of gold and pink, signaling the start of a new day. It's a poignant scene, the quiet around us a stark contrast to the chaos that had reigned hours before. This moment, shared in the embrace of each other's arms, feels like a quiet celebration—not of victory in a traditional sense, but of survival, of having endured.

Turning to face Emily, I see the reflection of my own emotions in her eyes—a mixture of relief, love, and an unbreakable resolve. It's in her gaze that I see the future we're stepping into, one not devoid of challenges but promising a new kind of strength, a new kind of purpose. The dawn of this new day mirrors the dawn of our new beginning, a symbolic alignment that underscores the serenity and hope now blooming in our hearts.

This chapter of our lives, while culminating in the dismantling of a dire threat, is more significantly a testament to the strength of our bond. It has been a pivotal moment, not just in the story of a town or of two people but in the narrative of human resilience and the power of unity. Our love, tested by the very brink of despair, has proven its resilience, its capacity to not just endure but to thrive amidst adversity.

Together, Emily and I walk towards, our steps light with the promise of new possibilities. We are ready to face whatever comes next, to build on the foundation we've laid through sacrifice and love. In each other, we have found not just a partner but a fellow warrior, a soulmate with whom the darkest of times can not only be endured but transformed into something profoundly beautiful. This isn't just the dawn of a new day—it's the beginning of a new life, our life, together.

New Beginnings

Emily

As I sit on the creaky porch of our temporary safe house, the morning air is crisp, the kind that refreshes the soul with each breath. A steaming mug of coffee warms my hands, its aroma mingling with the earthy scent of the dawn. The sunrise unfolds like a slow painting, streaks of orange and pink spreading across the canvas of the sky, illuminating a world that feels profoundly different from just a day ago.

The quiet is almost tangible, a soothing balm after the relentless pace of the past weeks. It's in this stillness that the full weight of what we've achieved begins to truly sink in. The militia that had cast such a long shadow over our town is no more, its members either awaiting trial or dispersed, their plots disrupted by our actions. It's a victory, certainly, but the calm also allows space for a deeper contemplation of the cost, the risks, and the sheer scale of what we undertook.

I sip my coffee, each gulp grounding me further into the moment. As I do, I can't help but let my thoughts drift to the many people whose lives will be irrevocably changed by what's happened. Families who will sleep easier, business owners who can now operate without fear, children who will grow up in a town not overshadowed by systemic threat. But there are also those who will carry scars from the conflict, visible and not. The healing process will be long, and for some, justice in a courtroom may offer solace but not complete closure.

"Big changes, huh?" Jake's voice breaks through my reverie as he steps out onto the porch, a second cup of coffee in hand.

I smile, shifting to make room for him beside me. "Yeah, it almost doesn't feel real. I keep thinking about all the 'what ifs.'"

He nods, sitting down, his shoulder brushing mine comfortably. "I know what you mean," he says, looking out over the horizon. "It's a lot to process. We took down a militia, Em. That's not exactly an everyday occurrence."

"We did," I agree, leaning into his warmth. "And now, we get to build something from the ashes. Something better."

Jake turns to me, his expression thoughtful. "Is that what you're going to write about next? The rebuilding?"

"I think so," I say, feeling a flicker of excitement at the prospect. "The story doesn't end with the militia's downfall. There's the aftermath, the recovery. That's where the real work begins. It's where hope takes root."

He chuckles softly. "Always the journalist, huh?" But his eyes are proud. "I can't wait to read it. You have a way of making sense of the chaos."

"Someone has to," I reply with a mock-serious tone, earning me a gentle nudge from his elbow.

Our conversation drifts then to plans for the day, for the week, for the future we're starting to reimagine together. It's a future filled with possibilities, and though we're both aware of the challenges ahead, there's a shared sense of readiness to face them, bolstered by our strengthened bond.

As the sun climbs higher, casting light on the new day, I feel a sense of purpose renew within me. The journey ahead is uncertain, but it's ours to shape, and I find immense comfort in knowing that whatever comes next, we face it together. This reflective awakening, amid the tranquility of a new dawn, isn't just a pause—it's a promise of a fresh start, for us and for our town.

The day's warmth spills into the quaint streets of our town, now echoing with a buzz that speaks of relief and renewed hope. Drawn by the need to witness this new chapter firsthand, Jake and I decide to visit the local café—a hub that, even in the darkest times, served as a meeting point for the community. Today, its role feels even more pivotal, a place for people to gather, share stories, and knit the fabric of our town back together.

As we walk in, the smell of fresh coffee and the sound of lively chatter greet us. It's busier than usual, the atmosphere almost celebratory. I notice faces that just weeks ago were etched with lines of worry now bright with smiles, their conversations animated and filled with laughter.

"Emily! Jake!" Mrs. Henderson, the café owner, spots us from behind the counter, her face lighting up as she waves us over. "I was hoping I'd see you two today. Come, sit down, have some coffee on the house. It's the least I can do after everything that's happened."

We thank her and take a seat at the counter. As I sip, I listen to the snippets of conversation around us.

"I heard they got the last of them yesterday," says a man at the table behind us, his voice a mix of incredulity and relief. "Can you believe it? After all this time, we can finally breathe easy."

His companion, a woman with young children in tow, nods vigorously. "It's like waking up from a bad dream. I'm just grateful it's over. The kids can play outside again without me worrying every minute."

The sentiment is echoed around the room, each story adding to a tapestry of collective relief and burgeoning hope. I pull out a small notebook, the journalist in me instinctively capturing these voices, these raw, honest accounts of a community finding its footing again.

"Seems like you're always working, even now," Jake teases, nodding at my notebook.

I smile, tucking the pen behind my ear. "Someone has to tell this story. Who better than someone who lived it?"

Jake grins, taking a sip of his coffee. "Just make sure you write something nice about me."

"Only the truth," I quip back, "the fearless hero who—"

"Hey now, we're all heroes here," he interrupts, gesturing around the café. "This town, these people—they didn't give up. That's the story. Resilience."

"You're right," I concede, my gaze sweeping over the café. "It's about all of us."

Mrs. Henderson joins in during a lull, leaning against the counter. "You two did a lot, more than you know. It's not just about catching those thugs. It's about showing us all that it's possible to stand up, to fight back. You've given us all a bit of your courage."

Her words sink in, a reminder of the ripple effect of our actions, how they've strengthened not just the physical security of our town but its spirit.

This visit, this mingling with neighbors and friends, serves as a vivid snapshot of the town's pulse—quickening with plans for recovery and reconstruction. These conversations, filled with plans for the future, reflect a shared vision for a rebuilt town, stronger and more united than ever. As we leave the café, the sense of community is palpable, a strong, reassuring presence that promises no matter what comes next, we'll face it together.

In the weeks following the disbandment of the militia, the courthouse becomes a focal point of the town's recovery. The rapid legal proceedings reflect the community's urgency for justice and closure. I find myself seated in the austere wooden pews of the courtroom day after day, a notebook always open in my lap, pen poised to capture every significant moment.

As a journalist, my role shifts from frontline reporting to careful observation, chronicling each hearing to provide a comprehensive narrative to the public. My series in the local newspaper aims not just to inform but to heal, offering a transparent view of the legal process that many hope will restore a sense of order and trust.

"The community needs this, Emily," Jake whispers to me one morning as we enter the courtroom together. His support is a constant as I navigate this new phase of storytelling.

"Absolutely," I reply, scanning the room filled with familiar faces—neighbors, friends, and families affected by the militia's reign. "They deserve to know everything is being handled fairly and justly."

The trials themselves are a procession of charges, testimonies, and legal arguments. The defendants, once menacing figures who wielded power with impunity, now appear diminished, confined to the defendant's box. As each one faces the consequences of their actions, I jot down notes, capturing quotes from the prosecution and defense, the reactions of the audience, the judge's rulings.

One afternoon, following a particularly intense session, I interview the district attorney, a key figure in the legal proceedings. "Our goal is to ensure that justice is served, not just as retribution, but as a cornerstone of rebuilding trust within the community," he explains earnestly, his eyes reflecting the weight of his responsibility.

I include his words in my next article, highlighting the broader implications of these trials for the town's psyche. "It's about setting a precedent that lawlessness won't be tolerated," I write, conveying the official's perspective alongside the emotional relief of the community members present.

Back at the café, where residents gather to discuss daily developments, my articles spark conversations. "Did you read what Emily wrote today? I'm glad they're not just sweeping this under the rug," one patron comments to another, her tone a mixture of relief and residual worry.

"Yeah, seeing it all laid out like that—it's tough, but it's necessary. Helps us all move forward, knowing there's some accountability," her companion agrees, folding the newspaper thoughtfully.

These interactions reinforce the value of my work, the importance of transparency in journalism. Documenting this legal reckoning becomes more than a professional task—it's a personal mission to aid in my community's healing process, providing a factual foundation to help stabilize the shaken ground we all stand on.

As the trials progress, the articles I write build upon each other, forming a detailed tapestry that depicts not just the fall of a corrupt power but the rise of a community's fortitude. My hope is that this written record will serve as both a reflection and a beacon—a historical document that speaks of a town that faced profound darkness and chose to light a path toward justice and renewal.

The quiet of our study is a stark contrast to the bustling energy of the courtroom and the café. Here, surrounded by walls of books and personal mementos, I find a different kind of sanctuary. This is where I lay the groundwork for a more comprehensive project: a book that will encapsulate the tumultuous saga of our town's confrontation with the militia.

Scattered across the desk are piles of notes and dozens of photographs—each a frozen moment in time, capturing the fear, the courage, and the unity our community displayed. As I sift through these materials, the magnitude of what we've been through settles deeply within me. Each document, each image is a thread in the broader tapestry of our shared experience.

Jake walks in with two cups of tea, placing one beside me before he leans against the edge of the desk, watching me work. "How's the book coming along?" he asks, his voice a mix of curiosity and gentle encouragement.

I pause, looking up at him with a thoughtful frown. "It's overwhelming," I admit. "Each piece of paper, every photo tells a story of fear, loss, but also incredible bravery. It's hard to know where to start."

He nods, understanding. "Just start with one story, one photo. The rest will follow," he advises, his hand reaching out to squeeze mine reassuringly.

Taking his advice, I pick up a photograph of a particularly large rally in the town square, a sea of faces united against a common threat. "This was when I realized just how much power there is in unity," I muse aloud, beginning to sketch out a chapter on community resilience.

As the days pass, my initial notes evolve into detailed chapters. I delve into the complexities of our fight, intertwining personal narratives with broader socio-political commentary. I explore not just the events themselves but their implications on community dynamics, governance, and personal identities.

One evening, as I type a particularly difficult section about the night of the final standoff, Jake sits beside me, reading over my shoulder. "You've captured it really well," he comments, his voice low. "It's painful to remember, but it's important that it's remembered."

"Yes, but it's more than just recounting events," I reply, pausing to gather my thoughts. "It's about understanding our reactions, our decisions. It's about recognizing that what we went through might serve as a lesson or a warning for others."

Jake nods, pulling me into a gentle embrace. "And it's about healing, too. For you, for me, for everyone in town," he says, and I can hear the underlying truth in his words. This project, while daunting, is proving to be a powerful tool for personal catharsis and community healing.

Each chapter I complete cements a piece of our history, offering insights and lessons learned. The act of writing becomes a process of reflection and understanding, not just for myself but for anyone who will read these pages. Through this work, I hope to honor the resilience of our community, the depth of our struggles, and the strength of our bonds.

This book, when finished, will be a testament to our journey through darkness and back into the light—a narrative imbued with hope, anchored in reality, and lifted by the collective spirit of a community that refused to yield. As I document these events, I'm not just preserving history; I'm framing a narrative of triumph, a celebration of the human spirit's capacity to overcome even the most daunting challenges.

One evening, after a long day of writing and reflection, Jake and I settle into the soft cushions of our living room couch, a bottle of wine open between us. The gentle hum of the evening and the soft flicker of candlelight create a serene backdrop for the conversation we are about to have—one about our future.

Jake pours two glasses of wine, handing me one with a soft smile. "I think we've earned a moment to just dream a bit, don't you think?" he says, raising his glass in a quiet toast.

I clink my glass against his, the crystal sound a bright note in the calm. "Dreaming sounds perfect," I reply, taking a sip and letting the rich flavor settle on my palate. "Especially after everything that's happened."

We both settle back, the wine warming us as we start to weave the tapestry of our future with words. "So, what do you think about moving? Starting fresh somewhere new?" Jake asks, his voice tinged with a mix of excitement and seriousness.

The idea stirs a mix of emotions in me. "It's tempting," I admit. "A new place could mean a new beginning. But then, there's so much here that feels unfinished. So much good we could still do."

Jake nods thoughtfully. "I feel that too. We've been through so much here. It feels like running away to leave it all behind, doesn't it?"

"Yes, exactly. It's not just about us. It's about this community," I say, gesturing vaguely towards the window, towards the town that has endured so much. "We've been a part of its darkest times, maybe we should also be a part of its healing."

"That's what I love about you," Jake says, his eyes reflecting the flickering candlelight. "You always see the bigger picture. So, you think staying here, helping rebuild—"

"—It could be our legacy," I finish for him, feeling a surge of purpose. "Not just rebuilding buildings, but restoring lives, nurturing hope."

Jake reaches over, his hand covering mine. "Then that's what we'll do. We'll put down deeper roots here. We'll be part of something meaningful, something bigger than ourselves."

The conversation shifts then to the practicalities—possible projects we could spearhead or support, organizations we could partner with, ways we could use our skills and experiences for the greater good. With each plan outlined, our future becomes clearer, a path marked not by the desire to escape but to engage more deeply.

"Our wounds might never fully heal," Jake says as we start to wind down, his voice soft in the quiet room. "But maybe that's not such a bad thing. They're reminders of what we've overcome, and why we're choosing to do what we're doing."

I squeeze his hand, strengthened by his words. "And as long as we're together, I know we can face anything. Our love got us through the worst; I can't wait to see what we can do with the best."

As we finish the last of the wine, there's a feeling of completeness, a sense of rightness to the decisions we've made. We are not just planning a future; we are committing to a life of shared purpose and mutual support. This conversation, simple yet profound, has not just charted a course for our coming days but has reaffirmed the unbreakable bond between us. Together, we're not just survivors of a dark past—we're architects of a hopeful tomorrow.

As I sit at my desk, the soft clatter of the keyboard under my fingers is a steady rhythm that accompanies my thoughts. The pieces

I'm writing now are more than just recollections; they are reflections, analyses of the deeper meanings behind our town's recent trials. With each sentence crafted, I aim to draw out the broader implications of what we've endured and achieved.

"This isn't just about a victory over the militia," I type, pausing to find the right words. "It's about what that victory represents—the reaffirmation of our community's commitment to justice and mutual support."

Jake walks in, a mug of coffee in his hands, and leans against the doorframe, watching me work. "Making any progress?" he asks, his voice soft, mindful of not breaking my concentration too sharply.

I look up, smiling slightly at his thoughtful gesture. "Yes, actually. It's becoming clear just how much our actions have impacted the town—not just in the obvious ways, but in how people see themselves and their neighbors."

He nods, understanding. "You're giving them a narrative to be proud of, a way to understand the chaos," Jake observes, coming over to sit beside me.

"Exactly," I respond, grateful for his grasp of my goals. "It's about encouraging a continued vigilance, not out of fear, but out of a renewed sense of duty to one another. We've shown that it's possible to stand up, to fight back, and to prevail. Now it's about maintaining that momentum."

Jake sips his coffee, considering. "And about not letting the darkness come back. Keeping the light we've fought so hard to uncover."

I nod, typing out his words almost verbatim. "'Keeping the light,'" I muse aloud, "I like that. It's exactly the metaphor this piece needed." Inspired, I write on, fleshing out the idea, connecting it to the tangible changes already evident in the community—the new community watch programs, the local government's transparency initiatives, the youth outreach programs that have sprung up in the wake of our collective ordeal.

As I continue, I weave in our personal narrative, how our relationship and our roles in this fight have demonstrated the power of personal integrity and courage. "Our story is proof that ordinary people can make extraordinary differences when they refuse to be bystanders to injustice," I write.

"Sounds like you're making it a call to action," Jake remarks, reading over my shoulder.

"That's the intention," I confirm. "If our experience has taught us anything, it's that vigilance and engagement are not just civic duties; they are the very fabric that holds our society together."

Jake nods, proud and supportive. "You're going to inspire a lot of people, Em. Just like you inspire me."

I lean back, allowing myself a moment to appreciate his words and the magnitude of what we're achieving together. "Thank you, that means everything to me. Especially coming from you."

Our conversation shifts back to daily life, to plans for dinner, to a walk we might take later, but the core of our discussion—our impact and our ongoing responsibilities—remains at the forefront of my mind as I return to my writing. With each article published, I hope to not only tell our story but to empower others to write their own chapters of engagement and change, ensuring that the light we've fought to uncover continues to shine brightly.

The crisp evening air wraps around us as Jake and I stroll through the quiet streets of our town, the familiar paths acting as gentle reminders of our shared history and recent trials. These walks have become a cherished ritual, a time to disconnect from the demands of our daily lives and reconnect with each other. Each step seems to stitch the fabric of our everyday lives back together, mending the tears wrought by months of tension and uncertainty.

"You know, these walks have started to feel like a bit of therapy," I comment, watching a couple of leaves flutter down from an old maple tree.

Jake chuckles, his breath forming a small cloud in the chilly air. "Cheap therapy, though, right? Just the cost of our time and maybe a hot chocolate if you play your cards right."

I nudge him playfully. "Always the deal-maker. But yes, it's the best kind of therapy. It's... restorative, being here with you, walking and talking without a crisis looming over us."

Our conversations during these walks meander from light-hearted banter to deeper discussions about our hopes and fears. Tonight, it's the latter, as we delve into how we've been feeling, the silent pressures we've wrestled with, and our hopes for the future.

"It's been hard, hasn't it?" I say, more a statement than a question. "Not just the physical danger, but the emotional weight of everything."

Jake takes my hand, squeezing it gently. "It has. But I think it's made us stronger, too. Not just as individuals but together. We've had to rely on each other in ways we never expected."

"And we've managed pretty well, I think," I respond, feeling the solidity of his grip, a tangible manifestation of his support. "We've seen each other at our worst and still came out stronger on the other side."

As we turn to make our way back home, our talk turns to plans for dinner, a simple yet significant act of normalcy. We decide on trying out a new local restaurant that's just opened up—a small, hopeful symbol of the town's, and our own, rejuvenation.

Later, seated at a quiet table near the back of the bustling restaurant, we share a meal, each bite a small celebration of survival and recovery. "Here's to us, and to everyone in town," Jake raises his glass in a toast, his eyes reflecting the soft candlelight between us.

"To us," I echo, clinking my glass against his. "And to healing, together."

These small acts—our walks, dinners out, and quiet evenings spent together—serve as the foundation upon which we rebuild our lives. They are moments of peace snatched in the aftermath of chaos, building blocks for a future we are piecing together with care and love. Our relationship, already strong from the forge of adversity, now deepens into something profoundly supportive, a mutual sanctuary from the wider world.

As we walk back home under the stars, I feel a profound gratitude for this journey we are on together. Healing isn't just about moving past the pain; it's about growing through it, and with Jake by my side, I feel ready for whatever the future may hold. Our shared experiences, once sources of pain, now form the bedrock of our deepest connection, each step forward a testament to our resilience and love.

***

As I type the final words of my series on the town's recovery, I pause to glance out the window, observing the tangible signs of transformation that have begun to redefine our community. The rhythmic tapping of the keyboard fades into the background as I take in the view—families meandering through the newly revitalized park, laughter echoing softly in the distance, and shop owners proudly standing by their storefronts, welcoming customers into spaces that speak of resilience and rebirth.

"Looks like your words have become reality," Jake comments, coming up behind me and wrapping his arms around my shoulders, peering out at the bustling street below.

I lean back into his embrace, feeling a surge of contentment. "It's incredible, isn't it? Seeing the town thrive again, watching people reclaim spaces that were once overshadowed by fear."

Jake nods, his chin resting on my head. "You played a big part in that, Em. Your articles—people read them and see not just the history but the potential for what's to come. It gives them hope."

I smile, touched by his words. "We did this together. It's not just my writing—it's our experiences, our fights, and our victories that I share. That's what resonates with people."

We decide to take a walk downtown, drawn by the allure of the new mural that has become a symbol of the town's journey. As we approach, the vibrant colors and powerful imagery depicting scenes of unity and perseverance come into full view. It's more than just art; it's a declaration of our collective spirit, a beacon of the community's enduring strength.

"Look at that," I say as we stop in front of the mural, taking in each detail. "Every brushstroke tells a story. It's like a visual diary of what we've been through."

"And a map to where we're going," Jake adds, pointing to the section of the mural that depicts hands joining over a rebuilt town. "It's about moving forward, but together, stronger for it."

We spend a few moments in silence, letting the mural's message sink in. A warm glow is cast over the painted faces, bringing them to life, and it feels as if the community's resilience is pulsating through the very walls of the town.

As we continue our walk, we talk about the future—about our plans and dreams, both for ourselves and for the town. The conversation flows easily, buoyed by the optimism that seems to infuse the air around us.

"I think we should get involved in the new community center project," I suggest, excited by the prospect of contributing to a cornerstone of the town's social revival.

"I was thinking the same," Jake agrees enthusiastically. "And maybe run some workshops? You could do writing, I could do... well, I'll figure something out."

Our laughter mingles with the ambient sounds of the evening as we make our way through the streets, each step reinforcing our connection to this place and to each other. The challenges of the past have not disappeared—they have been woven into the fabric of our identities, strengthening the threads of our bond and our resolve to contribute to our community's ongoing transformation.

As we head home, the last light of day lingering on the horizon, there's a profound sense of peace and anticipation. We are not just witnesses to this new beginning; we are participants, ready to play our part in shaping a future filled with promise and possibility. Together, we look forward, our hearts full of hope, our spirits buoyed by a steadfast belief in our shared future.

A Year Later

Epilogue - Emily

A year after the militia's disbandment, our town has transformed into a vibrant testament to resilience and renewal. As I look around at the streets bustling with new businesses and the laughter of children playing in the revitalized parks, a deep sense of pride swells within me. Jake and I have found our footing here, not just as survivors of a troubled past but as active participants in shaping a hopeful future.

Our home, too, mirrors this new beginning. It's filled with the quiet joy of anticipation, the walls adorned with pictures of our wedding—a simple, heartfelt ceremony surrounded by a few close friends under the sprawling branches of the old oak in our backyard. These images are constant reminders of our promises to each other, spoken softly but with unyielding conviction as the sun set around us, casting a golden glow that seemed to bless our new union.

The memory of our wedding day is etched in my mind with a clarity that time hasn't dimmed. The backyard, transformed with strings of fairy lights and delicate candles, radiated a warmth that complemented the soft twilight perfectly. Our close friends, who had become like family, gathered around, their faces alight with joy and anticipation.

As I made my way toward Jake, who stood waiting with an infectious grin, the murmur of our friends hushed in reverence of the moment. He looked every bit the partner I had dreamed of, his eyes shining with emotion.

"Couldn't keep me waiting too long, huh?" Jake teased gently as I approached, his words breaking the tension and drawing a laugh from me and the crowd.

"Never," I responded, reaching him and taking his hands in mine. The simplicity of our setting—a circle of friends under the open sky—felt just right.

Our officiant, a close friend who had seen us through thick and thin, started the ceremony with a few touching remarks about growth, love, and the journey ahead. Then, it was time for our vows.

Jake took a deep breath, his voice strong yet laden with emotion. "Emily, I promise to be your partner in all things, not possessing you, but working with you as a part of the whole. With these words and all the words of my heart, I marry you and bind my life to yours."

Tears welled up in my eyes as I took in his words, and I squeezed his hands, feeling the solid truth of his vow. "Jake, from this day forward I give you my hand, my heart, and my love, without condition, completely and forever. I promise to support you, to laugh with you, and to face challenges with you, embracing all that our life together offers."

As we exchanged rings—a visible sign of our invisible bond—our friend officiant said, "These rings are a symbol of eternity and the unbroken circle of love. May they forever remind you of your commitment to each other."

The moment we were pronounced married, our friends erupted in cheers, the sound filling the evening air with vibrant energy. Our first kiss as a married couple was sweet and promising, sealing our vows.

Afterward, as we mingled with our guests, our friend Mia pulled us aside. "You two really set the bar high, you know? How am I supposed to top this at my wedding?" she joked, her eyes sparkling with happiness for us.

Jake laughed, wrapping an arm around my shoulders. "Just wait till you see the dance moves we've got planned for later."

Throughout the evening, the conversations flowed as freely as the wine. Our friends shared stories, reminisced, and spoke of the future. "You guys are like the cornerstone of this community now," our friend Brian noted, a touch of seriousness beneath his teasing tone. "This town's going to look to you, just like it looked to you during the troubles with the militia."

"We're ready for that," I replied, feeling the weight and the honor of that role. "Together, we can handle anything."

The evening drew to a close under a sky now darkened to a deep velvet, the stars shining above as if in blessing. Our simple wedding, marked by laughter, heartfelt vows, and the company of friends, was exactly as we had hoped it would be—a celebration not just of a union, but of a shared future full of endless possibilities. As Jake and I finally said our goodbyes and turned toward our new life together, I felt an overwhelming sense of peace. No matter what the future held, we would face it as we had this day: together, surrounded by love.

Now, another layer of excitement has been added to our lives. The spare room, once my makeshift office filled with papers and photographs documenting the town's trials and triumphs, has been transformed into a nursery. The walls are painted a soothing sage green, the furniture soft yellow, creating a sanctuary for the new life we are about to welcome. Every so often, I catch Jake standing in the doorway, a look of awe and tenderness on his face as he imagines our future child playing or sleeping peacefully in the crib.

The nursery is bathed in the soft afternoon light that filters through the sheer curtains, casting a warm, comforting glow over the room. The walls, painted in soothing tones of green and yellow, create a serene backdrop for the simple white crib that stands ready for its new occupant. As I walk into the room, a sense of peaceful anticipation fills me, and I instinctively place my hand on my belly, feeling the gentle, reassuring kicks of our unborn child.

Jake follows me in, a smile spreading across his face as he sees me standing there. "How's our little adventurer doing today?" he asks, coming up behind me and placing his hands over mine, his touch warm and protective.

"Active," I laugh softly, enjoying the intimate moment. "I think we might have a future soccer player or maybe a runner on our hands."

He chuckles, bending down to whisper to my belly, "Hear that, kiddo? Your mom's already got big plans for you."

We spend a few moments like that, wrapped up in our little world, before Jake straightens and looks around the nursery. "I think we've done a pretty good job with the place, don't you think?" he says, his gaze taking in the stuffed animals lined up on a shelf, the gentle mobile hanging above the crib, and the cozy rocking chair in the corner.

"It's perfect," I reply, walking over to the crib and running my fingers along the soft, knitted blanket that my mother had made for us. "It's more than just a room. It feels like a promise—a promise of new life, new challenges, and new joys. It's a bit overwhelming, but in the best way possible."

Jake nods, understanding the depth of my emotions. "It's the beginning of an incredible journey. I can't believe we're going to be parents. I mean, I know we've been preparing for months, but it still feels surreal."

"I know what you mean," I say as we both sit down in the rocking chair, fitting together comfortably. "It's one thing to talk about being parents and another to actually be on the brink of it. But I feel ready—as ready as we can be. Especially knowing I have you with me in this."

"We're going to be great," Jake assures me, his confidence bolstering my own. "We've handled militia, rebuilding a town, and all sorts of crises together. How hard can a baby be, right?"

I laugh, the sound mingling with the soft creak of the rocking chair. "Famous last words, my love. But whatever challenges come, I know we'll face them like we do everything else—with a lot of love, a bit of humor, and together."

As we rock gently, the room around us feels like a small sanctuary, a bubble of calm before the whirlwind of parenthood descends upon us. It's these moments of quiet connection that I cherish deeply, knowing that they are the foundation upon which we'll build our family.

"Let's enjoy the peace while we can, then," Jake says, a twinkle in his eye, "because something tells me we're going to miss these quiet moments soon enough."

I lean my head against his shoulder, feeling a profound gratitude for the life we've built and the new life we're about to welcome. "Bring it on," I whisper, ready for the next chapter in our grand adventure, fortified by the love and partnership that have brought us this far.

"We're really doing this, aren't we?" he asks one evening, his voice mingling hope with a hint of nervousness as he joins me in arranging tiny clothes in the dresser.

"We are," I affirm, reaching for his hand and squeezing it reassuringly. "It's a new chapter for us, for the town. Everything feels... right, doesn't it?"

"It does. Better than right," Jake agrees, pulling me into a gentle embrace. "I think about where we were last year, what we were facing... It's like a different lifetime."

I nod, resting my head against his chest, comforted by the steady beat of his heart. "We've come so far, not just in putting the past behind us but in building something new. Something good. Not just for us, but for everyone here."

As we stand there, wrapped in each other's arms, the setting sun casts long shadows across the room, stretching the space with hues of orange and red. It feels symbolic, this light—like the promise of a dawn that is always on the horizon, reminding us of endless possibilities.

***

As I organize my notes for the upcoming community meeting, I think about the topics that have resonated most with my readers. Issues like community policing, the role of local governance in crisis management, and the importance of mental health resources in recovery efforts have all sparked significant interest and debate. These are not just local issues but universal challenges that communities face as they navigate the complexities of recovery and healing.

I am also mindful of the personal stories that have been shared with me, tales of loss and redemption, fear and bravery. These narratives have been the backbone of my series, bringing to life the statistics and broader socio-political discussions. They remind me that at the heart of all journalism are people—real lives impacted by the issues we write about.

As I continue to write, I plan to focus on these personal stories while also exploring the systemic changes needed to prevent similar situations in the future. My goal is to provide a holistic view that not only highlights the problems but also showcases the solutions being implemented and the lessons learned.

The community meeting later today is an opportunity to bring these stories and discussions into a larger forum. It's a chance to engage with local leaders, activists, and citizens in a dialogue about where we go from here. How do we take the lessons learned from our ordeal and turn them into proactive steps towards a stronger, more resilient community?

I draft a few questions to pose during the meeting:
- What are the key elements that helped our community recover?
- How can we strengthen these elements moving forward?

- What preventative measures can we implement to ensure the safety and stability of our town?

These questions are designed to provoke thought and inspire action, to move us from reflection to action.

As I finish my preparations, Jake comes in with a second cup of coffee, setting it down beside me with a kiss on the forehead. "Ready to change the world some more?" he asks with a grin.

I smile up at him, energized by his support and the collective spirit of our community. "One story at a time," I reply, my heart full of determination.

***

Just on the outskirts of town, housed in what used to be an old warehouse, is Jake's new venture—a state-of-the-art Tactical Training Facility that he built from the ground up. It's a place that buzzes with energy and purpose, the air often filled with the sound of instructions being called out or the muted thud of hands hitting training mats.

Jake has transformed the space into a hub of learning and development for law enforcement, military personnel, and security professionals. The large main room, with its high ceilings and spacious layout, is lined with all sorts of training equipment—mats, obstacle courses, and advanced tactical gear. It's here that Jake spends his days, teaching and guiding, his presence commanding yet approachable.

As I watch him one afternoon, leading a group through a complex maneuver designed to disarm an assailant, I can see the passion he pours into every lesson. He moves with precision and confidence, his instructions clear and his attention sharp on his students' movements.

"These skills are your toolbox," Jake often says to his trainees, his voice echoing off the high walls. "What you build with them can save lives, protect communities, and bring peace of mind to those you serve."

The fulfillment he derives from his work is palpable. After each session, as he walks among his students, checking in on their progress, offering tips, and sharing a laugh or two, there's a sense of satisfaction on his face that I've come to know well. This venture is more than just a job for him; it's a continuation of his commitment to service, a way to channel his experience and skills into something that empowers others.

His reputation as a trainer has grown quickly, the facility becoming well-known not just in our town but in surrounding areas as well. Law enforcement agencies have begun to send recruits regularly, and word-of-mouth has brought in private security firms seeking top-notch tactical training.

One evening, over dinner, Jake shares his vision for expanding the programs. "I want to introduce more advanced courses, maybe even some specialized workshops for crisis management and strategic planning," he tells me, his eyes alight with ideas.

"It sounds like you're really making a difference, Jake," I respond, admiration threading through my words. "You're not just training individuals—you're strengthening entire communities."

He nods, accepting the praise with a humble smile. "I hope so. I believe everyone deserves to feel safe, and if I can contribute to that, then I'll have done something worthwhile."

Back at the facility, as I observe him wrapping up a session, I see the respect and camaraderie he shares with his trainees. They look up to him, not just as a teacher but as a mentor who has walked the path they're on and who knows the weight of the responsibilities they carry.

Jake locks up for the night and joins me in the car. We drive home in companionable silence, each lost in thought about our respective projects but comforted by the shared journey we're on.

This venture, this new chapter in Jake's life, is not just about passing on skills or techniques. It's about building a legacy of empowerment and safety, about transforming potential into readiness, and about turning the lessons from past challenges into blueprints for future security. As he often says, "It's about preparing for the worst, hoping for the best, and being capable of handling anything in between."

As the day draws to a close, the setting sun bathes our bedroom in a golden glow, the light soft and warm, wrapping around us like a gentle embrace. The world outside seems to pause, granting us a moment of perfect peace as we find ourselves drawn together, a magnetic pull that is as natural as it is inevitable.

Jake's hands are gentle as they trace the contours of my face, his touch familiar yet always filled with new electricity. I reach up to meet his fingers with mine, our eyes locked in a dance as old as time. The air around us is charged with anticipation, each breath shared a stoke to the growing fire between us.

"Emily," Jake whispers, his voice husky, laden with emotion and desire. His words are a caress, as potent as his touch, and they send shivers down my spine.

"Jake," I reply, my voice a soft echo of his own, full of longing and love. We move closer, the space between us charged with the promise of what's to come.

Our kiss is deep and slow, a languid exploration that speaks of profound familiarity and endless discovery. There's a tenderness to the way our lips move together, a gentleness that belies the intense passion that underlies each touch, each sigh. As we pull each other closer, the rest of the world melts away, leaving nothing but the feeling of being utterly connected, heart and soul.

The gentle intensity escalates, a natural progression from tender kisses to more urgent, passionate caresses. Jake's hands roam over my back, pulling me closer, as mine tangle in his hair, each movement stoking the flames of desire that burn brightly between us. The connection is as emotional as it is physical, a testament to the deep, unshakeable bond we share.

We move together to the bed, the soft sheets a welcome contrast to the heat of our bodies. Every touch, every whispered word is a reaffirmation of our love, of the commitment we've made to each other. This is not just a physical union but a spiritual one, a merging of souls that have weathered storms and celebrated victories side by side.

The world narrows down to the room, to the bed, to the space where our bodies and hearts meet. The passion is a wave that we ride together, reaching heights that are made all the more intense by the depth of our emotional connection. It's a dance we know well, yet it feels new every time, each moment a discovery, each climax a revelation.

As we finally drift down from the heights of passion, our bodies tangled and our breathing synchronized, I rest my head on Jake's chest, listening to the steady beat of his heart. His arms wrap around me, a protective cocoon that speaks of safety and belonging.

"We have something special, Emily," Jake murmurs into the quiet room, his voice filled with awe and love.

"We do," I agree, my voice muffled against his skin. "And it only gets stronger."

This moment of intimacy, this steamy reconnection, is not just about fulfilling desire but about celebrating the unbreakable bond we share. It's a poignant reminder of our journey together, of the challenges we've overcome and the life we're building. In each other's arms, we find not just pleasure but peace, a profound sense of coming home. This connection, this love, is our greatest strength, and as we hold each other close, we know that together, we can face anything the future might hold.

In the quiet aftermath of our passionate reunion, as the soft afterglow of the sunset fades into the gentle embrace of twilight, Jake and I lie entwined under the light sheet, our bodies a testament to the closeness we share. The room around us feels charged with a serene energy, reflective of the profound journey we have traveled together.

Jake's hand finds mine, his fingers intertwining with mine as he turns to look at me, his eyes deep pools of contemplation. "Can you believe how much has changed in just a few years?" he asks, his voice a whisper that seems to fill the room with its gravity.

I shift to face him, my head resting on my hand as I look into his eyes. "Sometimes, it feels like a lifetime ago," I reply softly. "From the chaos and fear of the militia to this peace... it's almost surreal."

"Yeah," he agrees, his thumb tracing small circles on the back of my hand. "I remember how it all started—feeling like we were the only ones aware of how deep the problems ran. It was overwhelming, wasn't it?"

I nod, memories of those early days flooding back—the tension and uncertainty, the feeling of being on the brink of something either great or disastrous. "It was. But I also remember feeling that as long as we faced it together, there was nothing we couldn't handle. And look at us now," I say, a smile playing on my lips.

Jake smiles back, a look of pride crossing his features. "We made a pretty great team, didn't we? Took on a militia, rebuilt a community, and started a family."

"And won some battles with ourselves along the way," I add, thinking about the personal demons we had each confronted throughout our ordeal. "We've grown so much, not just as a couple but as individuals."

He nods, his gaze becoming introspective. "I think that's what I'm proudest of, Em. Not just the external victories, but the internal ones. Learning to trust, to hope again, to believe that we could make a difference."

"It's about resilience, isn't it?" I muse aloud. "About finding strength in places we didn't know we had it, about pushing through when everything seems against you."

"Exactly," Jake says. "And now, with our little one on the way, it feels like all those lessons, all that growth, is about to be tested in new ways. But I know we're ready for it."

I squeeze his hand, affirming his sentiment. "We are. Because if there's one thing we've learned, it's that together, we can overcome anything. And now we get to teach that to our child. To show them what it means to stand up, to fight for what's right, to love deeply."

Jake pulls me closer, and we share a quiet kiss, a seal on our promises and reflections. "I love you, Emily," he whispers against my lips.

"I love you too, Jake," I whisper back, feeling the strength of our bond, the certainty of our future together.

As we lie there, the night deepening around us, our conversation fades into comfortable silence. Our shared reflections on the changes we've navigated, from upheaval to peace, from uncertainty to stability, weave a stronger fabric for our relationship. In each other, we have found not only a partner but a fellow warrior in the battles of life—a bond that is unbreakable, ready to welcome and shape the new life we have created together. The night may fall, but our future is bright, illuminated by the love and lessons of our past.

***

The early morning air is crisp, a gentle herald of the dawn as Jake and Emily step onto their front porch, a blanket wrapped around their shoulders against the chill. The eastern sky is a canvas of soft blues and pinks, the first light of dawn just beginning to paint the horizon with the promise of a new day.

They stand in silence, hands clasped, a perfect unity of purpose and passion etched into the simple act of watching the sunrise. The world around them wakes slowly, the sounds of the town stirring to life a faint backdrop to the tranquil moment they share.

Emily rests her head on Jake's shoulder, her eyes fixed on the burgeoning light as it spreads across the sky, turning clouds into golden cotton on a canvas of awakening blue. "It's beautiful, isn't it?" she murmurs, her voice a whisper carried away by the morning breeze.

"It is," Jake agrees, squeezing her hand. "But not as beautiful as the life we're going to give our little one. A life filled with love, with peace... with hope."

Emily smiles, turning to look up at him, her eyes reflecting the dawn's light. "We've been through so much," she says. "Fought so hard for a future that, at times, seemed like nothing more than a distant dream."

"And now that future is here," Jake replies, his gaze returning to the horizon where the sun crests the distant hills, its rays spilling like liquid gold over the land. "A new day, not just for us, but for everyone we've brought with us on this journey."

They watch in silence, the beauty of the moment overshadowing the struggles of the past. The challenges they had faced—the darkness they had navigated together—had indeed molded them into more than they had been. Leaders, lovers, partners in every challenge and joy that life had offered.

As the full sun breaks free of the horizon, its light seems to flood the world with warmth, washing over them and filling the spaces around with brightness. This light, like their love, like their commitment to each other and to the community they've helped to rebuild, promises to chase away the shadows of the past.

"We have so much to look forward to," Emily says, her voice steady with conviction and joy. "So much to teach our child about the world, about fighting for what's right, about loving without reservation."

"And we'll do it together," Jake adds, his voice resolute. "As we always have."

With that, they turn back towards the house, their home, where new challenges and joys await. Their story, marked by resilience and a deep, unbreakable bond, closes not with an ending but with the beginning of a legacy—a new chapter in lives filled with potential and promise.

As they step back inside, ready to greet the day and all it holds, they know that whatever challenges may come, they will face them together, fortified by love and driven by a shared commitment to make the world a better place for themselves, their child, and the future generations that will follow. In this shared vision, they find not just hope for the future, but a profound sense of contentment and a readiness to meet the sunrise of their lives together.

Don't miss out!

Visit the website below and you can sign up to receive emails whenever Lilly Grace Nash publishes a new book. There's no charge and no obligation.

https://books2read.com/r/B-A-WUJHB-JCRDD

BOOKS 2 READ

Connecting independent readers to independent writers.

Also by Lilly Grace Nash

SEALs of Love Romance
Undercover Hearts

Watch for more at https://lillygracenash.com.